BLOWOUT

BREAKERS HOCKEY #6

ELISE FABER

BLOWOUT
BY ELISE FABER
Newsletter sign-up
This is a work of fiction. Names, places, characters, and events are fictitious in every regard. Any similarities to actual events and persons, living or dead, are purely coincidental. Any trademarks, service marks, product names, or named features are assumed to be the property of their respective owners, and are used only for reference. There is no implied endorsement if any of these terms are used. Except for review purposes, the reproduction of this book in whole or part, electronically or mechanically, constitutes a copyright violation.

ONE

Cas

I WAS a hockey player who'd had fun.

Lots of fun.

I liked women—curvy or slender, tall or short, breasts or ass or long, shapely legs, blond or black or brown-haired or a redhead. It didn't matter to me.

I just liked women.

But over the last months, I'd concluded that I liked one in particular.

She was smart and a hard worker. She had an ass that could make a grown man weep (and maybe it had brought a tear or two to my eyes once or twice, mostly because I was growing so desperate to see and touch and kiss the lush curves of Jules's ass that I was living in a perpetual state of blue balls).

Tonight was the night my balls got some relief—or maybe the night that they lived in even more agony for at least a bit more time...

Because tonight I was going to ask Jules out.

And if she said yes, then I'd be lucky enough to spend more time with her.

Which meant my balls would spend more time in her vicinity.

Hence, a lack of relief.

Hence, me almost wishing for my balls to continue their agony.

Hence...I was an idiot who was delaying.

I was *going* to ask Jules out.

It had taken me an embarrassingly long time to work up the courage—harkening me back to my high school days—to ask her to go on a date with me, but I was a professional hockey player, dammit. I'd dated plenty of women.

I could ask one more out.

Easy to think.

Harder to accept.

Because as I slid from the bustling barroom and followed Jules down the hall, my pulse was pounding in my veins, sweat was pricking on my nape.

Because...this meant something.

She pushed out through the back door and I followed, slipping into the evening air.

CeCe's, one of my favorite places to come—both because this woman worked here and because it had good food—was in a bustling part of the city.

Tonight was no exception.

Laughter punched through the night air, traffic buzzed in the distance, but here, behind the restaurant in the quiet alley that had dumpsters shoved on one end and a row of employee cars on the other, it was hushed.

"I come out here to think sometimes," she murmured, surprising me, not realizing that she'd heard me following her out.

Not realizing that she'd seen me there staring and not speaking.

Being an idiot.

Christ.

"When it gets to be too much," she said, voice still soft, turning toward me, her brown eyes rich, dark chocolate in the dim light.

God, she was pretty with those big eyes and gentle curves to her cheeks, her jaw. Her lips were plush pillows that I wanted to taste.

They'd be incredibly soft, I knew.

They had to be.

And she—

"You know," she whispered, insecurity creeping into her tone. "Because it's so loud inside the bar and busy and—"

"Will you go on a date with me?!"

It was an abrupt burst of sound, so it was no surprise that she jerked back in shock, the gentle smile that had been on her face while telling me about her need to find a bit of quiet disappearing in an instant.

I could have turned and punched the thick brick wall behind myself, pummeled it until my knuckles split.

She'd been giving me a little piece of herself.

An insight I could have held close, an opening I could have eased through.

I wasn't an idiot—or rarely outside of my interactions with Jules, anyway.

I could have taken that insight and used it to learn more about her, to understand the shadows that sometimes lived in her eyes, to find out what made her smile and why she had a need for quiet. Was it just the buzz of activity inside? Or because she was busy with work and school and being a mom that she needed to steal slices of silence?

Instead, I'd yelled at her.

And her face said she both didn't like the volume and what I'd asked...yelled...whatever.

"Jules," I began, being certain to modulate my tone this time, to not startle her.

To not yell. *Fuck.*

"I can't," she said before I got further than saying her name. "Not because of you." She reached out, squeezed my forearm, and hell if sparks didn't fly up my skin, skitter through my heart, grow into embers in my stomach, flames licking down toward my dick.

"I—"

"I'm not ready to date anyone," she murmured. "Again, not because of you."

Her fingers sliding away, and I didn't miss that they curled into a fist she pressed to her hip, her knuckles standing out in sharp relief.

Her lips pressed together, released. "I-I'm just—"

I reached over, captured her fist. When she went stiff, I crouched a little so that our gazes connected. "Don't worry," I whispered, smoothing out her fingers, hating the half-moon indentations on the palms of her hands, hating that I'd been the cause of them. "I get it. I just"—I brushed my thumb over the crescent-shaped hurt—"*Careful*, gorgeous."

Her inhale was sharp, and I let her hand go, stepped back to put more distance between us.

I wanted to leave, to find some privacy—some quiet—to introduce my fist to the bricks, but I didn't want things to be weird between us, didn't want Jules to be uncomfortable here.

Where she worked. Where she'd become part of *us*.

The Breakers.

The guys and I came in regularly.

She was taking careful steps toward friendship with Hazel and Pru and Kailey and Beth.

I didn't want to be responsible for fucking that up.

"The quiet," I said, waving my arm out toward the alley. "I get needing it."

Not a smooth transition in the least.

But disappointment was flowing through me in great waves that resembled tsunamis.

So, it was the best I could do at that particular moment, yeah?

Meanwhile, Jules was so still she resembled a statue, and as I watched her out of the corner of my eye, it seemed like she was hardly breathing. Tense. On edge.

Because of me.

Fuck.

"I'm one of four, so it was always noisy," I told her, barely able to resist the urge to rub my temple, to try to soothe the ache that was beginning to blossom there. I was fucking things up. *Royally.* "The oldest," I added, wanting to give her something of me, something that would make her know a piece of me, but also something that wouldn't make her feel uncomfortable. "Which means that my parents were always in my business growing up"—this time when I shot her a smile, I breathed a little easier because some of the tension had left her frame—"at least until my siblings started making trouble."

That sent the corners of her mouth turning up. "And *were* you?"

I lifted my brows in query.

"Trouble?" she asked, eyes dancing.

And now *I* relaxed.

Because she was Jules again.

And maybe I hadn't fucked this up quite as much as I'd thought.

Growing up, I'd actually been a pretty good kid overall, critically aware that my parents had been working to the edges of their physical and mental abilities to provide for our family. I hadn't wanted to add to their stress.

But I hadn't been perfect.

"No more than any other kid," I admitted and then laughed at her expression before adding, "Truthfully, I get into a lot more mischief nowadays with the guys. In my family, Sam"—a glance at her—"he's my younger brother and the ringleader of trouble. Now *and* then."

The pranks that kid had pulled...

Good God, it was no wonder our mother always complained about all her gray hairs.

"Yeah?" she asked, curiosity in those pretty brown eyes. "What'd he do?"

I opened my mouth, mind spiraling through the stories of my brother, filtering out the best ones, the ones that would make her laugh—

The door crashed open behind us.

A drunk couple, locked in an embrace that resembled two octopi going at it, stumbled out, giggling and pawing each other, their mouths creating so much suction that the sounds of their saliva exchanging bodies was going to haunt me for a good long while.

Jules shuddered—I assumed for the same reason—but the couple had shattered the relaxed mood I'd managed to coax her back into. Her shoulders tensed and she inhaled, held that breath, then released it in a rush of air.

I watched all of that in fascination.

Then her eyes came to mine...and I braced.

She was going to keep trying to let me down easily.

God, I wanted to touch her, to kiss her, to hold her close until the uncertainty in the dark brown depths faded.

But she didn't want that.

So, all I could do was leave her be.

"I get it, gorgeous." I smiled a smile that I'd perfected over the years, one that had disarmed my parents, turned their worry from me when they had too much on their plates and didn't need to focus on my petty, unimportant kid-drama. "No hard feelings. Promise." A wink, my lips curving further, tone lightening. "I'm used to rejection."

And, just like it had growing up, that smile paired with the light words worked.

Jules relaxed again, rolling her eyes and shaking her head at me. "I'm sure," she said dryly.

"It's true," I teased, tugging open the door (much more gently than the octopi couple) and waving at her to proceed ahead of me. "My heart has been stepped on so many times over the years, I'm sure that it's basically just pulp."

Her laughter filling the hall...filling my heart.

Then she shook her head again, her smile as she looked back at me joining that laughter in my heart, and gestured to my table as we strode into the busy barroom. "Go sit down and" —another glance over her shoulder that didn't do anything to assuage my need to kiss her—"if you behave, I'll bring you one of Cody's freshly baked cookies."

I had a sweet tooth.

And I loved Cody's cookies.

But I knew that tonight, it would sit heavy in my gut, no matter how tasty.

Because I'd shot my shot.

And I'd fucked it up.

TWO

Jules, Two Months Later

"IT'S BREAK TIME."

I glanced over at Beth, tucking the round, black tray under my arm as I did so...

And instant regret of that action.

Frosty drops of condensation from cold drinks, of spillover from the beers and sodas and just plain glasses of water dripped down my side. From armpit to hip and frigid enough that I bit the inside of my cheek so that I didn't squeak and squirm in response.

All these years in this job and I still spilled shit on myself.

Though, I supposed I should be happy that my habit of dumping trays full of food on myself had been limited to three times. Total.

Twice—my fault.

Once—an asshole patron (who'd been permanently banned).

Beth cleared her throat, brows lifting, pregnant belly

rounded and just visible when she was sitting at the high top table.

Right.

Beth had made a statement. Though, it was more of a question, even if the actual words that had come out of Beth's mouth had been absent of the querying tone.

I glanced at my watch. "Just about."

"Your tables all have their food and refills," Beth said. "No one new has walked in. You've been on your feet for four hours—"

"You guys have only been here for an hour," I countered, just on principle. Beth was awesome and kind and sweet, but she also had a strong personality and was good at railroading people. It was important to show a little spine, otherwise she would walk right over me.

An arch look. "Am I wrong?"

She wasn't, unfortunately.

But I wasn't going to admit that.

"So, you've been on your feet for four hours." Beth smiled beatifically. "And we happen to have an extra Sprite with your name on it."

I narrowed my eyes.

I hadn't brought them any Sprites. None of the girls, or the guys taking up space at a high top on the other side of the bar, their eyes glued to their women, drank them. And okay...all the guys were staring at their respective women...except for one of them.

Cas.

He was looking at me.

He'd done it a lot.

Before he asked me out.

And he still did it after I'd turned him down.

I was a single mom of a busy five-year-old boy. I worked

long hours and jockeyed babysitters and my budget—my super-power was robbing Peter to pay Paul, lasting a few more days so that I could scrimp and save and make sure we didn't go broke. I didn't have time for hockey players who dated women like they were the Daily Special (and one that was never repeated).

Clink. Clink.

I jerked, attempting to tear my gaze from the ruggedly handsome face, from the intense green eyes that were the color of the mature Douglas firs I'd grown up with, surrounding me on all sides.

The mountains and cold, crisp air.

The snow crunching beneath my boots, walking into the nearby resorts with my boots tied together and tossed over one shoulder, my skis strapped to my back, bypassing the tourists' cars, and making good use of my season pass (earned back then from my newly emerging superpower of scrimping and saving).

God, I'd *loved* being out there.

I missed it now.

But...life changed and people either adapted and moved on or lived looking back.

I wasn't much for looking back.

I had Ethan, and he needed a happy, steady mom, and that meant *not* looking back. Because sure as shit, if I spent all of my time focusing on my past and all the bad stuff that had happened, I wouldn't be happy.

Nor steady.

Nor able to give Ethan what he needed.

Clink. Clink. Clink.

A crisp demand for attention. *Beth's* crisp demand for attention.

Right.

Finally, I managed to focus back on the table (and made

sure to ignore Beth's arch smirk). The other woman saw too damned much.

Narrowing my eyes, I asked, "And who is the Sprite for?" A beat. "Because I know it's not really for me."

"You." A grin. "Courtesy of Matt." She inclined her head, red hair bouncing, toward the bar, where my boss was watching the table. When our gazes connected, he smiled and nodded at the table, silently telling me to sit down. He was always watching out for me, though thankfully, I could take care of myself nowadays—something that hadn't been true when he'd first hired me.

Hence the spilled trays.

Now, though, I was an expert level waitress.

But he still watched out for me—albeit with less frequency, considering he was busy with his own husband and baby and had handed off a lot of the management of CeCe's.

I was thrilled for him. He deserved to be happy.

"See?" Beth said, drawing my focus again, her lips turning up. "Even your boss says you need a break."

I smothered a sigh. Knew I'd been bested. "Are you going to share your cheese?"

The women came in, usually once a week, and indulged in Cheese Night Extravaganza—basically, they ordered any and all types of unhealthy cheese on the menu and went to town, pounding more food down than I had ever seen *anyone* eat.

And they still had things like waists (minus Beth, who was acting as a surrogate and carrying twins for Pru) and sleekly muscled arms.

Seriously.

I would hate them if they weren't so fun.

They were also highly protective of said cheese, going so far as to threaten with forks if anyone dared to so much as steal a mozzarella stick.

Stabby-minded mofos.

But—forks and stabbing aside—I liked them.

They tipped well, weren't assholes, and had come in often enough that I'd begun to consider them friends.

Not that I *had* friends.

I was too busy being a mom and working and going to school and trying to keep my life together to actually do something like have friends.

Was I lonely at times? Maybe.

But I also liked to think that I was too busy to be lonely, and plus, I was used to being alone. I'd been alone for most of my life.

That was the nature of being born to a man who'd lost his wife because of me, who'd descended into grief (that was laced with no little amount of resentment because *I* had been the one who'd caused the death of the love of his life), who'd been solitary by nature even before he'd lost his wife.

The trees and snow and animals had been friends until I'd gotten old enough for school.

Then I'd managed to have some *actual* friends.

But I'd lost touch with those friends years ago. Moving across the country would do that to the convenient ties formed through shared classes and proximity.

People grew up, had their own lives.

Went to college.

Worked every spare moment and went to school and were single mothers.

Daydreamed—

Chairs screeched and, jerking, I glanced up from where I'd been absentmindedly tracing the faux woodgrain pattern of the tabletop.

My gaze hit Beth's, who silently pushed a plate forward.

Smothered tater tots.

My stomach immediately growled. They were my favorite.

It was sweet—and unsurprising—that the thoughtful and detail-oriented Beth knew the dish was my favorite. The other woman was devious and prepared and had never met a bone she didn't like to dig her teeth into. And good luck breaking her hold on it.

Case in point, the plate sliding and the mischief in Beth's eyes and the slight hint of a smirk.

Because the food and Sprite had come with a side of hot hockey players.

(The result of the chair-screeching).

An *extra*-large side.

Smitty—one of the Breakers' defensemen—sidled close to his shy, sweet woman, Kailey. Oliver—a former player—looped an arm around Hazel's middle, nuzzling a kiss into the side of his wife's neck. Marcel—current star forward—slid his stool right next to Pru's, pressing their thighs together. Raph—quiet, steady, and great on the ice—began massaging Beth's back, an instinctual, caring gesture from the man who beat Beth out in thoughtfulness (and stubbornness) and took care of her seemingly without thought.

And the single ones, they came close too.

Squeezing stools into the already full table.

I released a thankful breath when it was Theo—another forward who made it clear he had absolutely *no* plans of ending his single status—who ended up next to me and not Cas—the steady defenseman...and my secret fantasy.

He was the regret I turned over in my head in the dark of night—something I had far too much time for because I worked the late shift, was up late five days a week.

Something I had far too much time for because every time Cas was close...

Well, I had a hard time remembering why I'd turned him down.

Eyes the green of pine needles, a temptation to find home in a man who might—

No.

The temptation to find home in a man was a stupid one.

I'd tried that, and though it had ended with me having the best thing in my life—that being Ethan—I couldn't do that again.

It hurt too much when it went wrong, when I would ultimately end up alone.

But when I looked up, my fork full of loaded tots, my belly rumbling with the urge to. Get. Them. In. My. Belly. I found it nearly impossible to ignore the calling of those tall trees, the winter cold air, the snow crunching beneath my boots.

Especially when eyes of forest green kept catching mine.

THREE

Cas

I WAS TRYING NOT to stare like a fucking idiot, attempting to not slaver over her like a dog.

Like I always did.

But fuck, she was pretty.

Deep brown eyes, shining blond hair. Hips I wanted to grip as I stroked home, stroked deep. An ass that called for my teeth, the slight sting in my skin from the crack of my palm.

Not interested.

She wasn't interested.

I, on the other hand, was nearing obsessed.

Even though I was trying not to be, was attempting to ignore the draw I felt toward her. But fuck, it was getting harder with each minute I spent in her presence. There was an inner light to Jules that caught my focus, shining brightly, bringing out my protective instincts.

I wanted to make sure no one ever dimmed it.

I wanted to be able to call her mine, to shelter that light, help it grow, make it so damned bright that it wasn't ever at risk of fading. Turn the incandescent to LED, harness the energy of the wind and sun and rivers, making it so that her bright wouldn't ever go out.

But she didn't want me.

So, I tried not to stare.

And I failed every fucking time.

"Well," Jules said then, and I didn't have to look her way, because—fuck—I'd been staring at her again, committing every single freckle to memory, the way her lashes curled up, framing those bright brown eyes. I wondered if her skin was soft as it looked, if the faint hint of flowers I'd sometimes picked up around her was from her shampoo or her perfume or her lotion or just *her*.

She glanced away, snatching up her empty soda glass and sliding out of her seat. "I should get back to work before Matt gets pissed at me for slacking off."

My anger was razor sharp, the question sneaking out before I could stuff it down. "What does Matt do when he gets pissed?"

Jules stilled, and her gaze finally came to mine, finally connected...and held.

The air tightened.

My nostrils flared as I sucked in a breath, desperate for a hint of her, of those flowers I'd scented behind CeCe's, in the hall, occasionally when she brought my food or drinks.

But then Jules laughed, and it made my lungs spasm as I tried to suck in more air, even though there wasn't room for it in my chest. Fuck, but it was a pretty sound, that inner light shining through, filling the space between us.

Almost as beautiful as her smile.

Her laughter began when she was looking at me, and my heart stuttered at the sight of her mouth curving, her eyes crinkling at the corners, the gorgeous tinkling sound. "He scowls at me." Another laugh. "Matt is a good guy." But I didn't get to soak her smile in, not for long anyway, because then she glanced away, nodding decisively. "Okay, then." A tap to the table. "I'll just make my rounds and then come back to close you guys out."

"Thanks, honey," Beth said, yanking me back into reality, into this moment, reminding me it wasn't just me and Julie, that there were other occupants at the table with me. Beth squeezed Jules's forearm. "No rush, yeah?"

Jules smiled again, nodding at Beth, at the table, but then she glanced back to me, just briefly, and fuck if my pulse didn't skitter in my veins. But I only got it for a heartbeat. Then I lost her smile, her light as it arrowed back to Beth and Raph.

I watched her expression warm, that smile soften. "Yeah, I'll bet you don't mind cozying up to your hot hockey player while you wait."

Beth laughed, leaned back against Raph. "Nope. Don't mind that at all."

With one last grin, Jules slipped away.

I clenched my jaw, flexed my toes in my boots, digging them into the soles of my shoes, keeping me in place.

When all I wanted to do was go after her.

To take her in my arms.

To whisper in her ear, inhale the soft floral scent, to feel her body against mine and—

Smitty laughed, the sound booming through the air, and I looked away from where Jules had disappeared into the kitchen and back toward my idiot teammate.

Who was smirking in a way that made me want to punch him in the face.

But Hazel was sitting there with Oliver, and she could make the worst miscreants behave. I wasn't a miscreant, of course, though I wanted to do bad, bad things to Jules, but I definitely had miscreant vibes, mostly because I wouldn't mind taking a pot shot at my boisterous teammate.

I loved the guy.

But swear to fuck, Smitty could get on my nerves.

Movement by the bar drew my focus, and I watched Jules slip back out through the swinging door, a heavy tray laden with plates perched on my shoulder.

Yup. I knew I was in deep as I watched her deliver the food. She was strong and confident, smart, and worked her ass off. Yeah, she was quiet compared to some of the girls—though with Beth and Pru and Smitty around, it was hard to imagine anyone getting a word in. Thus, it wasn't uncommon for the rest of our group to come from different places on the scale of Kailey (our shyest member) Quiet to Smitty Loud.

Of course, she was also beautiful and had that inner light and—

I *liked* her.

I just...couldn't have her.

Sighing, I smothered the urge to go after her, to help her with the heavy tray, the large number of plates. At the very best, I knew that would be a huge overstep (and look at me go with my critical thinking skills!). At the worst, it would be an unwanted comment about her abilities.

Truthfully, though, I was still tempted to risk it. I hated the thought of her on her own, even here, wanted to show her that I was there, that I was—

"Might want to stop mooning over her," Theo muttered, clapping his hand on my shoulder, "and start doing something about it."

Normally, Theo would be right about getting off my ass and doing something about it.

Normally, I lived my life by grabbing on to opportunities, by putting balls to the walls, by knowing that I'd miss one hundred percent of the shots I didn't take, by leaving it all on the ice, by—

Insert other cliché sports analogy here.

There would be no ball-walling or shooting or leaving it on the ice.

Jules had turned me down.

So, I wasn't going to be a dick.

She'd drawn a line. I wasn't going to cross it.

Sighing, I picked up my glass, started to drain it, but Theo smacked me on the shoulder again, nearly making me choke on the beer.

"Welp, on that grumpy expression of yours," Theo said, the asshole fucking beyond chipper as I tossed a napkin on the table then gave a jaunty wave. "I'm out."

Which was when I realized that the rest of the table had cleared out.

Right.

I'd been—as Theo said—mooning over Jules, and not doing it slyly in the least. Certainly not slyly enough to avoid my teammate, Smitty's, matchmaking laser. Nor sly enough to avoid Beth's newfound interest in the same subject if their disappearing acts were any indication.

Cuddling up to her hot hockey player my ass.

Another sigh. Another gulp of my beer.

They would pile on the shit in the locker room.

Not something I'd typically care about. I could take the teasing and could dish it out just as effortlessly.

But it was going to sting because I didn't have a shot with Jules.

All the teasing would be pointless.

Grumbling to myself when I spotted the signed credit card receipt on the table and realized that one of the guys must have gone to Matt while I was mooning and Jules was working and cashed our tables out, I drained the remnants of my beer. I stood, threw a hundred on the table because she was a single mom and I knew what it was like to be struggling for money. My parents were good people, had made it work even though things had been tight as they raised four kids. They were okay now because my siblings and I were adults (and I was in a position where I could help with things like college tuition). But I still had a soft spot for those who were hustling their asses off.

Jules was one of those people.

I'd caught her studying on her break, working to improve her future.

I'd seen her leave a shift early when her son was ill.

I'd watched her hustle during every shift, remaining capable and cheerful even with dark circles beneath her eyes.

Now, it was late. CeCe's had cleared out, and I was one of a handful of customers left.

I should go. Let her get out of here. Let her get home to her bed and her son.

Smothering a sigh, I soaked up one more look of her as she cashed out her final table and headed for the hall.

I'd get my ass on the treadmill, would run off this frustration.

Hands on the metal bar that would open the door that led out to the rear parking lot, I started to push through.

"Cas!"

FOUR

Jules

THE HUNDRED-DOLLAR BILL was crisp in my hand as I hurried down the hall.

"Cas!"

He stilled, hands on the door, and as I got close, I realized that he was big. Okay, I'd *known* that. He was a hockey player, and though not universally giant-sized, every single one of them was taller than my own five-three.

Usually, by more than a foot.

But the height differential was more than that when it came to Cas.

Hell, my nose barely reached his throat.

And suddenly, I had the insane urge to lean close, to press said nose to said throat, and to inhale deeply. Spice, I knew. He'd smell of spice and man and sometimes orange. I sometimes got a hint of the scent when it came off his beard, off his skin.

Would an inhalation at such close proximity bring out a

deeper variety of scent for me to roll around in? Maybe a hint of sandalwood, perhaps a dash of something fresh and astringent, like mint?

Which was another of those things I thought about in the middle of the night.

What would it be like to have his scent in my nose, filling my senses?

What would it be like to be surrounded by the heat and strength of him?

What—

"Did you need something, gorgeous?" he asked softly.

I blinked, gaze jerking away from his throat, darting up to meet his eyes, mine no doubt wide as the rough endearment slid over my skin. "I..." God, *he* was the one who was gorgeous. And he smelled good, and it was late already, the hour firmly in that soft cushion of night between evening and sunrise. There was something about the utter navy of the sky, the darkness only interspersed by streetlights or stars or the faint glow of the TV I fell asleep to every night.

Moonlight on snow.

The whisper of the wind through pine needles.

All of that being torn away—

I had a better life here, I told myself. Better for me and Ethan. But even as I held tight to those thoughts, I clenched my jaw, attempting to control the pounding of my heart, the painful pulse of those old memories.

I was in the light now.

I wouldn't let myself go back there.

Fingers on my cheek startled me, made me realize I'd drifted off again. He'd called me gorgeous and I'd—

Right.

A breath as I tried to ignore the fact that there was something familiar about his touch—and tried to ignore just as completely that it was probably because I'd dreamed about it every night since I'd first seen him.

And, God, it had been so, *so* long since a man had touched me.

Had wanted me.

At least of the non-drunk, non-creepy customer who was trying to seduce me into bed variety that usually made a move.

Cas wanted me—and not in a creepy way. He'd asked me out on a date, and it could have been—

Nothing. Because I was me and he was a playboy hockey player, and I didn't do men and I didn't do men who were hockey players especially and—

All of this was a moot point because Cas was somewhere I couldn't go.

I worked in a bar. I went to school. I worked my ass off.

I wasn't easy.

No matter what my dad thought.

And there was that dark again, the slicing pain, the disappointment and hurt and—

Stop.

I was still standing in front of the man I dreamed about, the man I wanted in my secret fantasies but would never let myself have. I was taking up his time when he'd clearly been trying to leave, and worse, I was staring at him like a dope and not *saying* anything.

Sigh.

I tugged the pieces of myself together, drew myself up another inch, even though it still didn't bring me anywhere *close* to Cas's height, and then lifted my hand that held the hundred. "You left this," I said.

His brows drew together and then his big, strong body went still.

So still he was all but playing statue.

Playing a very *unhappy* statue.

I inhaled slowly, got that spice and orange and *maybe* a dash of mint from the base of his throat. It made me shiver, but I held his gaze. "Oliver already paid for the tables," I said. "And tipped generously."

"Good," he said, then, incongruously, wrapped his fingers over mine.

I blinked.

And, *God*, his hand was warm and strong and a little rough.

A fact that made me shiver again, but then he was folding my hand closed. "I know they paid," he said, ignoring the part of my comment about tipping generously. "That's still for you." Fingertips trailing over the back of my hand, making me shiver for a third time.

Then his words processed.

For me?

Um...

"Cas—"

But he was releasing me, and disappointment was a blunt blade shoving home hard and fiercely and *fast*. Except, he wasn't backing away like I'd instinctively braced for, wasn't pushing through the door and leaving me. He was reaching behind him, tugging off his sweatshirt. "You're cold."

"I'm—" I caught a glimpse of taut, flat stomach, a hint of a trail of short dark hairs dipping beneath the waistband of the jeans that cupped his lower half, including his ass—and good God *his* ass was perfect, lush and bitable. An ass I'd found myself tempted, more than once, to get my hands on over the time I'd known him. But that peekaboo of tummy—and God, I sounded like an idiot calling a hockey player's stomach a tummy, but I *was* a mom—had my *own* tummy clenching.

And other things, too.

South of my tummy.

He reached for me and, startled, I rocked back on my heels, my breath catching. But he didn't take me into his arms, didn't draw me close so that I could steal my sniff.

Instead, he dragged the material over my head.

One second, I was staring at his shirt, at his stomach, at that expanse of skin, and the next I was covered in fabric that smelled of him, his hands tugging it into place, manipulating my arms, tucking them into the sleeves.

It was warm and there *was* a hint of mint in the fibers...and it was fucking wonderful to be surrounded by him.

Even better than the fantasies that crowded my head in the middle of the night.

Even better—

"And I know they tipped," he murmured, his voice just as warm as the material, just as rough as his hands. "It's still for you, anyway."

My eyes flew to his. "It's too much," I whispered.

"Keep it."

"I can't."

"You work too much," he whispered back. "*Keep it.*"

My eyes drifted away from his, inadvertently closing down, avoiding the argument. My gaze caught on a dent in the wall. It had been patched over and painted, but the surface wasn't perfectly flat.

Trauma did that.

Busted through barriers, left marks and divots, and sometimes it even took chunks out that had to be filled in and smoothed over.

But even repaired, it was never the same, never exactly like it had been before.

I'd had repeated trauma.

The repairs were too great.

I was held together with duct tape and glue and pure *will*.

I didn't have it in me to trust again.

"And you sleep too little," Cas murmured, brushing a thumb beneath one of my eyes. And then the other.

I shuddered because despite all of those thoughts swirling through my head, all the reasons to avoid this man...his touch felt good.

"And you're cold." His hand lowering, his other joining in, both rubbing lightly along the outsides of my arms, using friction and his body heat to try to warm me.

But I didn't need it. I wasn't shivering because I was cold.

I was shivering because I was burning up inside.

"I'm not cold."

"Then why are you shivering?" he asked.

My gaze shot back to his, cheeks blazing, and I knew he understood what my body was betraying because fire entered *his* gaze, blazing through the forest of his irises, sparking and spreading.

An inhale.

Mine.

Maybe his.

All I knew was that time seemed to have stood still. Every molecule in the air arrested, settling over us in a quiet sort of peace that shouldn't have been possible.

We were in a bar.

I was at work.

But in that instant, it was only me and Cas and my body wrapped in his warmth, his scent in my nose. Longing and need and all those dreams that I allowed myself to have in the deep of night. The fantasies that I would never allow myself to have in my *real* life.

Except my fantasy was standing right in front of me.

And it was better than anything I could have imagined.

Which was saying something because I'd imagined a lot.

"Why are you shivering, gorgeous?" he pressed.

My heart thudded hard against my rib cage. I should stop this, should pocket the money, turn around, and go back to my life.

But...

I couldn't make myself turn away from him.

My chin came up. I leaned a little closer and let myself get lost in the fantasy—for just one moment. "You know why." A whisper. A challenge. Almost a taunt.

One second, his body was separated by mine, a few careful inches between us. The next, he had me pinned against the wall, his torso pressed to mine, palms flat on the wall. "Why?" he rasped, body bending, head dropping, nose to my throat, not shy about the fact that he was inhaling deeply.

Jealousy coiled in my belly. He got to smell. I didn't.

Of course, I was wrapped in his sweatshirt that I'd decided I was never giving back, covered in his scent—

Teeth on my skin.

I sucked in a breath.

He flicked out his tongue. "Why?" he asked again.

My mind threatened to short out, but I liked this, liked his hold, his body close, his mouth. Stupid, but...I liked it, and suddenly, I didn't care about all the very logical reasons I should keep my distance and—

Ethan.

I thought about my *son.*

Cold water on my desire.

And somehow Cas sensed it.

Because the next instance he was straightening, his body separating from mine. Now, I shivered for real, and yeah, part of it was from missing the heat of him, but the rest was a result of the chill from reality washing over me. From risking doing something that would put Ethan in harm's way.

"Bye, gorgeous," he murmured. "Sleep tonight, yeah?"

I nodded.

Then he was pushing out through the door.

Then...he was gone.

But even though that stung—him leaving, what I couldn't permit myself to have—I allowed myself a small smile.

Because when he'd been close, I'd slipped the hundred in the pocket of his jeans.

FIVE

Cas

CRINKLE.

Frowning, I glanced down at the jeans I'd just dropped onto the floor of my closet, then bent and scooped them back up.

If there was one thing my mom was proud of instilling in me, it was the fact that I cleared my pockets before I did my laundry (of course, she'd be equally upset that my laundry typically spent most of its time on the floor *near* my hamper and not *in* it, but I couldn't hope to meet all of her high expectations all of the time).

But that habit of clearing pockets meant that I was usually aware when I had shit in them.

And I knew that I'd taken out my cell, my wallet, that I hadn't picked up any receipts at the bar.

Mostly because I'd been outmaneuvered when it came to paying for dinner.

Next time I'd pay.

For now, I reached into my front right pocket and—

Cursed.

The hundred-dollar bill.

"Stubborn woman," I muttered, crumpling the money into a ball before immediately smoothing it out again, folding it carefully and setting it on a shelf in my closet, then stripping down. I wanted to take a shower before going to bed. The hot water always settled my mind, helped me sleep.

Not that it would happen easily.

Because Jules returning my money?

Them's was fighting words.

Well, I was going to fight back, going to make her accept this money.

Fuck knew she'd more than earned it with the hustle she showed on a regular basis. Plus, I knew exactly how far a hundred dollars could go when things were tight. They weren't for me any longer—tight, that was. I made enough and was smart with saving and retirement funds and investments so that I would be set for the rest of my life.

My parents were, too.

I'd made certain of *that*, despite their recalcitrance to accept my help.

Further that, I'd ensured that my siblings were secure as well. As the oldest of four, that was my responsibility, especially considering that my youngest sister had just finished college and was working while she considered her options for more school, my little brother was working while getting his graduate degree, and my other sister was getting married.

I'd paid for Sam and Margot's tuition (and Kathy's when she'd gone) and would have paid for Kathy's wedding, but my parents were refusing to accept my contribution.

So, I was going to give it Kath as a wedding present.

Maybe she'd use it as a down payment for her house, or to

go on a killer honeymoon—God knew that none of us had been on vacation enough growing up. We'd all been worked too hard for too long.

Meanwhile, Jules had shoved the money back in my pocket. *Christ.*

Women, man. They were confusing as fuck.

Of course, as the guys liked to tease me, I sucked at understanding women, so maybe it wasn't a surprise that I was often left in confusion.

Like how a woman who was sweet and lovely could turn into a raving banshee who didn't respect boundaries. Or another who said she wanted to be in a relationship, but then immediately tried to pick up a teammate. Several who'd seen me just as a paycheck, another who'd been beyond clingy and wanted me to pay to let her attend every away game. And Chelsea.

Sweet Jesus.

She was a hundred times worse than *any* of them.

She'd taken crossing boundaries and turned it into an art form.

"Fuck," I muttered, rubbing my forehead as I moved into the bathroom, cranking on the shower, knowing that she'd get the hint soon. Christ, she'd *have* to. I didn't know how to make it any clearer.

Hell, I was convinced that she didn't really even like me.

It was more the idea that *I'd* ended things.

No doubt, she was beautiful and smart. But there'd been a sharp edge to her that had always rubbed me the wrong way, a need for control that had made it clear she wanted me to make her a priority but that the courtesy wouldn't necessarily go the other way.

Fuck, maybe I did have a bad *picker,* as the guys always liked to accuse me of.

Still, it was better that I'd found Chelsea wasn't right for me sooner rather than later—though I'd been dumb for long enough for me to take her to CeCe's, for her to be a bitch to Jules (and yeah, maybe *that* had been the final straw for me, the fact that Chelsea had gone claws out on Jules within two minutes of meeting her). But as the guys liked to point out in the time since she'd been unhappy with me ending things and started showing up at the rink and my house and the practice facility, I was an idiot for bringing her to one of *our* places. One of the spots the team liked to congregate because the staff were cool, and the patrons left us to our beers.

And another place I had to dodge her on the regular.

Soon.

She had to lose interest in me soon. Right? *Right?*

And yeah, that was a slightly hysterical edge to my internal voice. Chelsea didn't want to let go. Jules didn't show any interest.

Though, tonight had been...

It was the first time I'd seen a glimpse that perhaps she'd wanted me—or at least part of her had responded to me, my body, my touch—and she hadn't turned down my sweatshirt, hadn't refused the gesture or offered it back.

Maybe she'd keep it.

Maybe she would wear it to bed...with nothing underneath.

The idea of her sleeping in my sweatshirt, of the warm cotton touching her naked skin, had my cock going hard.

But that wasn't new.

I'd jerked off to the image of Jules more times than she could probably ever guess. My fantasies were never ending.

Slipping into her tight, wet pussy, feeling her clench around me. Licking the tightened buds of her nipples, tasting her skin. Her fingers in my hair, her legs around my waist, heels digging into my ass. What she would sound like when she came.

And all the various places I could *make* her come.

My bed. *Her* bed. The shelves in my closet. The shower. The couch. Hell, my stairs were carpeted. I could set her right on the top step, stroke into her from behind. Or halfway up, her body sprawled over several risers, thighs spread, pussy glistening.

"Fuck," I muttered again, giving into the urge and wrapping my fingers around my cock.

She'd taste sweet. I just knew it.

And maybe she'd be a little shy, need some coaxing to spread her legs, need me to get her wild with need before she'd follow all my orders, her cheeks flushed pink. What I wouldn't give to be the one to turn her to the dark side.

Or maybe she'd take charge.

God knew that she could handle a table of rowdy hockey players without breaking a sweat.

Maybe she'd be the one giving the orders, telling me to fuck her harder or deeper or at a different angle, at a different speed. Maybe she would push me back and climb on top, no hesitation in her actions as she ground down on me, taking me deep into all the tight, wet heat of her, fucking me until we both came hard enough that we couldn't breathe, couldn't think.

I didn't give a fuck which way she chose.

One or the other or both or something different.

I could get off on anything Jules.

Case in point, my orgasm coiling at the base of my spine, exploding out through my body, hot jets of my cum landing in a hand towel I luckily managed to grab in time.

Fucking teenager shit, coming in a hand towel.

Fucking teenager shit, jerking off all the time because I couldn't get the girl I wanted.

And it didn't even help.

My cock was still hard.

I still *ached* for Jules.

"Fuck," I muttered again—apparently the only word my brain could manage to get across my tongue. After cleaning myself up, I strode naked to the closet and made sure that piece of dirty laundry ended up in my hamper (because I wasn't a fucking animal).

Then I ignored my still-erect dick and stomped back into the bathroom, wrenching open the shower door.

Hot water.

Another round of jerking off because I couldn't keep my mind from Jules.

I was going to be chafed if I kept this shit up.

Thankfully, round two got my dick to behave, and I deliberately kept my mind from the stubborn, gorgeous Jules as I got dressed.

But as I started to leave my closet, I saw the money on the shelf.

I grabbed it, set it deliberately on my dresser, right next to my wallet.

Jules could start this fight.

But I was going to damn well finish it.

SIX

"READY, MOM?" Ethan called, his feet stomping across the floor.

And once again, I thanked the universe that we'd found a ground-floor apartment. Keeping on my neighbors' good side would be impossible with the way my little guy stomped around.

Elephants had nothing on him.

And his voice.

Sweet baby Jesus, I loved my son.

But at zero-dark-thirty (okay, at seven-thirty in the morning after I'd worked late), there wasn't enough coffee in the world to make the lack of sleep bearable. His little voice was nails on a chalkboard.

I wasn't a morning person.

I hadn't ever been.

Which had made the late nights with Ethan as a colicky

newborn and later, working at CeCe's, not a trial—or not as much as a typical mom, I supposed.

I could stay up through the night, and do it many nights on end, without turning into a lunatic.

But being coherent for the school drop-off line?

Yeah, that was fucking torture.

Unfortunately, I'd had to learn how to pull it together—couldn't be a zombie while dodging kids and operating a mobile death machine.

"Ready, bud," I called back, wrapping up the piece of toast I'd made for him. Wheat, since I had to throw something healthy in there because his breakfast of choice included copious amounts of butter and cinnamon and sugar.

I would eat when I got back home.

Or maybe I'd pass out in my bed until my alarm went and I had to be coherent for the school *pickup* line.

God, I loved my bed.

I wanted to crawl between the blankets, to sleep for a hundred years.

Either that or for the six hours Ethan was at school.

My son's pounding feet grew closer, and he skidded around the corner into the kitchen, hair mussed, shirt on backward (and swear to God, the kid had a fifty-fifty shot at getting it on correctly, but he chose the wrong fifty percent *every single time*). Ethan grabbed the toast, immediately peeled away the paper towel and took a huge bite, his next words muffled. "Why aren't you wearing your school shirt?"

I was in sweats and a hoodie, no bra. My feet were crammed into my ugly but supremely comfortable UGG knockoff boots. What I *wasn't* in was Ethan's school shirt—which was a whole different brand of ugly and reserved solely for volunteers—an orangey tie-dyed tee that was emblazoned with a dragon and absolutely dwarfed my frame.

"It's Reading Day, remember?"

Oh, fuck.

It *was* Reading Day—or, at least, the day I helped out wrangling kindergarteners through some grade-level books to improve their reading skills.

Which basically meant that it was Torture Day.

I didn't mind being in the classroom (minus the fact that it was *early*), but kids—mine, those in the class—were exhausting and I always left after my time sweaty and exhausted, my mind throbbing.

"Right," I said, thinking quick. "You grab your backpack and hop in the car. I forgot I needed my shirt."

Making sure Ethan actually *did* snag his bag on the way out to the car, I zipped down the hall, ripped off the hoodie, wrestled my boobs—too big, too annoying, too much always in the way—into a sports bra and then grabbed the shirt and yanked it over my head.

Thank fuck I'd done laundry yesterday and didn't have to look for it.

I'd known exactly where it was.

Boots swapped for sneakers, so I didn't sweat my feet off.

A zip-up hoodie covering my torso. My purse from the table in the hall.

The front door locked and my ass in the driver's seat.

Christ. I was already sweating, which was bad enough.

But what was worse?

My bed was going to have to wait.

"Julie?"

I looked up from the stack of books I was organizing by reading level, meeting the gaze of Ethan's teacher.

His expression was serious, and immediately my stomach clenched.

I was a young mom. I'd been judged for it far too often.

Serious expressions from people in authority often meant that I was fucking up.

"Yes, Mr. Philips?" I asked, rising away from the bookshelf, standing to face him.

"Randall," he said. "Please."

I inhaled slowly, forced my exhale to be just as slow, and nodded, but didn't commit to calling him by his first name.

He was just...

A bit too...*something*.

He smiled, eyes drifting to the open door for a moment, presumably checking with a glance on his class, all of whom were currently running their wiggles out on the kinder playground. Then they came back to mine and his volume lowered, his body shifting closer.

Too close for casual conversation at my son's school.

That. That was the something.

And it set off the churning in my gut.

Set my inner radar pinging. No, *alarming*.

I slid a foot back, but he'd boxed me in at the bookshelves, and I didn't have a lot of room to make space between us.

"I happened to notice that Ethan doesn't mention his dad" —his gaze slid down, stopping at my hands, which were clenched tight around the pile of books—"is...are you two okay?"

A seemingly innocuous question.

But I'd been down this road before.

I knew what a Ring Glance felt like, knew that this conversation was heading, imminently, toward disaster.

I was young.

I was decent looking.

There was something vulnerable about me, no matter how hard I fought to weld steel to my bones, to make myself appear capable and competent and having my shit together, that meant men always...did *this*.

Smothering an internal sigh, I slid the books a little higher.

And look at that, his gaze came back to mine.

Almost like I had eyes.

Or magical powers.

"Ethan's dad has never been involved in his life," I said matter-of-factly. "He wasn't interested, and I decided it was better for Ethan to only have people in his circle who truly want to be there."

It had been an easy decision, even though it had shredded through my insides.

I'd been stupid—young and certain our relationship had been something different.

Or, well, something different for me. Because I'd been all in. *I'd* loved Nate with all my heart. He just...hadn't felt the same, and he'd made that fact brutally clear.

See? Young. Stupid.

In love.

And Ethan had suffered because of it.

The guilt that always existed beneath the surface, bubbling up, waiting to boil over, water flowing over the rim of a hot pan, sizzling as it made its way to the stovetop.

But I'd gotten good at bracing, at waiting for it to turn to steam and disappear.

Of course, it always burned me on its way out.

But then again, punishing myself, scalding my insides with that guilt was the only way to bank it.

I'd chosen a man who wasn't kind, who hadn't been interested in being a father, had contested every bit of support I'd asked for, so much so that I'd yet to receive a dollar. It was all currently in a trust, tied up in litigation that continued to cost me money and left me stressed and sad and *angry*. I'd managed to get my hospital bills paid for, at least, because they would have been crippling, but only recently had the results of the DNA test—taken a full two years before—been accepted as coming from an accredited lab. This being a blood test taken after the saliva one hadn't been "gathered properly."

Try explaining to a toddler why I needed to hold him down for a pointless blood draw.

More hurts Ethan had suffered.

As I navigated reports of tersely worded emails and phone calls between my lawyer and his.

We were protected now—legally, I had full custody.

But I was still chasing Nate for child support.

And I probably always would be.

It was a fight I was going to keep up with, though.

The money was Ethan's—or should be, anyway—and hopefully, one day, I'd be able to collect enough to pay for him to go to college or to put a down payment on a house or...whatever he might need it for.

"Ethan is a good kid," Mr. Philips said, and I clenched the books tighter, bracing against his closeness, the familiarity, and I knew—*knew*—that whiplash was going to come my way.

I could feel it in the air.

"Yes, he is," I agreed.

"And you're a good mom." His lips curved. "I can tell, you know." Said like he was bestowing on me the greatest of all gifts —his approval.

That made my skin crawl.

"Well, thanks," I murmured. "I should finish with the books—"

Urgency flaring in his eyes. "I just wanted to ask—"

Multiple screams on the playground.

It made me jump and drew his gaze again, his brows dragging together, and when it came again, he half-turned, opening some space between us, giving me an escape route, and relief slid through me.

Maybe I'd read it wrong?

Maybe I was too cynical, too jaded, too uncomfortable with all men.

Shoving the books on the shelf—and no, they weren't perfectly in order, but I wasn't going to worry about that, not with the alarms still blaring in my mind—I scooted through the opening.

"I'll let you take care of that," I said, waving a hand to the noise that was still continuing.

The screams had been female, so I knew Ethan was fine.

"Julie—"

"Bye, Mr. Philips!" I called, booking it for the door, knowing that running wouldn't solve this, knowing that his interest, his familiarity, was going to become an issue that needed finagling.

Knowing that this was going to become another fucking thing to shoulder.

I hustled down the hall, slipped out through the office, and headed for my car, my eyes prickling.

Because the weights I carried were already so damned heavy.

SEVEN

Cas

"AND OUR COLORS are going to be peach and silver."

That sounded...well, like *something,* but I had been raised with a mom and two sisters. It could be said, I knew a *little* about women—or at least enough about women that I knew to look to Margot and my mom for instructions on how to properly react to Kathy's announcement about wedding colors.

Since they were both nodding vigorously, my mom going so far as to clap her hands excitedly, I smiled too, joined in with the "That sounds great"s of my brother and dad.

They were well-trained, too.

"What are you planning for food?" my mom asked.

"I think we might do a carnival theme," she said. "Corn dogs, pretzels, a flavored popcorn bar, and a whole spread of fried things."

My arteries cried out in worry, even as my belly gave a happy growl.

"And then," Kathy said excitedly. "Johnny suggested a Pop-

Tart bar, and we're going to have those instead of cake. All sorts of flavors and toppings, so it'll be like a sundae bar but with *Pop-Tarts!*"

In case it wasn't obvious, my sister loved junk food.

But her doing jazz hands over Pop-Tarts was *next* level, even for her, and when I caught Sam's eyes through the screen of the video call, it didn't matter how much experience I had being raised with a mother and two sisters, keeping my laughter in was impossible.

Kathy glared at me through the camera. "No Pop-Tarts for you."

I grinned. "You know you love me, and you know I love your food ideas. Even if I'm going to have to do a shit-ton of workouts to make up for it."

"Hmph." Her scowl was adorable. I'd seen it from almost the moment she'd been born, and it was no less cute now that she was a grown woman.

"And you know," I said, "considering the amount of county fairs we attended as children, that I'm down for fried anything"—though my favorite was a fried peanut butter cup—"just like you know that all the strawberry Pop-Tarts are mine."

A sniff. "Maybe we're not getting any strawberry," she told me churlishly. "I'm only getting you brown sugar cinnamon ones."

Fake retching, I glanced at Margot on the screen. "Talk some sense into your sister."

She reclined back onto the couch, video feed bouncing as she got comfortable on the cushions. "Nope," she said with a smirk. "You know brown sugar cinnamon are my favorite too."

I glared.

She blew me a kiss.

"Evil siblings," I muttered. "Picking on your older brother."

"That's how our family shows love," Sam chimed in. "None of the sappy shit."

"Lies!" Margot said. "You're sappier than the rest of us combined."

Sam shook his head. "Not a chance in hell."

"Do I *need* to bring up the book of poetry you wrote after your breakup with Jessica Sullivan?"

Kathy cackled.

I would have been lying if I said I didn't do the same.

"Let's hear more about Kathy's wedding," my mom said before the conversation could devolve further. She glanced toward me on the screen—something she'd only recently perfected because she'd only recently figured out how to get her and Dad on the camera without me and my siblings getting a lovely upshot of her nose. "There will be strawberry Pop-Tarts"—toward Margot—"*and* brown sugar cinnamon"—to Sam —"*and* s'mores, so no more complaining."

Suitably chastised—and, I supposed, suitably provided with the proper amount of Pop-Tart motivation—we shut up and listened to Kathy tell us about the rest of the details she and her fiancé had decided on.

My younger sister was getting married.

Christ, that was wild.

As was the brutal reality that I was single and apparently equipped with a bad picker.

Then we listened to Sam talk about his new job—he was really liking the position and his new manager, and even with school, it was manageable. Margot's update was that she was still slogging through grad school applications while working as a barista and focused on the art of making the perfect latte.

My parents were settled and happy (this being communicated by my mom while my dad—man of few words—sat back and listened).

The only time I had heard my dad say more than a few words was when I had paid off their house. He was equally pissed-off and touched, mostly because after he'd initially refused the money, I had gone around his back and taken care of the remaining mortgage directly with the bank. My parents worked hard. They'd sacrificed for me.

It was easy to make the decision to live a bit smaller than some of my teammates for a couple of years after getting my first big, non-rookie contract (and bonus after winning the Cup).

And it wasn't a sacrifice to live in a decent house and have one nice car (rather than several very nice cars and a mansion).

My life was good.

But seeing the expression on my parents' faces when they'd learned the house was free and clear was a hundred times better.

Which meant that even with Kathy's wedding expenses, they were still going to be able to take a cruise this year.

Something my mom had dreamed of for as long as I could remember.

So, we talked about that (and I managed to sneakily get the name of their travel agent—I'd see what kind of upgrades I could arrange for them) and then it was my turn to be on the hot seat.

"Not much," I told them when they asked me what was new. "Doing some on-ice conditioning, getting ready for the season." I shrugged. "The usual."

"Are you still dating that girl?"

"Chelsea?" I asked.

"The blond one with the pinchy face," Margot supplied.

Yeah, I supposed that sounded about right. Chelsea had made it very obvious when she wasn't pleased...and made my life pretty unpleasant when she wasn't. Now that I thought about that, she hadn't been shy about showing that during the one interaction she'd had with my family, either.

"No," I said. "We broke up."

I didn't miss the relief on multiple faces.

And seriously, my picker *was* broken.

"Anyone else have any updates?" I asked, wanting the eyes off me and onto someone else. *Anyone* else.

Because the woman I really wanted—and probably the first woman my family would actually like, damaged picker or not—wasn't interested in exploring the spark between us.

"Tell me about the woman who's put that look on your face," Kathy said.

"What look?" I went for innocent.

It didn't work.

"The kicked-your-puppy look," Margot said. "I can feel the pathetic through the call."

"Seriously, *this* is how you treat your big brother?" I grumbled. "What happened to respect?"

"I lost it the time I saw you puking up *Three Musketeers* after trying to tell me you could eat a dozen of them," Kathy said matter-of-factly.

Christ.

I'd forgotten about that.

My stomach hadn't, apparently. It churned as the memory tried to surface.

I turned to my mother. "Why do I get the dating inquisition when they all get to talk about other stuff?"

"Because," Margot said before our mom could reply, "we've all heard enough about sticks and pucks and how you like your skates sharpened."

"It's called a radius," I corrected. "And I prefer—"

"Five-eighths," Kathy said, rolling her eyes. "Please save us the time spent waxing poetic about your skate blades and tell us when our highly successful and attractive older brother is going to stop playing the field and settle down."

If they only knew.

That I *did* want to settle.

That I wanted to find that settle with Jules, or at least to explore what we had together. Because she was funny and smart and worked her ass off. Because she was beautiful and I'd caught her gaze on me as often as my eyes were drawn to hers.

But I didn't want to talk about Jules.

I understood why she'd turned me down—well, I didn't *really* understand it, not when her stare tangled with mine so often, not when she was always friendly and stopped by my table to say hi and chat, even if I wasn't sitting in her section. Those brief moments of conversation only lasted a couple of minutes, but they were the best parts of my day.

My week.

And she didn't want to date me.

So, none of it really mattered.

Not the conversations, nor the way our gazes caught hold. Not the way my body focused on hers whenever she was in the vicinity, an inner Jules Detector that had my fingers itching to touch, my pulse speeding, my nose searching for any scent of her. Not even the way she intrigued me, made me desperate to know every secret and memory and thought in her mind.

That made me sound like a sociopath.

But I couldn't help it.

Jules was a puzzle I wanted to solve.

All of that was a fact that I didn't want my family to know.

The nosiness, the pressure from them if they did...fuck—

No. I'd rather talk about wedding colors—and all the merits of the various shades of peach—than share the fact that I wanted a woman who didn't or couldn't or *wouldn't* want me back.

So, I tried to come up with an answer that would prevent any further questions.

Unfortunately, despite my trying, I was drawing blanks.

"I'm not dating anyone," I said.

And the tone was wrong.

All wrong.

Which was why every single pair of eyes on the screen suddenly focused on me with laser precision.

Damn. I'd set off *all* of my family's internal alarms.

"But you *want* to be dating someone," Margot said softly. "The woman who put the kicked-puppy look in your eyes."

Fuck.

Because I did.

I wanted it so badly that I was jerking off a good three times a day, fantasizing about her for most of the rest of the day. And even *when* I managed to stop thinking of my dick, I was still thinking of Jules—planning all the questions I'd ask her if I got two uninterrupted minutes with her at my table. I wanted to know about her son, her past, her family, her dreams and hopes, if she'd ever been to a hockey game...and if not, if she'd like to go.

Which was back in date territory and crossing that barrier she'd set.

But maybe she wanted to take Ethan, wanted to take her son, and—

"It's clear you do want to be dating someone," Kathy said gentle too, joining in with Margot for their familiar one-two attack to dig out every juicy detail. "Dish, big bro."

Was it too much to think *fuck* again? It had been a constant litany in my mind of late.

Probably it was too much, but I thought it again, anyway.

"Kath—"

"*Dish*," she repeated.

"Baby," my mom said, and hell, I was a grownup and she could still make my feel like a little kid. "You might as well just tell us."

I glanced at Sam, who just lifted his brows, telling me that he wanted to me to *dish* too. A look at my dad told me the same —well, my dad didn't want me to *dish*, but he wasn't going to wade in and save me either. He was too familiar with his wife, his daughters.

"Traitors," I muttered.

Sam smirked.

"*Cas*," Kathy pressed.

"What?" I asked loudly, taking the only out I had. "Sorry, I think my connection is bad—"

"Don't you dare," Margot began.

"Luca!" my mom exclaimed, telling me I was in big trouble because she'd used my first name and not the nickname bestowed on me almost at birth.

"You're all frozen." I tapped the screen, all in on the deception. "Sorry, I can't hear—"

I hit the button to end the call, closed my laptop.

There would be hell to pay for my avoidance.

Without a doubt.

EIGHT

Jules

HIS LITTLE LEGS were practically a blur as he barreled toward me, backpack bouncing as he ran, his metal water bottle swinging from side to side in his hands.

It was only a few weeks into school and the bottle looked like it had been shoved into a garbage disposal.

Repeatedly.

Dings and scratches marred the sides, and the bottom was so dented it would be a miracle if it survived to Christmas break.

How my child managed to destroy a supposedly indestructible bottle was one of those mysteries of the universe that would never be solved. I loved Ethan, but the kid was definitely a bull in a china shop.

Case in point?

His run toward me ending up in a tangle of limbs, backpack straps...and that bottle flying out of his hand to collide with the concrete and roll steadily down the path in front of school.

Well, I supposed that solved the unsolvable mystery of Ethan's water bottle.

Moving toward him—steadily, but not running because he wasn't crying and didn't appear to be injured—I went to pick up the water bottle—

"Julie."

Christ.

It was Mr. Philips.

I'd successfully avoided him since the uncomfortable conversation from a couple of days before.

Not any longer, apparently.

I snatched the bottle, glanced up to see that at least he'd helped Ethan up and hadn't just stepped over my child like he was an obstacle to bypass.

Ethan liked him, but he'd only been in school for weeks, and there was a real possibility that the shine would wear off—especially if Mr. Philips couldn't take a hint, and then it affected how he interacted with my son.

Then I'd have to go mama bear and things would get complicated.

Mr. Philips squeezed Ethan on the shoulder as I straightened. "All good, Ethan?"

A nod. "Thanks." Ethan spotted me. "Mom!"

Then his arms were wrapping around my waist, and he was squeezing the air out of me...and it was glorious.

My bull in a china shop, *my* little boy who was growing too fast, *my* loving and generous son was in my arms and hugging me tight.

God, I loved him.

More than anything.

"Thanks for the assist," I told Mr. Philips cautiously, squeezing Ethan as he rotated in my arms.

"No problem." A smile that almost made me forget the

earlier awkwardness. "I know a little of what it's like to have two left feet." He ruffled Ethan's hair, then glanced up at me, lips still curved. "How are you?"

His question brought that awkward right back into the forefront of my mind.

"Can I talk to you privately for a moment?" He tilted his head slightly to the side.

"Umm..." *Shit.* I was going to have to do this, wasn't I? Make it clear nothing could happen. A stifled sigh as I caught the determination in the teacher's eyes. Yup. I was going to have to do this. Scanning the area, I spotted one of Ethan's friends running like a madman on the grass. "Can you go play with David, bud? I just need to talk to Mr. Philips for a minute."

Who would hopefully get the clue that he was only Mr. Philips and would *always* only be Mr. Philips.

"'Kay," he said and dropped his backpack and bottle at my feet before running off.

Yup. That was definitely how his water bottle looked like it had been gnawed on by a gremlin.

Mr. Philips stepped off the path, toward a section of grass that wasn't full of people.

Gut churning, I followed him, trying to fill my mind with ways to let him down easy, even as I spiraled with all the ways this was certainly going to go wrong.

I was going to have to be in the principal's office. Or speak to the school board. Or—

"Thank you for talking with me," he said. "I hope I'm not keeping you."

Except from running away from this conversation I wanted to avoid.

Which I was quite desperate to do.

"It's fine," I said. "What did you want to discuss?"

He stepped a little closer, managed to rattle my world further while simultaneously making me realize I'd been wrong about the interest I'd thought he had. "It's about Ethan's dad."

My MIND still spinning a few hours later—and not because Mr. Philips had been too familiar and made me uncomfortable, but because of what he'd told me—I still had to go to work.

Still had to *focus* on work.

I'd gotten Ethan home and settled with an afternoon snack. We'd blazed through his homework (twenty minutes of reading and one math handout). Then I'd sent in *my* homework for the online classes I was completing.

Then dinner was ready, and Ethan was bathed and in jammies and ready to spend a couple of hours with Mary, who'd showed up at my door just as I had finished changing into my CeCe's uniform—that consisting of a CeCe's T-shirt, a pair of dark wash jeans that hid any inadvertent stains, and comfortable shoes.

I'd answered the door, said goodbye, gotten my last Ethan Hug of the night, and left, confident that Mary—who I'd met a few years before in an English class we'd both been taking at the local community college, and had moved in next door the previous year—had Ethan covered.

She was invaluable, short on cash as most college students, and Ethan loved her.

I thought she was great, as much family as anyone had ever been.

Mary would put Ethan to bed and stay at the apartment until I got home, spending her time studying, watching trash TV, and then eventually passing out on the couch until I arrived and woke her up to walk her next door.

All of this was the normal routine, one I could complete with my eyes closed. But this afternoon, it was a routine I'd completed with my mind a jumbled mess of thoughts, and considering my brain was still full of worry, I didn't think the evening and post-shift one would go any better.

What the hell was I going to do?

What—

Loud laughter shook me out of my head, thankfully before the soda I was refilling could spill over the edges of the glass. Quickly, I pulled it away from the machine, set it on the tray. Focused.

Because the Breakers were in the house tonight.

And their women were in the house tonight.

And it meant...that *Cas* was in the house tonight too.

Also, why did I suddenly sound like I was a DJ in a club?

Everybody throw your hands up! Sexy Breakers players in the house tonight!

Losing it. Clearly, I was *losing it.*

And I needed more sleep and to spend less fantasizing about a certain hockey player and his yummy ass and his sexy, soft, rasping voice murmuring in my ear, his rough hands on my skin, his mouth brushing my skin, and—

Cold liquid on my hand.

"Shit," I muttered, yanking the next glass I'd been refilling away from the machine and using a paper towel to wipe the sides. Disgusted with myself, I set it on the tray, washed my sticky hands in the sink.

"Need some help?"

It was a question voiced in a sexy, soft rasp I instantly knew, a rasp that slid down my skin. Phantom lips trailing over my abdomen and belly and *lower.*

My head jerked up, eyes colliding with Cas's.

They immediately filled with concern. "Are you okay?"

I tore my gaze away, went back to refilling glasses. "Yeah," I said. "It's just been a long week. Did Smitty decide to get another pitcher after all?"

Silence.

For so long that I found myself looking up, my stare tangling with Cas's again.

And braced.

He wasn't going to let this go. Men never did.

They pushed and demanded and pounced when I wasn't prepared, tearing me to shreds, leaving me wounded and trying to pull myself back together and—

"Yeah," he said so softly I almost couldn't hear it. "Smitty decided he wanted another pitcher."

For a second, I couldn't respond.

Because I had been mentally preparing for that argument surely heading my way.

But Cas didn't rush me as I slowly computed his response, just kept leaning against the bar, one strong forearm resting on the wooden surface. Springy, dark hair covering the olive skin there. Not so much that meant he'd be a full-on grizzly every-where else, but enough that there was no doubt he was a *man*. Ropy muscles, thick blunt fingers I'd like to slip between my thighs, press up into the slick heat of my pussy, fucking me fast and hard before he fucked me with his—

His hand flexed, those fingers pressing against the bar top, and I jerked again.

Shit.

I didn't need another thing to fantasize about in the middle of the night.

"Want me to come back?" he asked.

"N-no," I stammered, putting those fingers out of my mind, snagging a pitcher and filling it, forcing myself to focus so it wasn't all foam. That only took a few moments, and I used that time to stop thinking about him finger fucking me into glorious oblivion.

Because it would be glorious.

I had no doubt about that.

I shivered, clenched my teeth together until my jaw protested.

Then rounded the bar, intending to bring the pitcher over to the guys' table, so focused on trying to stop myself from fantasizing about Cas, I nearly mowed down the man himself.

"Whoa," he said, catching my arms, steadying me—and then the pitcher—before I could dump it on both of us. "I was going to offer to carry it over for you," he said, dropping the hand still on my arm and the other that had steadied the pitcher. "Since I'm heading out anyway."

That didn't make sense.

The exit wasn't by the bar, by *me*, but I wasn't thinking all that closely with him so near, with the scent of him in my nose, the imprints of his touch on my skin.

The heat of his body wrapping around mine.

Oh.

That was his hand, settling on my waist, sliding up to my arm, my hand, tugging at the pitcher.

"Here," he murmured. "I'll take it."

I inhaled.

This was...strangely intimate considering the surrounding people, the noise, the complete lack of privacy. And yet, just like before, when we'd talked, our bodies close in the hallway, I felt as though we were alone, the rest of the world a blurry background.

"Jules?" he murmured, his voice very close to my ear.

"Hmm?"

God, even his beard was sexy.

How was his beard sexy?

Another tug and the pitcher disappeared from my hand.

Fingers brushed lightly over my cheek. "Try to get some sleep tonight, yeah?"

I inhaled. Sharply.

Not because of the soft, rasping question.

But because of the touch. That light caress that had lightning bolts sliding through my veins. I was still reeling from that as he spun and walked away, holding that pitcher, giving me a view of that glorious hockey player's ass.

An image that was burned into my mind for the rest of my shift, right along with that soft, rasping question echoing in my ears.

An image and a question that firmly made their places at home inside my mind when I closed out and found a slightly crumpled hundred-dollar bill tucked into the front pocket of my jeans.

I didn't have to think hard to know where it came from—or *whom*, rather.

None of my big tabs had paid in cash.

And none of the others had paid in bills that large.

It was Cas's.

Amusement and annoyance tangled.

But all I could think was this was war.

NINE

Cas

"COME ON, SPARK," I muttered when my elderly ass dog tried to stop and sniff another freaking bush.

Spark was Sparky.

My golden retriever, who was closing in on sixteen and was still one of the best presents my parents had ever gotten for me.

All I'd wanted growing up had been a dog.

But I'd stopped asking when I'd gotten old enough to understand that pets were expensive—food, vet bills, toys, treats, beds, crates, collars, leashes, and all the other paraphernalia that came with them.

Then, for my thirteenth birthday, my parents had packed us all up in the car and we'd met a woman from our father's work at a park. Her dog had played Houdini, escaped the yard, and returned home knocked up. A few months later, they'd had eight tiny puppies they needed to find homes for, and...

I had gotten first choice.

The shock and happiness from that day still filled a large part of my heart.

Because Sparky was the shit.

Even *if* my thirteen-year-old self had let then seven-year-old Margot give him a dumbass name.

Spark ignored me, taking his time sniffing that bush, clearly discovering myriad new smells he'd never been lucky enough to have in his nose before despite his sixteen years' experience of sniffing. Cat piss. Dog piss. Flowers. Bugs. Maybe a soda dumped in the plant so someone didn't have to carry it to their car. Bird poop. Dirt. Other shit that dogs got off on, if Sparky's intent smelling was any indication.

God, I remembered when I'd barely been able to hold back my exuberant pooch, when Spark had made it his mission to pull my arm out of the socket to get sniffing.

Hell, being dragged around by my pooch in my teenaged years was the best off-ice training I'd ever had.

Now, at fifteen (well, sixteen next month, since at this point I rounded up), Sparky was moving much slower.

Mostly, I coaxed him around the block and then called it good.

Less exercise.

More of Sparky sniffing himself into blissful oblivion.

Eventually, Spark managed to tear himself from the bush, and we continued meandering our way down the sidewalk at a snail's pace, eventually turning into the park. Soon enough the path would be cold and covered with snow, but today, with the sun shining and the sky a clear blue overhead, it was filled with kids running on the grass, clambering on the playground equipment. Some adults were tossing a football around. A soccer practice was being held in the distance.

Spark's ears pricked, but where once, he would have been

quivering to join in on the excitement, today he wagged his tail a couple of times and ambled toward another bush.

Which was when I heard it.

"I know, bud." Her voice slid like fingers down my spine. "But we can't always get everything we want."

A knot in my gut, that statement hitting too close to the childhood memories of my parents struggling. Those memories and how they'd still found a way to give me so much clung to the edges of my mind, and that paired with the *voice*—a voice I knew as well as any of my teammates, as any of my family, had my fingers tingling.

I looked up from where I'd been watching Spark sniff his thousandth bush and watched Jules walking toward me with a boy who must be her son. The little boy held her hand as he skipped by her side, and I couldn't help but frown as I tried to ferret out the resemblance.

The boy was stocky where Jules was thin. His hair was dark, a deep brown that rivaled my own, not the light blond of Julie's, and his skin tone more olive than the peach of hers.

But when they came closer, the resemblance became obvious.

His coloring was similar to mine, but his face was Julie's.

They had the same lips and eyes and nose. They even wore the same expression—serious as it was. Drawn brows, flat mouths, though only Jules had the shadows in her eyes.

Fuck that shit.

The thought rippled through my mind like a rock splashing into a lake, crashing into the water with a huge impact, radiating fault lines, and then, eventually, settling to the bottom, an ever-present reminder.

I was processing that feeling, the intense *promise* that had just sewn its way into my soul, when Spark barked.

Drawing both of the Blackstars' attention.

The serious expression disappeared from Jules's face, the shadows evaporated, and her lips turned up as Sparky pulled at his leash, tail wagging, a glimpse of that puppy energy from long ago.

"Look, Mom!" her son cried. "It's a golden retriever!"

Now those lips turned up higher. "Yeah, bud, it—" Her words cut off as her gaze rose, sliding up, reaching mine, her smile and pace faltering so abruptly, it was almost comical.

"And he's got a handkerchief!"

Of course he did.

Sparky needed to look good when he went out, and his bandana was quite dapper in my opinion.

"Mom!" He tugged on Jules's hand when her feet slid to a stop and she didn't reply. "Mom, *look!*"

Jules *was* looking, just not at Sparky. She was looking at me and, fuck, I could just spend all day doing the same, staring back at her, noting every minute change in her face.

So fucking beautiful.

"Can I pet him, Mom?" Her son tugged at her hand. "Can I?"

"He's friendly," I said, moving toward them, not going to be an idiot—not this time, anyway. I was taking the opening, but I was doing it slowly. Carefully. "If your mom says it's okay," I added quickly. "Spark would love to have some scratches."

Wide guileless eyes pointing up toward Jules. "Mom, *can* I?"

A long moment of quiet. Then her shoulders rose and fell on a breath, and she nodded. "Okay, Ethan, but just do it the slow and steady way that I taught you, all right?" The little boy had started to drop down already, was reaching for Sparky (not that Spark would have minded—he loved people, but he loved kids most especially and didn't mind them crawling all over him), but Ethan stopped at the first mention of his mom's *but*, had waited for her to finish. Then he nodded.

A good kid.

A good mom.

Easy enough to see.

Especially when Ethan slowed down his movements, crouching to Sparky's height and holding out a fist so that Spark could smell.

Once he'd passed Spark's inspection, Ethan began scratching him under the chin.

Which led to Sparky *kissing* him under *his* chin.

Boyish laughter in the air. Ethan's smile wide. Sparky's tail going crazy.

"Why's his face white?" Ethan asked, having moved on to scratching Spark's head and ears (and making the pup practically drool in pleasure).

"He's old," I said, bending down and stroking a hand along Sparky's back, the soft hair parting and flowing through my fingers. "Almost sixteen in human years, which is like ninety in big dog years."

Ethan glanced up at me, eyes wide pools of dark chocolate. "Really?"

"Really," I said solemnly.

"Whoa." Then he was giggling again because Sparky got tired of standing and just plopped down in Ethan's lap, taking them both to the ground.

"Oh, shoot, sorry," I told him, steadying him so he didn't tip backward. "Spark gets tired sometimes."

Brows furrowing, but not seemingly in any discomfort because of the takedown, Ethan hugged Spark and endured more licking before resuming his scratches again. "His name is Spark?" he asked, and it was clear that he didn't approve.

"Sparky," I said. "But don't look at me. I let my sister name him."

"You have a sister?" Ethan asked.

I nodded. "Two."

Ethan scowled. "My mom won't let me have one of those."

The scowl. The statement. Fuck, this kid was going to make me laugh.

"It's not as simple as going to the store and just picking up a sister," Jules said dryly. "As I just told you."

Ethan's scowl didn't ease. "*Chase* has a sister."

Now I *did* chuckle—they were both funny—and earned a scowl from Julie.

"It's not funny, Cas," she muttered, closing the distance between us and bending to scratch Sparky. That bend was... *chef's kiss*. A glimpse of curves, a brush of her body against mine a hint of flowers in my nose.

"Who's Cas?" Ethan asked.

"That's Cas," Julie said, pointing. "I know him from CeCe's. He comes in and eats with his hockey player friends sometimes."

Wide eyes and enough awe in his voice that my ego pulsed with joy. "You play for the Breakers?"

Biting back a grin, I nodded solemnly.

"Whoa," Ethan said again.

My lips turned up. "You like hockey?"

"It's the *best*," Ethan breathed. "Mom sometimes lets me stay up late to watch you guys play."

"Does Mom watch too?"

The wry question had Jules going still beside me.

"Yup! Every game."

I glanced at her, saw her cheeks had gone pink and she wouldn't meet my eyes.

Hmm.

But Ethan had perked up again, clearly already over the awe. "She said I could be a hockey player when I grow up if I practice hard."

My brows rose. "You play?"

A nod that was almost bobblehead-esque. "Yup," he said, the p at the end popping.

I opened my mouth to ask what position, but Jules straightened, announced, "We should let Cas get on with his day." One more scratch to Sparky's head. "Come on, bud."

"Maybe we can go skating sometime," I blurted, seizing the opening less than gracefully (though at least it wasn't a yell this time). "Shoot some pucks around," I said, "and I could give you some pointers if you want."

"Really?" Ethan asked, his eyes wide, the awe back. "You and me?"

"Yeah."

"Whoa."

I grinned, full-out. "How about your mom and I talk it over, okay?" I said, catching a look at Jules's expression and knowing this would take careful navigating on my part. "See if we can come up with a time and day that works."

"*Whoa.*"

That final *whoa* finally unstuck Jules and she laughed softly, shaking her head. Though the look she shot me told me it wasn't *all* amusement in her reaction. She knew she'd been had, at least in this situation. And I, for my part, was trying to not fist pump like a moron at having secured a little more time with her. Plus, Ethan was fucking cute, and I liked kids, liked teaching kids, too. It wouldn't be a trial to spend a little time on the ice with him.

"Come on, bud," she said, brushing off her hands. "Cas and I will talk later. But, for now, you have a date with your homework and then the bathtub."

"Aw, man," Ethan muttered, but he still scooted away from Spark, who seemed to have fallen asleep under his careful attention, and stood up.

Sparky didn't move.

"What are you going to do now?" she asked after I had tugged lightly on the leash, called my pooch's name, and Sparky still didn't bother to so much as open his eyes.

I shrugged and did what I always did when my pup had had enough of his walks—

I bent and scooped Sparky up.

Jules laughed, and it was a real one this time, and it was so fucking beautiful that every nerve in my body shot to attention.

Ethan's eyes were wide, and he said his trademark, "Whoa," though this time it was a whisper.

"You do this *every* time?" she asked.

I shrugged again, albeit with arms full of golden floof. "He's old, and he gets tired."

A softening in her face, one that set my heart pounding.

She leaned in.

I held very, very still.

She pressed her lips to Spark's head and my pooch sighed in contentment.

Then she looked up at me, studied me for a long, long time, and her face went a little soft (I thought, I *hoped*) as she said again, this time softly, "We'll talk later."

A moment after that, she and Ethan had gone.

Only then did I allow myself a tiny fist pump.

"Good boy, Spark," I whispered.

Sparky's tail thumped against my abdomen...and then I took my pooch on the remainder of his walk, Spark's fluffy body warm in my arms.

TEN

Jules

I hefted the bag of trash out through the backdoor of CeCe's.

It was late.

Last call had been made.

And all I wanted was to get home to Ethan.

Plus, if I made it home before three, I wouldn't have to pay Mary for another hour. Mary was awesome, but money was always tight, and with Ethan in big kid school now, things were only going to get more expensive.

My baby was getting bigger.

Which meant the kid was eating more, and he was outgrowing his clothes and his shoes, and—

Every hour I wasn't spending on childcare meant more money to save for clothes and food and hockey gear, and, heaven help me, college one day.

I dropped the trash bag to the ground, tied it off, and then rose on tiptoe to push open the top of the dumpster, having to do it a couple of times before it banged back against the brick wall and stayed in place. Then I waited, eyeing it warily.

It had fallen down and crashed onto my head too many times to count.

But when it remained resting against the wall, I bent for the bag, hefting it up and launching it into the dumpster.

The rim of the dumpster was high, and I was short, so even with practice, that still took me a couple of tries to be successful in my bag launching. A leap had my fingers reaching for the top, sending it crashing down, and I turned back for the bar, brushing my hands off as I went.

All I had left to do was close out a couple of tables, bus a few others, and then I was going to clock out and head home.

Smiling, I tugged open the door to the hallway.

And just that quickly, my smile faded.

I sighed, my head falling back, gaze hitting the ceiling. "Jesus Christ, not again."

Cas's ex.

The woman's name was...Chester? Charmaine? Colette? No. *Chelsea.*

It was Chelsea.

And that woman was a Do Not Engage Zone.

Thus, I didn't say anything, just started to brush by her. I'd learned my lesson the last time Chelsea came in. The daggers that woman had thrown my way...yeah, I didn't want any part of *that* crazy.

I needed to focus on Ethan. On the new clothes he was going to need. The shoes. The hockey gear. The college fund.

All of which would be really difficult to give my son if I got my ass fired.

Talons gripped my arm, yanking me roughly to a halt.

Okay, so truthfully, they were really long *nails*, but they might as well have been claws, digging in with surprising strength considering the lithe, slender blonde seemed to barely weigh a hundred pounds.

God, Cas could have crushed her.

Cas was big and strong and dwarfed *me* and—

Was why I was in this predicament.

Right. *Focus.* Mentally sighing, I tugged at my arm. Unfortunately, the talons didn't release, Chelsea holding firm.

"Let go of me," I ordered, keeping my temper in check.

Barely.

Chelsea's eyes narrowed at my tone, furious sparks in the depths, snapping out, "You need to—"

"I don't *need* to do anything." I was patient. I had to be. I dealt with drunk assholes on the regular, had a kid I loved, but who tried my patience—also on the regular. But I had no room in my life for this kind of bullshit. I knew, *knew* Cas had been clear that he didn't want to see Chelsea anymore—he'd said as much the previous three—yes, *three*—times that the other woman had shown up at the bar when he'd been here with his teammates.

He hadn't played any games.

The last time Chelsea had appeared, he'd given her the blunt truth, and he'd done it in front of the table—instead of walking her into the hallway (where I had shamelessly eavesdropped on them) as he'd done on previous visits.

All that being said, I knew this wasn't some game-playing nonsense from a hockey playboy. He'd been kind on visit one. Firm on number two. Blunt and a little frustrated on visit three. So, there was no reason for Chelsea to be here, thinking she had a chance and generally fucking up my night.

As thus, my temper flared. "Let go," I growled, "and *back* up."

"I said, you need to—"

"Again, ma'am"—too polite, probably, but I was hanging onto the dredges of my patience by my fingernails—"I don't *need* to do anything." I tugged at my arm again. "Except for my job, which"—I glanced down at the talons digging into my skin and sending pain shooting up my arm—"you're stopping me from doing. So...*you* need to back up."

Outrage across a beautiful face. Those nails digging deeper. "Did you just *ma'am* me?"

Wow.

Not touching *that* one.

Instead, I tugged at my arm. Again. And this time, I finally succeeded in freeing myself. Although the action hurt like hell and left me with nail marks—several of them bleeding—on my forearm.

Great. Good times.

Sighing, I stuck out my arm when Chelsea reached for me again, nearly clotheslining the other woman, but at least she slid to a halt...and seriously, there was a whole lot of crazy in the other woman's eyes.

"You need to go home," I tried.

"I *need* Luca—"

My patience snapped.

I was bleeding and my arm hurt and, dammit, it was fucking *late,* and I was tired. I wanted to go home to my bed, wanted to sleep. But, most of all, I wanted to be done with this fucking conversation.

"Who's Luca?" I snapped, my back to the barroom that I needed to get back into...once I could turn away from the clawed woman in front of me.

A talon-tipped finger jabbing in my direction. "*You* know who he is. Cas. You always flirt with him and then he watches you and I *know* you're in love with him." More crazy in those eyes. "I know it and I hate it, and you need to leave him alone because. He. Is. Mine." She pushed against my arm. "*Mine!*"

Apparently, Cas was Luca.

That was...a development.

But I couldn't focus on it. I needed to get home and save that hour of babysitting. Stat. And maybe I also needed to get away from this woman who saw what I had been trying to hide, saw that I wanted Cas, saw...too fucking much.

Because I *couldn't* have it.

Because—

"Jules?" Matt asked from down at the end of the hallway. "You okay?"

And seriously, now I could *kiss* my boss.

"Not really," I called.

A heartbeat later, he was at my shoulder, heat drifting along my spine, soaking in through my clothes, his male scent filling my nose.

"What the fuck?"

I froze.

Because...not Matt.

Oh. *Boy.* That wasn't Matt.

I whipped around, saw Cas standing there. But I'd already known that it was his heat soaking into me, his scent in my nose. Beyond his big, strong frame, I saw that Matt was pushed against the wall, as though he'd been shoved there and was now regaining his balance.

Because Cas had been in a hurry to get to me.

Me.

I inhaled, my insides going melty. They'd begun to thaw at the sight of him crouching in front of Ethan, talking about hockey, offering up his time. That melt had continued when he scooped up Sparky and carried his sleepy pooch just because his dog was tired. And now—

"What. The. *Fuck?*"

Thoughts of melting disappeared.

Because...*shit.*

"Luca, baby," Chelsea began.

I turned back and saw that Chelsea's gaze had gone...oh, man, it sent a prickle down my spine. It had been crazy before, but now it had gone really, *really*...bad. This was not a woman who was going to give up easily.

Not now that her prey was in her sights.

Right. On that note, I was out of there. Clearing my throat, I inched along the wall, said, "I'll just go—"

Cas's fingers wrapped around my wrist, and he started to pull me toward him.

Gently, but angling his body so that I could stand behind him, so that he was between me and the crazy in front of him.

And *that* settled somewhere deep inside, sanded off the rough edges, warmed me, set the melt going again. But before I made it all the way behind him, he went tense and something scary—or *scarier*—emanated from him, filling the air, filling the hall.

On instinct, I froze.

Cas lifted my arm, and the scratches, the blood dripping along my forearm hit the light, suddenly much more visible, suddenly much more obvious, and that scary in the air increased. It looked worse than it was. Yeah, it hurt. For sure. But the dripping wounds looked...ghoulish.

And Cas's face...

Was frightening.

"What the fuck?" he said a third time before he finished drawing me behind him.

"Cas," Chelsea began, "I need to—"

Cas—*Luca*—spun us around, propelling me down the hall, leaving Chelsea still talking behind us, but I barely heard another word because then I was inside the women's restroom and my arm was in the sink, and Cas was turning on the faucet.

Warm water on my skin.

The volume increasing in the hall...then abruptly cutting off.

And all the while, Cas didn't seem to notice.

His fingers were gentle as they smoothed soap over my skin, rinsing it with the warm water. Then washing it again.

Like him shifting me behind him in the hall, talking with Ethan, dealing with Sparky, his actions settled deep.

Even though they probably shouldn't.

Even though they probably didn't mean anything except that he was a good guy looking after someone who was hurt because of him.

Not that I was blaming him (or reading too much into what he was doing, for that matter). I was just acutely sensitive to it because I'd never had that type of care growing. No mom. A resentful, angry father. Getting my booboos gently tended hadn't been something I was used to—

The water shut off.

Cas blotted my skin with a paper towel.

Gently. *So* gently.

"I'm okay, you know," I whispered. This hurt was...nothing.

His head tipped up, gaze hitting mine, eyes still furious.

But he didn't say anything, just kept blotting until my skin was dry. "You need to be bandaged up," he said, shifting my arm from side to side as he stared at my skin, "but I don't think any of these need stitches."

"I'm fine," I told him. "Promise."

His eyes flickering.

His fingers tightening.

Then slowly, *oh* so slowly, he lifted my arm, pressed his lips to the inside of my elbow well above the cuts. After, he inhaled deeply enough that I shivered.

"You're cold," he murmured, lips still on my skin.

I still had his hoodie from the last time he'd presumed that. Hadn't been able to bring myself to return it. Not when I'd begun sleeping in it—wrapped in his warmth, his scent.

"No," I whispered.

My voice was husky.

"No?" he asked, heat in amongst those flickering eyes, and I knew, like last time, he read between the lines, that he knew exactly what I was thinking.

Mutely, I shook my head in answer.

"So, if not cold then..." He trailed his lips a little higher, pushing the sleeve of my tee up, dragging his mouth along the inside of my biceps, and I shivered again. "Warm?" he asked silkily.

Another shake of my head.

"Hot?"

Yeah, okay, *that* was the one.

And even though I didn't nod, I knew he felt the answer. Because I shivered again and then melted against him. Oh God, that was good—his hot, hard body all along mine.

"Hmm." He dropped the sleeve of my T-shirt, pressed his mouth to my throat, tongue flicking out, just the slightest bit, tasting me.

I wished he'd keep doing it, wished he'd taste in other places.

And now I wasn't just hot.

I was *molten*.

"Jules?" he asked against my skin.

My pulse was thundering beneath my skin, leaving me weak and shaking, my thighs trembling, my body slumping against his. I couldn't remember any of the reasons I'd thought exploring this pull between us was a bad idea, why I'd been avoiding it. Not when this was so, so *good.* "Hmm?" I managed.

He lifted his head.

Green, green eyes on mine.

Lips parting—mine, *his*—and he leaned down, his lips growing closer.

Hot breath on my skin. Spicy male in my nose. His mouth right, *right* there.

Oh God, he was going to kiss me.

Oh God, I wanted him to.

Oh God—

His lips hit mine just as...

The door to the bathroom slammed open.

ELEVEN

Cas

I SHOULDN'T BE KISSING her.

But, *goddamn*, was it *good*.

The moment our mouths touched, I'd said fuck all to every boundary and inch of distance she'd erected.

Instead, my mind was focused on the way she felt in my arms, how sweet she tasted, her lush lips pillowing against mine. I was focused on how her face had softened when she'd looked up at me, my arms full of Sparky. I was focused on the way she'd stared at me in the hall, eyes hot when my mouth was at her neck. I was focused—

On the way she kissed me back.

Right *then*.

Her fingers wove through my hair, short nails biting into my scalp, making me want her to score them down my naked back, to dig into my ass as I fucked her deep.

My hand slipped under the hem of her T-shirt, just brushed the silken skin of her belly—

The door flew open, slamming into the wall behind it.

Jules jerked, tearing her mouth from mine, but I didn't have it in me to let her go, not when she still had her fingers in my hair and her body was all flush against mine and—

"Jules?" Matt said.

I didn't like the other man, didn't like the way he looked at Jules, didn't like how close he was. Yes, I was fully aware that was because I was a dumbass considering that Matt wasn't even straight, but I hated that she smiled at the other man, that she touched his shoulder or arm or occasionally hugged him.

She was mine to protect.

She was *mine*.

She—

Slowly, her fingers slid from my hair, her body inched back.

Yup. I hated Matt. Most of all for interrupting.

Especially as I watched her lick her swollen lips, blink her heavily lidded eyes. As I watched her press her hands to pinkened cheeks, and—

As I watched her...back away from me.

Moving toward the door.

I tucked away my temper, glanced up at her boss. "You have a first aid kit?"

Did my voice sound like I'd scrubbed down my vocal cords with steel wool? Maybe. But I wasn't letting Jules get away from me. Which sounded bad, I knew. The problem was that my dick was controlling too much of my mind at that moment. I just didn't have it in me to make it sound good or smooth.

And I needed to make sure she was okay.

Needed to make sure I hadn't just fucked up all that had begun to grow between us.

And maybe I needed to kiss her again.

Focus, Castillo.

I inhaled silently, let the breath out just as quietly.

Then lifted my brows at Matt, wondering if the fucker was going to answer me.

A long, searching look from the other man before he glanced back at Jules, and I knew the moment Matt spotted the scratch marks on her arm because his jaw went tight, a muscle began ticking in his cheek. His gaze flew back to mine, disapproval evident.

Which killed me.

Because that disapproval was well-earned.

My fault the psycho kept showing up here. *My* fault that Jules was hurt.

"I've banned your woman," Matt said icily.

Your woman.

That stung, but it also had my temper spiking, as stupid as that was. I didn't have the right to be pissed, not when I was the cause of this situation. I opened my mouth to grit out some gratitude, but Jules spoke first.

"She's not his woman," she said softly, stopping at the door, her escape pausing, at least for the moment. "And"—she waited for Matt to look at her—"none of this is Cas's fault. We've all heard him make it clear that he's not interested. So, it's *not* his fault Chelsea can't get a clue."

Considering that I didn't believe the reassurance myself, I didn't hold it against Matt when the other man's face didn't soften, when he didn't ply me with a bunch of bullshit about this situation being okay.

It *wasn't* okay.

My drama had bled into Jules's life.

Literally.

Jules had bled.

Because of me.

Clenching my jaw until my teeth practically groaned in protest, I strived for calm. "Where is she?" I asked.

Matt's brows dragged together. "Last I saw, she was screaming at security, and they were threatening to call the cops."

"Don't threaten," I said. "*Call* the fucking cops."

Jules took a step back toward me. "I—"

Finally, a glimmer of approval. Not that I cared. "He's right," Matt said, tugging his phone out of his pocket. "It's time to stop fucking around with this." He shot a glare in my direction. "I'll get security to detain her." His glare intensified. "Get Jules cleaned up and then her ass into a chair."

"But—" Her blond ponytail swung behind her as she started to shake her head.

Matt turned to her, speaking in a way that was far too familiar for my peace of mind. I didn't like that Jules and her boss could communicate with a glance. *I* wanted to be the one she turned to, the one who was staring into those dark brown eyes, sharing the inner thoughts that were currently clouding her gaze. "I've got a friend on the force," Matt said, the words soft. "We'll get you home as soon as possible." His voice dropped until I had to strain to hear him. "I'll pay you for the extra time."

Home.

To her kid.

More guilt ravaged my insides.

A soft sigh, but she nodded and then Matt left (though not before the fucker squeezed Jules's arm).

She turned, started to follow her boss.

My question was a burst of sound as I closed the distance between us. "Is Ethan all right?"

Jules's head jerked, brows forming a tight V as she spun back to face me. "Yeeesss," she whispered, dragging the word out and making it almost a question.

"But it's late," I said stupidly.

Those brows lifted. "*Yes.*" Still drawn out. Still a question.

"And he's little."

Then clarity slid onto her face, relaxing the lines, sending the confusion to the wayside. "My neighbor watches him while I'm at work. If it gets too late, she goes to sleep on the couch."

"Oh," I murmured. "Okay."

Somehow, my stupidity had her face gentling further. "Ethan's okay," she said and laughed softly. "Sometimes I think he likes Mary more than I do."

That couldn't be right.

Jules was the most fascinating woman I had ever met, the most beautiful, the most—

And I needed to get my shit together.

She had paper towels wrapped around her arm, was probably still bleeding from wounds that my ex had inflicted on her, and...I wasn't doing jack shit about it.

Pulling it together, I gently touched my knuckles to her cheek, relief sliding through me when she held still, when she leaned into me for a fraction of a second. Then, of course, she was straightening, retreating, and her skin no longer against mine.

"Where's the first aid kit?" I asked, shifting around her, tugging the door open.

"I'm fine. I can—"

"Where's the kit, gorgeous?"

Eyes on mine. Her lips parting slightly on an exhale. "In the kitchen," she murmured.

"Okay," I said, sweeping an arm forward, silently gesturing for her to proceed me out. "Bandages. Sprite. Talking to the police. Then home and sleep."

She stared at me, not moving, not saying anything, so I dared to slide my arm around her shoulders, dared to touch her again, was thankful that she leaned in again, when she allowed herself to be tucked against me.

I led her down the hall.

Into the barroom, which was now empty, the lights dim.

Guided her forward, led her into the kitchen, and propped her up on a stool. Thankfully, the kit was bright red and mounted to one of the walls (thus, easy to spot) so once I was sure she was steady, I opened it, started to pull out some bandages.

But when I went to put on the first one, she placed her fingers on my wrist, the touch scorching up my arm, burning a path right down to my cock.

"Wait," she said.

My tending or my cock?

One was a little easier to control than the other.

"They'll need to take pictures," she said softly, answering the question. "There's no point in covering them." She forced a smile, but it wasn't real in the least, not when her eyes were full of dark, of shadows, of *pain*. "Plus, I like my arm hair," she said, still smiling, still faking, making the light tone she'd adopted ring all too false. "I'd like to avoid waxing by Band-Aid."

"Don't," I whispered, setting the bandage down and carefully linking our fingers together.

Her brows in that adorable V again. "Don't what?"

I brushed my thumb over the inside of her wrist. "You don't have to pretend with me, gorgeous."

TWELVE

Jules

HOW THE FUCK he could tell I was pretending to be okay, I didn't know.

I also didn't like it.

Many a year had gone into building my mask and no one was allowed to see through it, thank you very much.

He brushed that slightly rough thumb over my wrist again, making me have to clench my jaw so that I didn't shiver.

Okay, so I failed at the whole not shivering thing.

Which, of course, he noticed, releasing my wrist, leaning back and started to strip off the sweatshirt he was wearing.

Goody, my inner demon thought. *Another sweatshirt to steal.*

Then my inner demon cackled because one, it wanted more stripping, and two, it really liked that with his movements, Cas's shirt lifted, giving me a glimpse of skin, of his flat abs.

I sucked in a breath, but then I was assaulted by the heat of him, the *power of him* as he carefully tugged the sweatshirt over my head, gently moving my arms into the sleeves, slipping my hands through the cuffs. Just like before, my head spun when I was surrounded by his scent. Floating up into my nose, covering up the remnants of the odor of heavy bar food, of the busy kitchen that rarely ever stopped being frantic from open to close and reminding me of spice and man and the forested mountains that were in Cas's eyes.

My pussy clenched.

And seriously, *what the fuck was that?*

I didn't do need and desire and *men*. Remember?

When I got the occasional itch—rare, because I existed in a state of exhaustion that only occasionally required me buzzing friend to help scratch it—I definitely didn't seek out men. For one, I spent too much time away from Ethan as it was. For another, I wasn't willing to let another man into my body.

Not after it had all gone so wrong after I'd ended up pregnant—

And...*nope.*

Not what I needed to be thinking about right then.

But what excuse could I give to throw him off my track? I inhaled deeply, holding it for long enough that my lungs began to burn, that my head began to swim. I was tired, that was it. Tired and emotional and just...upset that his ex had gone full-on eagle talons on me.

Yeah.

That last one.

Except, when I opened my mouth to spit out that excuse, to spew the others, he slowly lifted his hand, his thumb brushing against my lashes.

To my horror, I realized that there was a tear there.

That somehow some of the emotions I kept so carefully bottled up inside me were escaping, and worse, that they were manifesting themselves in tears.

Cas leaned in.

I sucked in another breath, more emotions, more roiling.

Because the kiss in the bathroom? It had been the best I'd ever had. *Ever.*

His lips hit my forehead. "I'll be right back."

Then he was backing away from me, slipping out through the swinging door, leaving me in the quiet kitchen.

I heard glasses clink, the rattle of ice, the swoosh of the soda machine, and it didn't surprise me in the least when he pushed back into the kitchen, a glass filled to the top with Sprite, bubbles skating up the insides, bursting at the top. He placed it in my hand.

"Drink."

A soft order.

And then he was rooting through the bag again. Considering all the bandages were on the steel countertop and the antibiotic ointment was sitting next to it, there wasn't really anything I needed.

Then he held up the small packet of ibuprofen and my heart squeezed tight.

How he knew my arm was beginning to throb, I didn't know. Or maybe he was just assuming that the gouges had to be hurting...because that was what any normal person would assume. It wasn't anything special about me or him or our situation.

He just was a thoughtful human being.

That was all.

Except then he paused, the packet grasped in between fingers and thumb. "Have you eaten tonight?"

And right on cue, my stomach grumbled.

I *had* eaten—Matt had shoved something at me during the beginning of my shift, convinced that I never ate enough.

A few years ago, when I'd first gotten a job here, that might have been right.

Things had been *Tight*, with italics and a capital T, because between the move and medical bills and getting my apartment set up and childcare and security deposits and—

Yeah, I'd skipped more than a few meals.

Thus was the life of a single mom who seemed to make a career out of getting fucked over by men.

"I ate earlier. I'm sure it'll be fine," I said, holding my hand out for the packet.

Cas shoved it into his pocket, then turned away from me and moved to the big walk-in fridge. Curious, I didn't protest, just sat there and watched him survey the contents for a long moment before he reached in and...

Pulled out an apple.

That hit the counter next to him and then he was reaching up to the top shelf, shirt riding up again and making more clenching happening between my legs.

For fuck's sake.

I needed to get a grip, but it was hard as hell when his scent was surrounding me, when I was fascinated by his movements, by what he was going to do next.

A plate on the counter. A cutting board next to it.

The apple was in slices in a few seconds.

Then he was scooping into a jar he'd retrieved from the top shelf, filling a little ramekin that he set on the plate. More searching, reaching for a small container from Matt's rack of spices.

Before I could figure out what it was, he'd used it and put it back, was picking up the plate and walking over to my stool.

"Eat," he ordered softly.

My gaze went to the plate, simple slices of apples arranged

neatly in a circle, the ramekin filled with peanut butter. I leaned in, sniffed.

He'd topped the apples with cinnamon.

Just a little.

Oh *shit*.

My heart did that squeezing thing again.

No one—outside of Matt—took care of me. *No* one. It wasn't Ethan's job, and I was going to make damned sure that he never expected it to be. My father had stopped any care the moment he'd found out I was pregnant, and any protection or guidance or *love* before that had been strictly bare minimum and loaded with resentment.

Don't die care.

Food in the fridge. A bedroom and clean clothes (that latter at least until I'd turned eight and had started doing my own laundry). Shoes on my feet. Doctors and dentist appointments once a year until I could schedule them myself. Heat in the house. Hot water. A TV that, more often than not, was blaring a sports game.

Blaring a *Sierra* game.

I shoved that memory down, not willing to go there.

Because if I hadn't been close with most of the local guys who played hockey, hadn't worked my ass off in the rink where they'd practiced, renting out skates and serving concessions and generally coordinating chaos, I would have thought all hockey players were assholes.

But they weren't.

Hell, most of them *were* nice.

Like Lake Jordan—my only true friend growing up—and the man who'd later been the only reason I'd been able to make a life in Baltimore for me and Ethan in the first place. He'd given me means to make the move, encouraged the distance and fresh start. He'd even helped me find a place to stay until I got on my feet, and had made the connection with Matt, who was the son of a family friend, so I had a way to provide for me and Ethan.

Lake was a good person, a good man who had wanted to do more for me. But...I had too many memories, too much pain linked to him, to the past and present he represented. So, I'd had to let him go, had to pull back and limit our communication.

Plus, his career had been taking off, and he didn't need me to drag him down and...I couldn't be tied to a hockey player.

And...now I had found myself mixed up with hockey players all over again.

Smitty and Oliver and Raph and—

Cas.

Cas who'd sliced apples and sprinkled cinnamon and scooped peanut butter and...

And it was just who *I'd* picked who'd been an asshole.

The rest of them were good.

Fingers on my wrist, bringing me back into the present, to the big, beautiful man with soft eyes watching me. "Eat," he ordered again and then he lifted a slice of apple to my lips.

My lungs inflated. "Cas—"

He slipped the piece between my parted lips, taking advantage of me speaking, and I bit down, the juicy, ripe fruit bursting to life on my tastebuds.

I chewed, swallowed. "Cas—"

He simply dipped the slice into the peanut butter, scooped up a dollop, and shoved the fruit into my mouth again.

Another bite.

The tart and sweet interspersed with the creamy nuttiness of the peanut butter.

God, it had been a long time since I'd had something like

this, and while it was a simple snack, it was delicious and filling and—

I couldn't lie.

What I like most about it was that Cas had made it for me. I liked that *he* was feeding me.

I should stop him, should feed my damn self.

But for some reason, I didn't...or couldn't...or...

Maybe tonight I didn't want to take care of myself.

Just for tonight.

THIRTEEN

Cas

IT TOOK everything in me to not kiss the juice that had turned her mouth into a glistening temptation, to not lean in and taste the mix of tart and sweet on her tongue.

She was hungry.

That was the only thing that stopped me from kissing her a few minutes before, from kissing her in that moment—the fact that her stomach had rumbled, that she was hungry. She worked too hard and barely took breaks and I hardly saw her eat. Plus, she was hurting and needed the medicine. And to take it, she needed something in her stomach.

So, I kept feeding her apple slices dipped in peanut butter.

Because I couldn't make the cuts disappear.

But I could get food in her belly, soothe her hunger. I could do that one small thing for her.

She was just finishing the final slice of apple coated in peanut butter when the door to the kitchen pushed open and her boss and a cop walked in. Matt's eyes narrowed at me as the police officer strolled toward us, pad and pen in hand, expression serious.

I hated that the softness that had crept into Jules's body immediately disappeared.

She was tense, her body going stiff next to me, and—ah, the hell with it—I slid an arm around her shoulders and drew her against me. Something her boss really didn't like, considering that the other man's scowl was fierce and intense and—

"Can you tell me what happened?" the officer asked.

Jules recounted her interaction with Chelsea (and seriously, for fuck's sake, how was the other woman so fucking *dumb?*). But any amusement that I might have felt—and it was damned limited in the first place—dissipated when I heard how Jules had gotten those marks.

Chelsea was a fucking bitch.

So, I sat there seething as the officer finished with the statement. I figured that I was going to have to convince her to press charges, but she didn't argue when the officer asked, just agreed, and held out her arms so that pictures could be taken of the marks.

Which meant she'd straightened away from me, stood so that I couldn't hold her any longer.

But she'd let me hold her for a time.

So that was...something—it was *more* than something. It was...*right.*

Matt huffed out a sigh, reached between us to snatch up the plate, muttering to himself as he strode across the kitchen and dropped it into the sink. The water went on. The muttering continued, but then Jules wavered slightly, and I moved close to her again, slipping an arm around her waist, tugging her back against my chest. "She needs to get home and sleep."

The officer's eyes hit mine before drifting up and over my

shoulder, no doubt going to Matt's—who was still muttering, though this time it was punctuated by the sound of the water going on and off, the plate clanking into the dishwasher, the ramekin joining it.

Not happy I was here.

Not happy I was touching Jules.

Well, the other man was going to have to fuck right off.

I tugged Jules a little closer when she trembled. "She can take your card and call you if she remembers anything else."

Silence.

Another glance over my shoulder.

Then back to me after a long moment. "I'll run with this," he told Jules, "and then be back in touch with you soon."

"Okay," Jules whispered.

Goodbyes were exchanged and then Matt and the cop left the kitchen, the door swinging shut behind them.

I shifted, used the bandages I'd laid out earlier from the kit and gently smeared antibiotic cream on her skin before I covered the cuts with the Band-Aids then gently wrapped her arm in gauze to keep everything in place and protected.

A kiss to the inside of her elbow.

A silent apology.

She was shaking slightly, fatigue clouding her eyes, so I kissed that swathe of silken skin again before straightening. "Let's get you home."

"Right." A breath.

More trembling and...fuck it.

I swept her up into my arms, holding her against my chest, hating that she was shaking, despising the lines of exhaustion on her face, furious at the dark circles beneath her eyes. My fault they were getting worse. *Her* fault for allowing them to get bad in the first place.

"I can—"

I pushed out the swinging door, carried her down the hall and into the staff room. "Where's your stuff?" I asked.

"I'm fine, Cas," she said, pushing at my chest—something I might have listened to if not for the fact that she was shaking so hard that her teeth were clacking together, if not for the fact that her shove against me was weaker than a fucking feather trying to shove back an elephant.

"Where's your stuff?" I repeated.

Her stare to mine, eyes assessing.

Then she sighed, probably understanding that there *wasn't* any assessing that would change the fact that I was going to see her home.

Not her arguments.

Not Matt.

Not the late hour.

I was going to get her safe and *then* I'd torture myself with all the fucked-up shit that Chelsea could have done to Jules. Then tomorrow, I was going to get my lawyer on making sure that Chelsea stopped fucking around with Jules, and I didn't care how nasty I had to get.

After a long standoff, Jules sighed and pointed to a row of lockers. "Mine's on the end."

I walked there, glanced from the lock and back up to Jules's eyes, lifting a brow.

"Let me guess," she muttered, "you're going to want me to open it from here."

"Either that or you can tell me the code," I muttered, keeping her close.

Her eyes flashed with annoyance, but it was better than her trembling from earlier. "You going to escort me to the bathroom, too?" she asked tartly.

I shrugged—which, no lie, had the pleasurable side effect of rubbing her body against mine and, yeah, I was just desperate enough for that to feel really, *really* good.

Just call me a pervert and be done with it, okay?

"If you need an escort to the bathroom," I said, ignoring my inner monologue. "I'm there."

She shook her head. "Right-left-right, 35-12-9."

"Got it," I muttered, carrying her to the locker, and also yeah, it wasn't the smoothest thing to try to open a combination lock while she was in my arms, but I also wasn't ready to let her go.

And plus, I'd managed to open my locker while making out with my high school girlfriend loads of times.

This wasn't nearly as hard.

It also had the positive of bringing my lips and nose close to her skin, since I had to look over her shoulder to put in the numbers.

And, oh look, I had to kiss that skin. Yup, *had* to.

She shivered, relaxed against me.

My tongue flicked out.

The door banged open, causing Jules to go stiff in my arms. And seriously, for fuck's sake, Matt needed to butt right the fuck out.

"Jules," Matt said tersely. "I'll drive you home."

The lock opened and I shifted Jules enough to tug the metal door wide, to grab out her jacket and purse. I set the jacket gently over her, then placed her purse on top. "I'm taking her," I announced.

And yes, it *was* an announcement.

Not necessarily to Jules, because I was guessing she got that already. But it was definitely an announcement to the other man, who was glaring at me, looking like he wanted to rip Jules out of my arms.

I wasn't going to play tug-a-war with the woman I wanted.

But I also wasn't going to let Matt put his hands on Jules. Not right then. Not when she was my responsibility, *mine* to protect.

Something *I* communicated very clearly with *my* glare.

Basically, it boiled down to *touch her and die.*

Matt's eyes narrowed.

I held his gaze long enough that I braced for a fight.

But then Jules lifted her hand, rested it on my chest. She didn't speak to me, though. Her words—*word*—was directed at her boss.

"Matt," she said softly.

Matt's glare disengaged from mine, face softening as he looked at Jules.

Then his shoulders hitched up and he sighed before spinning on his heel and disappearing out of the room.

"I didn't expect you to be a caveman," Jules muttered when we'd pushed out into the alley, headed to her car. Yes, I knew that she drove a boring little sedan that got great gas mileage. I also knew that she wasn't a fan of signals, drove with a lead foot, and it was filled with crap—trash, zip-top bags, balls, and general kid junk.

No, I wasn't pulling a Chelsea.

I just...paid attention to every single time when she was in my life, whether it was on the periphery or right in my face.

"Grab your keys," I ordered, moving to her car.

A shiver ran through her body.

Fuck. Too damned cold out here.

But she didn't move to get her keys—or not quickly enough, anyway. Because she was too busy yapping. "You're going to let me drive?"

Fuck no, I wasn't.

She was shaking. Exhausted.

I'd drive her home and come back for my car later. She'd need hers to get Ethan to school in the morning.

Ignoring her question, I reached into her purse, snagged her keys, and unlocked her car. A moment later, she was in the passenger's seat and I'd buckled her in and the door was shut, and then I was in the driver's side with my knees practically in my armpits.

Christ, I'd forgotten how little she was.

Mostly because she took up so much space in my heart and mind.

I jammed the key into the ignition, shoved the seat back, readied to pull out of the spot.

"I guess you're not going to let me drive."

FOURTEEN

Jules

HE'D CARRIED me like he never wanted to put me down.

And then he...

Then he'd buckled me in the passenger's seat.

He'd *buckled* me in.

That alone had my heart thudding against my rib cage, my palms going sweaty. Because...it meant too much.

So, I went with sarcasm.

That clever tool had been my constant companion for years past.

And as far as coping mechanisms went, it wasn't the worst.

My tone was dry when I said, "I guess you're not going to let me drive."

The incredulous look he shot my way made my thundering pulse settle, had amusement bubbling up and boiling over. I couldn't stop myself from giggling...and I couldn't stop the warmth growing in my belly, drifting up to encase my heart at the way his face changed when I laughed.

He dropped one hand off the steering wheel and reached toward me, brushing his thumb lightly over my bottom lip. "You are so fucking beautiful."

I wasn't.

Really, I wasn't.

Okay, so I didn't think I was ugly. I *liked* the way I looked—sleek blond hair that didn't take much work to make look silky and shiny (which was good because I didn't have time to do more than wash it on occasion and throw it into a ponytail or let it air dry); dark brown irises that reminded me of chocolate syrup, a nose that was maybe a bit too proud, but it was my mother's nose, my one connection with the woman I'd never known and yet who so dramatically affected every facet of my life. My skin was clear and sun-kissed from playing outside with Ethan so much, and while my body wasn't perfect and I'd never fully lost the baby weight leaving me with a good rack, which, yeah, was inconvenient and got in the way, but even I could admit the extra weight there looked good on my frame. Plus, I *was* in good shape—a side benefit of having a busy kiddo and a job where I was on my feet all day every day.

So, I was happy in my own skin and body.

But I wasn't beautiful.

"Cas," I whispered, shaking my head.

One more brush of his thumb along my lips, the simple action doing everything to remind me of the kiss.

Of *how* he'd kissed me.

It should have been icky, bustling me into a bathroom and kissing me with the toilets all too close. But it was the way he'd held me and washed my cuts that had melted me, had made me desperate to taste him.

And instead, he'd tasted *me*.

And *oh*, had it been good.

"I'm driving you home."

And since I was firmly in dream kiss land, this time I couldn't even formulate the smallest protest or dry comment. He knew it, too, the fucker, his mouth tipping up before he retracted his hand and placed it back on the steering wheel, confident and capable as he pulled out of the parking spot and turned onto the quiet streets.

Not a lot of cars on the road after three in the morning.

And considering it was even later than normal, that wasn't a surprise.

A hand on my jean-clad thigh, drawing my gaze from the empty street to Cas—or rather, to his hand. His palm was strong and broad and almost covered the entire expanse of my thigh. And the touch was *hot*, almost shocking, as the heat of his hand soaked through the fabric of my jeans. Hot. Strong. A little rough. I could imagine that hand drifting over my bare skin, sliding *up* my naked thigh, dipping into the damp heat pooling between my legs.

God, it had been *so* long since I'd had sex.

Not that it had been all that good with Nate. I'd had a few tinges, a few moments of pleasure, times where I'd *thought* I was coming because it felt good. *Thought*, because it wasn't until I'd gotten a vibrator and did a deep dive into my body that I'd understood what I'd had with Nate wasn't close to everything.

There was more—*oh,* how there was more.

And I'd bet there would be more—*much* more—with Cas.

It wouldn't require a deep dive or toys or severe concentration on my part and intense focus on his.

He'd *know*.

How did *I* know this fascinating little tidbit? Because every single time he touched me—whether it be on my face or my hand or my leg—I felt it in my pussy.

So yeah, he'd *know*.

He already knew how to touch me and make me feel good.

The only problem was that if I allowed all that *good* to continue, it would ruin everything.

"Wanna tell me where to go, gorgeous?" he said softly, and I shoved the inconvenient attraction from my mind, used another corner of my brain to schedule an appointment with my vibrator, and then put the rest to work on the getting home portion of my evening by providing Cas with directions.

Luckily, I didn't live far from CeCe's, so it didn't take a lot of focus to tell him when to turn (thank God, since my mind was full of thoughts of Cas and the vibrator and the things *he* could do with it—which, of course, would be eclipsed by the all the better things he could do with fingers and cock and tongue) and to point out my apartment when we'd pulled into the complex.

A little while later, we pulled into my parking spot.

Right.

Vibrators, *shoo*. My brain no longer allowing any thinking about what Cas could do to my body.

I grabbed my jacket, my purse, reached for the handle of the door.

It opened before I could fully grasp it, but when Cas would have swooped me up again, would have held me against his big, warm body and carried me inside, I put my hand up, shoved against his chest.

"No," I said, patience finally snapping. I was exhausted... and I was capable. Of a lot of things, but most certainly of walking the ten feet it took to make it into my own apartment. "I played along with the caveman thing because that was easier at the bar," I told him. "But I won't do it in my own home."

His teeth clicked together.

I braced for an argument.

But, to my surprise, he just stepped back, let me get out of the car (and get to my own feet). "Keys," I said, softening my tone because he was listening and because...apples and cinnamon and peanut butter, gentle fingers smoothing bandages on my arm, soft lips coaxing mine open, a hot, slick tongue dancing along mine.

He held them out.

I took them.

And look at that. Those ten steps up to my front door took no time at all, and then I was unlocking it, turning the handle and quietly letting myself into my apartment.

Cas followed me, but I didn't protest that particular development.

First, I had to make sure Mary got safely into her apartment. Then I would call Cas a Lyft so he could get back to his car at the bar.

Then I would sleep.

Glorious, *glorious* sleep.

Flicking on the hall light, I moved to where Mary was sleeping on the couch, knelt at her side, and gently woke her.

It took a few minutes because Mary was a deep sleeper, but eventually, I managed to get her up off the couch, to gather her things, and to get her into her own apartment next door, Cas making the task a bit easier by unlocking it for me (always the hardest part of the task since Mary's body seemed to suddenly be full of sand rather than bones).

"Thanks," I murmured. "Can you wait outside?" I whispered when he went to lift Mary off me. "She's a little nervous of new people. I know she's asleep, but I don't want—"

"Of course." He touched my cheek, slipped back outside.

I closed the door, hauled Mary down the hall. My sitter roused herself enough to kick off her shoes and stumble toward the bed, and I supervised, making sure that she didn't crash into any other piece of furniture (or any of the crap that was littered around the bedroom floor). Yawning as I tugged the covers up and tucked her in, I hoped like hell that Matt and the police and Cas got the shit that Chelsea was pulling settled down so there were no more nights like this.

I slipped from the bedroom, down the hall, and stepped out onto Mary's porch.

Cas was sitting there. Not on his phone. Not looking impatient or annoyed. Just waiting and watching for me.

I inhaled.

Apples and peanut butter and cinnamon.

Gentle touches and scorching hot kisses.

Was I *sure* I didn't want more of those?

Because just thinking about not having them made me feel *real* dumb. Who turned down a man like Cas, who was nice and thoughtful and sexy and strong and kissed me until I stopped thinking? And who wanted me. *Me.*

No one really wanted me.

No one had *ever* really wanted me.

And I knew that because I'd been wooed and wowed before. Because I'd thought a man was all of those things before.

And while I'd gotten Ethan out of it...I'd also had Nate.

Who'd left my heart in tiny little shards, who'd broken me until I couldn't trust my heart with anyone.

Because I'd laid that unprotected organ at his feet and he'd...

Stomped on it.

FIFTEEN

Cas

I SAT on the small set of steps that led up to her door, waiting for Jules to emerge from the apartment next door.

She'd all but carried the younger woman, brown hair mussed and face creased with sleep down her stairs and up to the adjacent set that led to the apartment next door. Then had somehow kept the other woman upright as she struggled with the getting the key out and attempting to unlock the door.

Which had been the point I'd lost my ability to sit back and watch her struggle.

So, I'd taken the keys, gotten the door open, held it for her to shepherd the other woman through.

And then, though I wanted to help, wanted to carry Mary—whose name I'd only caught because Jules had had to use it quite a few times to rouse her—I hadn't gone inside. Even though I didn't like that Jules was struggling. Even though I knew it would be faster for me to just carry Mary into her bedroom.

Jules had asked me to back off.

I wasn't going to make the mistake of not listening to her.

I wasn't that guy.

Ha.

So said the guy who'd all but bullied her into her car so I could drive her home.

Well, I wasn't going to make the mistake of not listening to her in this instance. She'd been pushed far enough and—

Footsteps on the stairs next to me.

I glanced up, expected to watch her walk into her own place, to shut the door, to end our evening.

Certainly, I'd pushed her far enough to test the patience of even the most saintlike of saints.

But instead, she surprised the shit out of me by sinking down onto the steps next to me.

"What?" she asked after a few moments.

(Probably because I was basically staring at her like she was a bug).

"Nothing," I said, shifting enough so that I could watch her without getting a crick in my neck. She was surprisingly little, despite the fact that she took up a lot of space in my mind, my heart. Actually, sitting next to her, towering over her even though we were sitting on the same step, reminded me how tiny she was.

And breakable.

"*What?*" she asked again.

And strong as hell.

And she'd been hurt because of me.

"I'm sorry that Chelsea—"

"Don't," she said, reaching out and taking my hand, lacing our fingers together. Her skin wasn't like silk there—it was a little rough, calloused on her fingers, on her palm. I liked it, though. It reminded me how capable she was, how tough and strong. "It's over—hopefully." A gentle smile to soften the fact that this might *not* be over. "And while I'd prefer not to be in the crosshairs of your ex again, I know it wasn't really about me."

No, it wasn't about her.

It was about me—

Except it *was* about her.

Chelsea had been infuriated when we'd gone to CeCe's, had hated even more that I'd talked to Jules.

I had always thought Chelsea was being unreasonable.

Now, I understood that I probably hadn't done a good job of hiding what I felt for Jules, understood that wasn't good boyfriend material and made me a bit of a dick. But...that was still no excuse for Chelsea pogo-sticking so far over the fucking line it wasn't even funny. She'd *hurt* Jules, made her feel unsafe at her place of work and no apology I could make would undo that.

Still, I found I needed to give it to her, would apologize for an eternity if it meant that she'd feel better, wouldn't have nightmares, wouldn't hurt.

"Jules," I said. "You're being really cool about all this, but I'm still—"

Her fingers squeezed around mine, cutting me off. "So, your real name is Luca?"

I blinked at the sharp left turn. "What?"

She turned our hands over, slipped her fingers from mine, and my stomach clenched. I wanted to keep touching her. Wanted her to keep touching *me*. Not to pull away.

But before I could maneuver more touching, she spread my hand out, began tracing her finger over the lines of my palm, and I relaxed because...touching. "Your first name isn't Cas or

Casian or...some over C name that begins with *Cas*? Instead, it's Luca?"

I held very still, not wanting to startle her, to have her pull back. To have her stop touching me. "My first name is Luca, but no one calls me that." I shrugged. "Luca is my dad. I've been Cas for as long as I can remember."

"Oh," she murmured, the tip of her finger sliding over my skin, raising the hairs on my arm, my nape. "I never knew."

I touched her cheek. "How would you?"

She went still at the question, or maybe at my touch. Then her shoulders lifted and fell on a breath. "I guess," she said on a soft laugh, "I *wouldn't* know."

"Exactly." I gave myself one more second of that silken skin before pulling back. "And anyway, I should say that I've been Cas for as long as I can remember with everyone except for my mom. I'm always Luca with her because"—I made air quotes—"she didn't spend nine months carrying me and twenty hours pushing me out to not call me by my given name."

She giggled. "I think she earned it."

"Yeah," I said. "She did. So, I put up with Luca because she's awesome."

"It sounds like it." Sad in her eyes, in her voice.

The silence dropped between us like a curtain separating the actors and the audience—a slow, steady descent until it was there and nothing but the most determined bout of applause could bypass the barrier.

I didn't have acting chops, wasn't going to break the quiet of the evening, the peace I felt with her sitting next to me by smacking my hockey-player-sized palms together like an imbecile.

But I couldn't let the silence sit between us.

I knew that her sitting quiet and introspective and more

open than she'd ever been before might be my best chance to find out more about her.

I danced my fingers along her forearm, lightly stroking skin that *was* like silk there, that was so soft it almost felt like a crime to touch it, let alone to have a portion of it obscured by bandages and wrap. "Did you always go by Jules? Or is that strictly a Breakers' addendum to your life?" I asked.

Her smile...was so beautiful it lit up the space between us. "When Beth heard that I had never had a nickname"—she glanced down at my hand and I hated that I'd lost my view of her face, but her voice was soft and *Jules* and almost as good— "she decided to remedy that." A peek up, giving me a glimpse of those gorgeous eyes. "Luckily, she chose something tolerable."

"It's beautiful."

Her head lifted further, her mouth tipping up. "It's not Commando," she said, referring to the name Beth had recently tried to christen Smitty with—a reference to the fact the man lived to be naked and didn't care who knew it.

I touched Jules's cheek again, soaked in the feel of that silky skin. "True," I said, grinning at her. "Jules is beautiful, like jewels."

Confusion in her eyes. "Like topaz," I whispered, brushing her lashes. "And garnet," I added, running my thumb over the apples of her cheeks. "Rubies." I touched her bottom lip.

"Garnet?"

My mouth turned up. "My mom is big into birthstones. I always thought that knowledge was just taking up space in my head." Instead, it was helpful, giving me the words I needed.

At least, I thought that until I saw the flicker of sad in her eyes.

"What?" I murmured, thumb running lightly over her bottom lip.

She shook her head. "It doesn't matter."

"It *does* matter, gorgeous. I want—" I cut myself off before I said something stupid and too much (like *I want to know every single thing about you*). Before I continued pushing. Always pushing her too far. Because, in this, I needed to play it cool, to not send her running.

"What do you want?" she asked, barely audible.

"You."

Okay then. Apparently, playing it cool was out of the question.

But...she didn't run.

Her fingers tensed, wrapping around my hand, flexing tight.

But...she still didn't run. Instead, I watched as the pink grew on her cheeks, the ruby red of her mouth darkened, her lips plumping, her tongue darting out to moisten the lush pillows I wanted to taste again. Somehow, I managed to hold still, though. To wait and see what she would do.

And it just about killed me.

Because her hand slid up the inside of my forearm, my biceps, to my nape, weaving into my hair. Her body arched, and she lifted so that her mouth came close enough to mine that I could feel her breath on my skin.

One long, taut moment.

Her lips were *so* fucking close.

But then her hand dropped, and she scooted away and I lost all of her—the warmth, the heat, the curves, the sweet scent of her.

"No?" I asked softly, my heart thudding, my hands aching to touch.

A long pause. "No," she whispered.

My pulse was thundering, but, thankfully, my voice was calm. "Too much?"

Teeth pressing into her bottom lip. "No," she whispered again.

I needed to shut up, needed to take my win and just go. But I still couldn't stop the question from rolling off my tongue. "You didn't like it?"

A small smile, a self-deprecating shake of her head.

"That's the problem. I like it too much."

SIXTEEN

Jules

I SHOULD JUST GO INSIDE.

It was late.

I was exhausted—emotionally and physically.

But I couldn't bring myself to get up, to walk into my apartment.

I couldn't bring myself to leave him.

Cas's head tilted to the side. "What do you mean, gorgeous?"

Yeah, well, I'd walked right into that one. I could have avoided this, *could* have left him, gone to bed. But, as always seemed to happen when I spent time with this man, I couldn't tear myself away.

Not when his gaze was on me, making me feel like I was the single most important thing in the universe.

My inner cynic snorted.

That wasn't exactly a surprise, was it?

It was the middle of the night, and we were the only two people awake in the vicinity.

Which was a nice excuse, a nice idea to hold on to in order to keep my heart safe.

If only he didn't make me feel like the only woman on the planet *all* the time—in a crowded bar, when I was chatting with the girls and stealing bites of cheese, when I was working my ass off to handle demanding tables, in a quiet kitchen taking care of me, and in the hushed softness of night here on my porch.

"I can't go there again," I said, because I had to give him something.

A pause that was long enough to settle heavy on my chest before he eventually asked, "Go where?"

I glanced away from those piercing eyes, stared up at the dark sky. "Get involved with a hockey player."

Since I wasn't watching him, I couldn't see him go still. But I could *feel* it, knew it with the same part of me that always knew what he was doing—laughing with a teammate, almost able to hear his rough chuckle, no matter where I was in the bar; sensing the warm weight of his gaze on me as I moved through my tables, feeling the slight rasp of his stubble on my cheek, the heat of his breath, the strength of his body.

"Someone from the team?"

His words were quiet, but there was a note in them that sent a thrill through me. Jealousy. Winding through each word and making me feel...

Stupid.

I'd dealt with jealousy before, with possession, with a man wanting me above all else.

Until I'd actually given myself.

And then he'd—

"Not from the Breakers," I whispered.

He went even more still. I felt that in my bones. "From where?" he asked.

"It doesn't matter."

Quiet.

Pulse of protectiveness in the air. "*Gorgeous*," he warned.

I couldn't keep my eyes off him, found my body shifting back to face him, even though it was smarter—safer—to not look at him.

But, as I'd already pointed out, I was *real* dumb when it came to this hockey player.

"He plays on the Sierra now."

A muscle flickered in Cas's cheek.

"He didn't then," I whispered. "We were kids. I was the hometown one. He was the junior player living far from home." A breath. "And I worked at the rink, so I knew all the guys." I felt my lips turn up. The memories of that time crowding into my mind, washing away the hurt that had followed my time with Nate. "I was a rink rat even though I didn't play." Even if I'd been *remotely* athletically inclined, my father would have flipped his shit. "But I loved being there. The rink became my home when my real one wasn't..." Christ, how did I encapsulate everything into a few sentences? In the end, I decided to just lay it out there. I'd never hidden from the truth. I had never been able to. Not when my dad had made it so fucking clear that I was unwanted, that I was basically a murderer. "My home life wasn't good. My father loved one person in his life— and that was my mother." A sigh. "Who I killed."

Cas sucked in a breath, reached for me, and tugged me back against his body, enfolding me in strong, warm arms. I didn't resist, *couldn't* resist—not when this old truth hurt so fucking much. "*Jules*."

"It's true," I whispered, giving in, burying deeper into his hold.

A hand smoothing down my arm. Cas didn't say anything, but the touch centered me, and his hold kept me here in the present. "She died giving birth to me," I whispered. "And from the time I was old enough to know that fact, he made sure I never forgot it."

His arms convulsed. "*Gorgeous.*"

That cracked open my chest and settled deep inside, and under the quiet of the cold, late night, I gave him the rest of it. "The rink was my sanctuary, and the hockey boys were my best friends." A sigh. "And I was young and stupid, and he was..." More of that stillness in Cas's frame, and it distracted me for a moment. It truly was impressive that he could control his big body so completely. Then I knew I had to keep going, that he had to understand. "He seemed to like me for me."

Lake had warned me that Nate wasn't a good guy. And they'd been playing on the same junior team, so he would know.

But Nate had been pretty and funny. And he was the one everyone wanted and...he'd wanted *me.*

No one had ever wanted me.

And Nate hadn't really either—or not for long, anyway. He'd gotten what he wanted and moved on, and then when I'd turned up pregnant...

He'd made my life hell.

Of course, that had only been until my father had found out.

Upon which, my knowledge of hell had been expanded.

It had only been because of Lake that I'd survived, had made it this far.

I knew he wanted to do more—then and now—but...it was all too mixed up in my head: him and Nate, hockey players and what they meant for my heart, my life.

I'd needed to pull back.

Lake had let me.

"What happened?" Cas asked, making me realize that I'd been lost in the past, in the painful memories.

"I got pregnant," I whispered.

His arms convulsed again.

Then grew even tighter when I whispered, "My dad kicked me out when he found out. I went to Nate and—"

A jerk of his body and I realized I'd made a critical error. I didn't like to think of Nate, to talk about him, let alone to even mention his name. I preferred to go full Voldemort.

But the critical error?

Cas played against the Sierra, would know the rosters.

"Nate Miller?" It was a growl.

Shit.

I tried to backpedal. "Things didn't end well between us."

The understatement of the year.

"What did he do?" Another growl.

More than I wanted to talk about right then. I'd already revealed way too much, but I gave him the rest, anyway. How Nate had shattered my heart and Lake had helped me get set up. How I'd felt stupid and alone and had sworn off hockey players.

Except, that Lake had kept checking in.

Except, that Smitty and Cas and the Breakers had taken me under their wings.

I bared my soul and didn't know how the hell to feel about it and, as I was trying not to freak out about that fact, I yawned.

Not on purpose, but his reaction to it made me file that away for later. A card to play. An escape route that played on his need to take care of me.

Right then, though, he stood up, drawing me to my feet. "You should go to bed," he murmured, pressing his lips to my forehead before nudging me toward the front door.

"Yeah." I needed to be smart—at least for one moment that night. But after I'd taken a step toward the apartment, I stopped and turned around, remembering that he didn't have a car. "How are you going to get home?"

His expression was soft as he pulled his phone from his pocket, held it up. "Don't worry, gorgeous. I'll call a Lyft."

Emotions skittered through my belly.

Because I couldn't leave him to wait for his ride on my porch.

Not in the cold, dark night.

Not—

"Why don't you come inside and wait for it?" I blurted.

His face went even softer, and he brushed his knuckles down my cheek, along my throat. "That doesn't help you get to bed, gorgeous."

"Yeah." My gaze dropped to my feet. "But you can wait in the front room, and I'll just go on to sleep." I pointed to the keypad above the lock on the front door. "Just hit this button to lock up after you go out. Or if you forget something or the car is late and you need to come back in, just hit 1622."

His finger under my chin, tilting my head up. "Jules, I'm *fine*—"

"Just do it, okay?" I said, tapping my toe, and then because I instinctively knew that he was going to continue to argue, I gave him the truth. "Because if you don't, I won't be able to sleep worrying about you being out here freezing your ass off."

His teeth clicked together, and he sighed.

But thankfully, that meant he stopped arguing.

And followed me inside.

SEVENTEEN

Cas

I SOAKED in all the details, all the insights into her life, catching more on a second look now that it wasn't all new.

Ethan's shoes on the rack by the door. A large winter jacket on a row of hooks, its smaller twin hanging next to it. A train-themed backpack sitting on the bench beneath them, a toy truck at its side. Jules had dropped her purse there and now she paused, hand on the wall just above the plain black leather, toeing off her shoes in an unconscious movement that gave me even more insight.

I could picture her doing the same every night, could imagine her doing it in *my* hallway.

A push from one foot tucked the shoes fully beneath the bench.

Then she turned for the kitchen, flicked on the lights, and tugged out a stool. "I can make you a cup—"

There were colorful canisters on the counter, a bunch of bananas on a hanger shoved into a corner near the sink. Some sort of craft project in process on the island. And, Christ, there were even drawings held up by colorful magnets on the fridge.

I caught her arm, drew her against me.

I shouldn't do it.

I *shouldn't.*

But I couldn't stop my head from dipping, from my lips brushing over hers.

She was just so damned *wonderful.*

"Go to bed," I whispered, lifting my head, forcing myself to release her, to not taste her again. "I'll be okay."

"I—"

A breath, but then she nodded.

And then she moved down the hall.

A door *clicked* shut.

My gaze caught on a drawing of a dog on the fridge.

Of *Sparky* written in childish scrawl beneath it.

Christ, I was in deep.

And I didn't give one fuck.

"Thanks, man," I said a while later, hopping out of the back of the car, making sure the door latched before taking off for my SUV still parked in the lot.

It was the only car left.

Which wasn't a surprise, considering the sun was just beginning to rise in the east, a narrow strip of light filling the horizon. Late. Much later than I normally stayed up, and the team's schedule meant that I regularly kept odd hours, especially with travel and trying to wind down after games. One of which I had that night and that meant I needed to sleep at some point, to rest up and focus on my actual job.

Not on what my mind wanted—which was, for the record (in case anyone was unaware of the fact), *Jules.*

Sighing, I reached into my pocket for my keys and froze when I encountered a thick, crumpled piece of paper. "What?" I muttered, tugging it out.

And suddenly, I wasn't tired.

My body was exhausted, yes. Was telling me it was time to get in bed and sleep.

But now I was mentally wired.

Because Jules was playing with me. I grinned at the much-abused hundred-dollar bill. She was playing with me, and she'd shared—

Something that had the smile sliding right off my face.

Because *what* she'd shared made my blood fucking *boil.*

She'd been with that douchebag, with Nate *fucking* Miller, prime asshole in the league and one of the top producers on the Sierra.

And she was living in...

Well, I wasn't so much of an asshole as to describe her apartment in negative terms. It was a home, and it was clean and bright and cheerful. She'd created a great place for a kid to live. But it *was* small, and a bit worn down, and she worked her ass off into the wee hours of the morning on a regular basis.

Hands clenching into a fist, one around the hundred-dollar bill, crumpling it further, the other around my keys that sent a sharp bite of pain up my arm.

"Fuck," I muttered, yanking open the driver's side door and dropping into the seat.

Nate *fucking* Miller.

God, the man was a jackass—a cheap fucker on the ice and apparently off it as well, considering that Jules had to hustle hard, and she and Ethan were living in that small apartment with the worn cabinets and cracked plaster in the corners and—

I was going to crush that motherfucker the next time we played.

A jab at the button to start my car. A quick movement to back out of the spot.

And then I was driving home.

Or maybe I should rephrase that.

I *should* be driving home.

Instead, my car just sort of...pointed itself back in the direction of Jules's place.

She would have barely gotten any sleep at this point and Ethan had to wake up to go to school and—

None of that was my problem.

And yet, knowing that, I still found myself driving back across town to Jules's.

I'd just hang out for a few minutes, make sure that they were up and moving so that Ethan wouldn't be late for school.

That was just...being neighborly (my house wasn't all that far from Jules's).

And her night had been rough because of me and—

Well, that was pretty much the point I stopped trying to make excuses and just gave into the urge to check up on them.

Insane?

Yup.

But I still drove to the apartment building, still parked at the curb.

Still waited, the sun growing higher, the sky brighter.

Even as there wasn't a single sign of movement in the house.

No lights on. No movement through the windows.

I was spying on her and that was creepy as fuck, and who really cared if Ethan was late for school one day?

Except...I knew that *Jules* would care.

She'd beat herself up.

One interaction with the pair of them in the park, coming to know her at CeCe's over the years, and I *knew* that she would hate that her son was late for school because she forgot to set her alarm or overslept or—

"Fuck it," I whispered, turning off my car and getting out.

I'd just...

Well, I didn't really have a plan, other than it involved making sure that Jules didn't have anything else in her life to make her feel sad or disappointed.

I made my way up to the front door, pressed the buttons on the keypad to unlock the door (doing this while ignoring the sliver of guilt—*it was for her benefit!*), and...

Then I walked back into Jules's house.

EIGHTEEN

Jules

SUNSHINE WAS STABBING at my brain through my eyelids.

Too early.

Not enough sleep.

Not enough—

Wait.

Sunshine was stabbing at my brain through my eyelids.

Sunshine shouldn't be shining into my eyes, not until I was making Ethan breakfast and running around like a chicken, trying to get all the last-minute things together.

That it was stabbing in through my eyelids *now* meant that...

"I'm late!"

Shit.

Pulse pounding in my veins, my stomach immediately in a tight clench, I sat up, tossing the comforter to the side and scrambling out of bed.

My bare feet hit the cold floor and then I was running down the hall toward Ethan's room, *my* feet pounding on the floor instead of my kiddo's for a change. "Eth, buddy! We have to—"

I skidded to a halt in front of his bedroom, pushed the door open, and—

It was empty.

"Ethan?" I called. There was no way he'd gotten out of bed without me nagging him fifteen times. To *Get. Up!*

A clatter from down the hall.

Had miracles happened, and he'd gotten ready?

I wasn't going to look a gift horse in the mouth.

Rushing into my bedroom, I threw my hair up into a ponytail, yanked socks onto my feet, then snagged my phone from the side table. Thirty seconds later, I was hustling down the hall, skidding into the kitchen, and—

Screeching to a stop.

What.

The.

Fuck?

"Hi, Mom," Ethan said, his little legs swinging back and forth as he sat on a stool pulled up to the counter. Next to Cas.

What. The. Fuck?

Cas flipped the spatula—and that was a mind fuck right there, Cas standing in my kitchen, next to Ethan, holding a fucking *spatula*—and a pancake appeared on the plate that was positioned in front of Ethan.

It was already coated with syrup and I immediately saw why when my son picked up the bottle, doused the pancake on his plate with copious amounts of the sweet, sticky liquid and jabbed the soaked pancake with his fork.

It disappeared into the black hole that was Ethan's stomach.

Hell, I wasn't even sure my kid chewed.

Cas turned to face me, and the *balls* on the man to not even have one ounce of guilt on his face when he extended my own plate full of steaming pancakes.

Huge balls.

Huge.

"Eat, gorgeous," he said quietly.

There were dark circles under his eyes. Hell, there were dark circles beneath the dark circles.

Had he even slept?

I was pissed that he was in my house, with my kid, worried about the exhaustion drawn so deeply into the lines of his face, and—*hell*—my heart was squeezing over the fact that he was in my kitchen cooking pancakes for my son.

It was a scene...

Well, hell, it was *fatherly.*

And *that* wasn't something Ethan or I had ever experienced.

Cas bent a little, meeting my eyes. "I'll explain later," he murmured. "Just eat now."

Explain.

Right. He needed to explain why he was in my house.

And yeah, maybe *I* needed to explain why I wasn't freaking out about him being in my house, cooking pancakes, loading my kid up with sugar, and *in my house.*

But instead of freaking out, I grabbed a fork, cut off an edge of the pancake, shoved it into my mouth...and holy sweet baby Jesus, that was absolutely divine. "Mmm," I groaned, immediately scooping up more of the pancake and scarfing it down. Ethan was doing the same...because I didn't raise a fool.

Carbs.

Sweet, glorious carbs.

Okay, *that* was why I didn't kick Cas out—and kick his ass for the intrusion.

The carbs.

Not because my heart was pounding against my ribs and warmth was in my belly and—

Cas dropped another pancake onto my plate.

Right.

I should eat the pancakes.

Or...school—I should focus on being a mother and getting Ethan to school, not on my stomach, no matter how delicious the pancakes were.

"I made his lunch," Cas said quietly, opening Ethan's train-themed lunchbox and showing me the contents. A sandwich, a plastic container with cut-up veggies, a banana, and a pack of gummies. What I'd pack.

"Ethan helped me," Cas said, zipping it back up. He winked and embers flared in my belly. "Even with the veggies."

"I cut up the carrots, Mom," Ethan said through yet another pancake. "And I got dressed on my own."

Which explained the raucous riot of colors that formed his outfit that morning.

"That's really good, buddy. Did your alarm wake you up?"

"Nope." More pancake into his mouth. "Cas did."

"I heard it going off," Cas said quietly. "Just poked my head in to make sure he was up and moving."

"Heard it because you were in my house?" I asked dryly.

Pink on his cheeks, his eyes darting away. "Something like that."

"Right."

His brows lifted. "More pancakes?"

I wanted to refuse, solely on principle. But my stomach rumbled, stealing that from me. The bitch. Except, even as I thought that, my lips twitched and I nodded. "Did you get any?"

He shook his head. "I'm good."

There was something a little edgy about that statement, but I didn't get a chance to push it because then he asked, "I have a couple extra tickets to tonight's game. Do you guys want to come?"

I nearly dropped my plate.

Because that was *not* fucking fair. Because that explained the *edgy*.

Because Cas had to know that Ethan's reaction would be—

"Yes!"

It was almost a shriek, paired with the plate clattering to the counter and his little body jumping up and down on the stool. "Yes! I want to go. Can we go, Mom? Can we—"

"That was mean," I mouthed to Cas.

Who just lifted his brows again and steadied Ethan, so my son didn't tumble off the stool as he expressed his excitement. "I can leave the tickets at the box office so you guys can come when it's convenient." He poured batter into the pan before tugging his wallet out of his pocket and slipping a card out from the inside, extending it toward me. "Here's a parking pass for the private lot. That way, if you need to leave early for bedtime, you can avoid the traffic."

"We won't have to leave early, right Mom?" Ethan asked, still bouncing, though it was now in between even more pancake consumption. "You always say that good stuff happens at the end."

That had the result of drawing Cas's gaze back to mine.

And damn, did the man see—and *hear*—too fucking much.

"We can go," I said, tearing my gaze from Cas's, moving to my son, and ruffling his hair. "*And* stay till the end."

"Promise?"

Damn.

My kid knew me, knew I wouldn't go back on my word.

"Promise," I repeated.

"And promises are meant for keeping," Ethan said, finishing the statement I'd taught him over the years.

Thankfully, I wasn't working that night.

Something that Cas probably knew, given that he was sneaky and in my house making pancakes and had made the offer in the first place.

"And get snacks?" Ethan asked me innocently.

Sweet Christ, arena prices. *That* was going to kill me, if the big, sexy player making pancakes in my kitchen didn't first.

But I stifled that thought—or *thoughts*, rather—and embraced that I was going to get to give my kid something he wanted desperately and something I couldn't give him by myself. Free tickets from big, dark, and sexy meant I could swing arena prices for snacks. "Yes," I told Ethan as I snagged his syrup-covered plate. "And a souvenir, too. Now, you've got to get your shoes and jacket on, and we need to hustle so we're not late for school, yeah?"

No hesitation. Just, "Okay, Mom!" Then he zoomed out of the room, his pounding feet echoing all the way through the hall.

The plate disappeared from my hand, was replaced with my own. "Eat, gorgeous."

"You play mean," I murmured, scowling up at Cas.

A shrug. A nudge with the porcelain disc. Another order. "*Eat.*"

Since the pancakes were delicious and my stomach told me that I hadn't had enough carbs—thank you very much—I obeyed the order, no matter how pernicious, and ate. "You're not off the hook," I grumbled, forking bites in at a rapid clip. "You know that, right?"

"You can take it out on my ass later," he said lightly, picking up the pan and bowl and taking both to the sink. The water came on, sizzling in the pan, and he turned back to face me, voice going serious "I can pay for the food—"

"No," I said quickly.

His expression said he wanted to argue.

But, as I'd established, he was smart and presumably saw that I wasn't going to budge on him paying for our food and Ethan's souvenir.

"You weren't planning on it," he pointed out. "I know it's hard when expenses pop up out of nowhere."

He was right. I hadn't planned on taking Ethan to a Breakers game.

But I was going to buy my kid expensive chicken strips and popcorn and cotton candy and one of those maniacal wave-shaped stuffed mascots as well, anyway.

Because Ethan didn't get opportunities like this very often.

So, I was going for it—even though it came from a man who had broken into my apartment...and made pancakes.

"You know I'm going to change the code, right?" I told him archly.

A grin that should have melted my clothes right off me before he turned back and began scrubbing the pan, the bowl, Ethan's plate and fork. "You'll tell me the new one."

I narrowed my eyes. "And you know I don't date hockey players."

That grin didn't fade as he set the dishes on the drying rack. "Who said I want to date you?"

Ouch.

But I didn't let that hurt show, just went to my purse, words more than a little terse when I said, "I'll remind you that *you* asked me out."

He shut off the water, dried his hands on a towel. "Yeah,"

he said. "I did." He closed the distance between us, the warmth of his body searing me through our clothes, the spicy scent of him in my nose. "I *don't* want to date you, gorgeous," he murmured, trailing his knuckles over my cheek, even as his words sliced through me.

Ouch again.

"I want to *keep* you."

Those words weren't a slice.

They were warmth, no heat, no...an *inferno*.

I shuddered, my body leaning against his. "Cas—"

His lips brushed mine.

That inferno exploded, a sudden gust of oxygen, gasoline on flames, fuel for the fire burning in me.

I rose on tiptoe, pressed my mouth to his, got a taste of tongue and teeth and *need*.

But when I went for more, he pulled back, brushed his knuckles over my cheek. "You need to get Ethan to school, gorgeous."

No.

I needed to kiss him again.

My fingers gripped his T-shirt. "Cas—"

A press of his lips to my forehead and then he was gone, the front door closing behind him a moment later.

"Shit," I whispered, trying to get myself together by smoothing my hand over my hair, my shirt, the front of my sweats.

I felt something crinkle.

Reached into my pocket.

And pulled out that damned hundred-dollar bill.

NINETEEN

Cas

"ER-HMM."

I glanced over at Smitty, who coughed again, then picked up his water bottle and took a long swig.

Fucker better not be getting sick and spreading that shit through the locker room. There was always one patient zero and then pretty soon everyone was hacking up a lung.

Kind of hard to play hockey when you could barely breathe.

"Er-hmm."

Another glance toward Smitty, this time with narrowed eyes.

But all my teammate did was take another sip of water and continue on with tying his skates.

Okay, that was less patient zero and more full-on annoying Smitty-ness.

Case in point?

"Er-hmm!"

"Jesus fucking Christ, *what* Smitty?" Theo snapped—something that was uncharacteristically Theo, who was usually pretty easy-going.

Although, I had seen my friend and teammate cornered by a certain sports blogger and journalist turned television color commentator, had witnessed that easy-going disappear into a proverbial *poof* of smoke.

Eva Moreno was smart, took no shit, and had a body built for sin.

Exactly Theo's type.

If their personalities hadn't combined like oil and water.

And yet...I kept spotting them together.

Hmm.

Smitty, meanwhile, wasn't bothered by being snapped at—then again, the troublemaker was probably used to it. He just straightened, took another swig from his water bottle, and then set it on the bench, lifting his brows...and turning a smirk in my direction.

Shhhhiiiittt.

"Er—"

"I swear to God," Theo muttered.

"Hmm." Sock balls were launched in Smitty's direction, but he just ducked and then smirked at me again. "I hear that a certain favorite waitress is coming to the game tonight."

More smirks turned in my direction.

"With...her son."

Now raised brows joined the party.

Fuck.

"On Cas's tickets."

My groan was mental, but I was almost certain the rest of the room heard it because smirks turned to grins and Smitty said, "Finally got Jules to agree to go out with you, Cassy boy?"

Yeah, not exactly.

But I *had* finally made some progress, and I wasn't going to fucking backtrack. And I especially wasn't going to backtrack on it because of *these* nosy, pushy fuckers who wanted to know every single detail of each other's lives.

"Leave it alone, Smitty," I warned.

My teammate just laughed. "You know we're not going to leave it alone, so I don't know why you're bothering to try to issue orders."

Fucking hell.

That was *it*.

I jumped up to my feet—well, to my skates—and marched across the room, jabbing a finger in Smitty's face. "She's been hurt, fuckhead, so don't mess with her."

Now, Smitty might be an annoying asshole half the time (although so loveable the rest of the time that everyone forgot about his annoying nature), but he also had a protective streak that was a mile wide. At my words, his expression immediately changed, and his voice became a growl. "Who hurt her?"

That wasn't my information to share—but that wasn't to say that I wouldn't drop a few hints before the next time we played the Sierra, would make sure that Nate Miller got his due. And just to be clear, that *due* was ensuring that Nate Miller spent most of the game on the ice and slammed against the glass.

Smitty corralled (for the moment), I dropped my hand. "I'm taking care of it," I muttered. "Same as I'm going to take care of Jules."

"Does *she* know that?" Smitty—rightfully—pointed out.

I pressed my lips together, glared. "She knows enough."

Laughter in that big, burly chest. Laughter that echoed across the room. "Good luck to you, man."

"Right," I muttered.

I didn't need luck.

Jules was worth any amount of trouble or bad luck she'd dropped into my lap.

"It'll be worth it," Smitty said, like I was bestowing the most sacred of knowledge.

"I know that," I snapped, striding back to my station. "I don't need you to tell me that," I grumbled, slumping onto the bench. "She's fucking amaz—*ow!*"

I glared at Theo, who'd decided to launch a sock ball at my face. "What, asshole?"

"You're supposed to be less cranky when you finally get your picker on straight."

That was just...really...

"If I never hear that word again," I grumbled, scooping up the sock and launching it back at Theo, feeling a little better when it ricocheted off his forehead. Ha. Fucker. "It'll be too soon. My *picker* isn't broken or crooked. It's perfectly—" I broke off, scrambling for a word that didn't sound...well, sexual.

My teammates weren't so concerned with that.

"Hard?" Smitty chimed in.

"Long?" Theo asked.

"Thick?" Raph.

"Steely?" Marcel.

"Girthy?" Walker.

The room froze, and then a collective groan filled the space.

"Too much?" Walker asked with an innocent expression.

"*Way* too fucking much," Smitty said. "And coming from me, you know that's true."

"Girthy is a totally reasonable description for a picker."

Christ. I needed out of this conversation.

As thus, I sped through the rest of getting dressed, ignoring the comments and conversation flowing around me, not acknowledging any of the parts that had to do with me. No way was I getting drawn in to that. I wanted to focus on the game. I needed to show Jules...

Hell, I needed to show *off* for Jules and Ethan.

Hello ego.

But it was the truth, and I wasn't going to shy away from it, wasn't going to shy away from *any* of it.

I shrugged into my jersey, shoved my arms through the sleeves, yanked my head through the opening, taking the opportunity to glare at my teammates. "I'm bringing Ethan down after the game, so make sure you fuckers stay around to sign stuff for him."

"Whatever you say, boss," Smitty said, saluting.

Fuckers.

"And play some decent fucking hockey tonight, yeah?"

"Want us to set you up for a goal too, grumpy?" Raph called. "Make you look good for your giiirrrl?"

Yeah. That'd be fucking nice.

Not that I was going to admit that.

No need to give them any further ammunition.

"Fuck you guys."

"Ah, no need for that," Smitty hollered. "You know we'd make love to you."

I shoved my helmet onto my head.

"He means we love you," Theo said.

"You mean you love seeing me be tortured by a woman," I grumbled.

"Well, yeah," Theo said, grinning as he snagged his own jersey. "That's the best part."

The annoying bastard.

And because of that, I made a mental note to do some digging into my friend and the sports blogger. Turnabout was fair play.

"Good luck with Jules," Marcel said lightly, though my quiet friend was smirking just as widely as the rest of them.

I narrowed my eyes.

"Yup." Smitty waggled his fingers. "Good luuuck!"

"Like you're not going to be laughing your ass off the entire time."

"Oh, I will." A beat. "But I'll still have your back throughout the entire wooing process."

Wooing process.

Sigh.

But the having my back? That was good. That was what made the teasing, as light-hearted—and girthy—as it was, bearable. Because the guys were my friends, my family. Teasing came with hockey, and as much as I might grumble about being on the receiving end of it, I could dish it out just as well.

And I would.

Would!

Fuckers.

"Shut up and finish getting dressed," I ordered, moving out the door and snagging my stick off the rack.

It was time to play some fucking hockey.

And hopefully impress the girl I was crazy about.

TWENTY

Jules

"WHOA," Ethan breathed as we walked across the street and approached the arena.

I knew the feeling.

It was huge and brightly lit and surrounded by people who were dressed in the trademark royal blue and black of the Breakers.

Ethan and I didn't have jerseys like so many of the fans approaching the entrances had, but I'd managed to track down a beanie for him at a local secondhand store that morning. For myself, I had settled for wearing Breakers colors—blue top and earrings, black scarf and beanie. We both wore our thickest coats, which, luckily for my attempts at team spirit, were both black.

Easy to match the home team's colors.

But I'd chosen black coats for a reason—they were utilitarian. Plus, the color meant that it was easy to hide the stains.

Ethan tugged on my hand, and I realized that I'd slowed

down to practically a crawl, trying to see everything, trying to take it all in, trying to commit it all to memory. And, yeah, maybe I was also trying to glean every bit of insight about what Cas's life was like, what it was like for him to play here, to *work* here.

He knew my biggest secret—or maybe not secret, since it wasn't like I was hiding Ethan, hiding that he was mine. I just... didn't talk about where he came from. But now Cas knew that Nate was his father, that he'd broken my heart and faith in myself. Knew that my father had disowned me and blamed me for my mother's death and thought I was a slut. And he knew that I wouldn't have been okay without Lake's help, but I couldn't bring myself to allow him to get close to me again.

But parts of me had been permanently broken by Nate.

All of which I'd told Cas, had given him my biggest hurts, my deepest pains.

And I knew next to nothing about him.

I'd heard him talk about siblings, and he'd mentioned two sisters to Ethan. I knew he was close to his parents and his teammates. I knew what kind of beer he drank and that he ordered a burger as often as he got a salad. I knew his laugh and how his arms felt around me. I knew that he listened to what I said and that he actually saw me, and he treated me with care and sprinkled my apple slices with cinnamon and cleaned up after making pancakes in my kitchen—

But I didn't really *know* him.

Except, *didn't* I?

I knew some big important things. I knew a lot of small ones and—

"Mom!" Another tug. One that jarred me out of my mind and sent me jerking into motion.

"Sorry, buddy," I told Ethan. "I'm just impressed."

"It's *so* cool!" he said, doing a little dance.

While he was completing his jig, I took the moment to remind myself that I didn't *need* to know Cas.

I wasn't dating hockey players.

Not even yummy ones? the self-destructive part of my mind asked.

Nope. No. Never.

No more hockey players. No matter how yummy they were.

A nod to myself (and ah, wasn't delusion great?), and then I'd spotted the box office so led Ethan that way.

One hockey game.

For Ethan.

No more hockey players.

Ever.

***

"Whoa, Mom!"

I was feeling the same thing.

The inside of the arena was bright and huge and cool, the air tightening the skin on my cheeks as we walked carefully down the concrete stairs, following the usher who was leading us to our seats.

"Here you are, Ms. Blackstar," she said, pointing toward a pair of chairs on the aisle that was obscenely close to the glass. Just—I counted quickly—six rows back.

Expensive seats.

Oh, I was going to *kill* him.

"Thank you," I told the usher.

"He can go down"—the woman nodded at the row of kids gathered next to the glass—"and watch the players warm up so long as you guys are in your seats at puck drop."

Wide, excited eyes on mine. "Can I, Mom?"

I nodded. "Yeah, honey," I said, the words barely out of my mouth before he was scrambling down the steps and pressing himself into a free spot on the glass. I'd need to wrangle him away from the ice at some point, get the kid some food, but he'd been too excited for me to torture him by making him wait in the long food lines.

And not that I would admit it, but he'd wasn't the only one who was too excited to wait in line.

Smothering a grin—and thinking that it was convenient to have a kid to blame my impatience on—I watched Ethan chatter excitedly with a kid next to him who was decked out in Breakers gear from head to toe.

That was my boy, able to make friends anywhere.

A rush of noise drew my focus back to the ice, and I found my breath catching as the teams began to enter the rink. I'd served hockey players at CeCe's on a regular basis for years now. I was used to their height, to how big most of them were. But like *this*—on their skates, flying rapidly around the ice—and I felt tiny, like an insignificant speck in the universe as all the crazy bright planets and moons and meteors flew around me.

Tap. Tap. Tap.

My gaze focused, and I saw Smitty grinning at me, waving a big hand. He pointed down at the kids, presumably asking which one was mine.

I pointed at Ethan.

And that was when my heart cracked open because he crouched enough to stare into my son's eyes, mouthing something I couldn't see, but a moment later, he'd straightened and tossed a puck over the glass to Ethan.

Shit. Now my eyes were damp.

But even through that dampness, I saw that Smitty took a few more moments to toss pucks to each of the kids gathered around Ethan.

Such a good guy.

But even as I thought that, my gaze was skipping beyond Smitty, going to the players fanning out behind him. Marcel was there and Raph, Theo, and Walker, a few of the other faces were familiar as well, but none I knew as well as Cas's.

Even from across the rink—he was standing on the bench at the far side of the ice—I could feel his gaze on mine, warm and searching and—

The connection was broken as he turned away to talk to one of the people on the bench.

Then he straightened and hopped over the boards, skating across the ice.

Coming toward me.

He paused in front of Ethan, grinning when my son held up the puck Smitty had given him, waving at the other kids who mirrored Ethan's actions.

But then his gaze was back, and it was heavier and hotter and more intense than anything I'd ever experienced.

I saw how much he liked that I was there, that Ethan was there.

He *wanted* us there.

And...a piece of my heart unlocked.

Another piece.

A dangerous piece.

Yet, I couldn't even summon a modicum of panic because the moment it began to gather in my belly, to grip the back of my throat, a voice called my name from behind me.

I glanced up, saw another employee of the arena, only this time his arms were full. He held a huge tray of nachos and pretzels, a tub of popcorn, two drinks, some boxes of candy, a hot dog and a huge, wrapped sandwich that smelled so delicious, it immediately had my stomach rumbling.

Before I could say that I hadn't paid for any food, he was setting the tray in my lap, was slipping away—

No slipped *back*.

To make room for the other employee who was standing behind him.

Holding two *huge* bags emblazoned with the Breakers symbol.

Those were tucked at my feet.

Then both employees were gone, and I was staring at them, my mouth hanging open, trying to process what in the fuck-all was going on.

"Whoa! Is this for us, Mom?" Ethan said, using his superhuman skills to scent food to magically reappear at my side.

"I—"

Tap. Tap. Tap.

Gasping, my head jerked up, eyes finding Cas's again.

Intense green eyes.

Stubborn green eyes.

Oh, I was *so* getting him back for this.

"Yeah, bud," I muttered. "It's for us."

TWENTY-ONE

Cas

SMITTY NUDGED ME.

"I don't think you're going to get good service at CeCe's for like...an eternity."

"Shut up," I muttered, shoving my teammate away and at least going through the motions of warming up.

It was hard, even though I'd been doing it for so many years that it should be pure instinct at this point.

But aside from ignoring the shit-giving that Smitty was no doubt going to continue to toss in my direction, most of my focus wasn't on the puck or my skates or stick. It was on Jules and Ethan, on the latter's smile and how I wanted to keep that in place forever, and on the former's frown and how I was quite desperate to kiss it off her face, to turn it into that gentle upturn of her lips that she'd given me when I'd filled her plate with pancakes and when I'd made that snack of apples and peanut butter and cinnamon.

Small things.

Small ways to take care of a woman I cared about.

But she'd reacted to those small things like she'd never had a bit of kindness before—and I supposed, based on what she'd told me, she *hadn't* had them.

Ethan had, though.

One look and it was easy to see that her kid was comfortable in the fact that he was loved and cared for. Not selfish or spoiled, but at ease with the fact that he had a mom who loved him and did everything she could to make his life great.

So, yeah, it wouldn't be hard to find the effort to make him smile, to make that great life even better.

For him...*and* his mom.

And I would bet that Jules wouldn't be able to hold on to her mad for long, especially if I spent my time trying to make Ethan happy.

I'd already watched her expression soften in the face of Ethan's excitement.

Yeah, she was Ethan's mom so her heart belonged to her kiddo, but in truth, a person would have to be dead to not be swept up in Ethan's excitement. It was pure and filled with joy and, yeah, I had only spent an hour over pancakes with Ethan that morning, but hell if the kid hadn't already sewn his way into my heart. Ethan was only five years old, but he was funny and smart and kind, and I loved his mom.

The truth was that I was falling for them both.

Especially when Ethan had shown me a picture he'd drawn for Sparky. Yup *for* Sparky. Not a drawing of my pooch to put on Julie's fridge, but a drawing for Sparky for *my* fridge.

Christ, that had killed.

And I hadn't even cared that Ethan had dominated the conversation by talking about school and friends and hockey, hadn't cared that Ethan had asked a million questions or that he'd reminded me of my promise to take him to skate and shoot (and promises were made for keeping—to which I had assured Ethan that I'd talk to Jules about days and times). Then, just as quickly, he'd pivoted back to questions and had asked me how a stove worked.

And then the fridge.

And how shoes were made.

Switching between topics in almost dizzying fashion. Peppering me with questions, most of which I didn't have the answers to. Expending so much energy even though he'd practically been a zombie before I had gotten him to wake up enough to get dressed and brush his teeth. But once Ethan *was* up, he'd been going eight million miles an hour.

I had been raised in a busy house—lots of noise and activity and people talking over each other.

That was just inevitable when a person had three siblings and parents who were together and friends who came over all the time and family that visited and generally were just part of a big, busy group of people who loved each other and did that noisily and without compunction and with no little amount of chaos.

So the questions and conversation didn't bother me in the least.

I just needed to start doing some YouTube research if I was going to keep up with the kid's inquiries.

My knowledge of how things worked was sorely lacking.

"Cas!"

I blinked.

Normally, the crowd noise was just that. Just *noise* that I couldn't distinguish, a low rumble to a loud roar that fueled me, that sent me skating faster, hitting harder. But I heard my name like Ethan was right next to me, talking to me over pancakes in Jules's kitchen.

Turning toward the crowd, I felt the emotion pound into me harder than that fucker Lake Jordan, who played for the league's newest team, the Sierra, and could check like a fucking Mack truck.

Ethan's smile was *huge* and when he saw I looking, he spun and showed me the back of the jersey.

I'd had them put Castillo on Jules's jersey because...well, I couldn't lie. The devil in me had wanted to see my name on her back. But I hadn't given instructions for Ethan's. I'd thought to leave it blank and then get Ethan's favorite player put on—that favorite player likely not being me.

But someone had put Castillo there.

And that made me feel...

Fuck, the kid had dug himself in deep.

"Shit," I whispered, my heart pounding like I'd taken too long of a shift, was hauling ass to the bench to take a break.

And that was before my gaze went to Jules.

Because when it did, I swore to fuck that black crept in on the edges of my vision.

Because she was wearing the jersey and the smile she gave me wasn't perturbed, wasn't annoyed because clearly I'd been pushing when she'd ordered me to back off. It was soft and gentle and sweet...and then she spun to show me the back.

Slam.

Another crushing hit.

Fuck, I needed to keep them both.

She turned again and was still wearing that smile and I knew that she was going to give me hell for the spoiling, but I also knew that it meant something to her.

Something big.

Like the cinnamon and peanut butter and ibuprofen and apples had.

Like the pancakes and feeding her son had.

And I knew that I'd do anything to keep putting that look on her face.

Because I'd never met a woman who deserved it more.

TWENTY-TWO

Jules

BOOM!

I jumped, clamped my hand to my chest, thinking that hockey was not for the faint of heart as I watched the Breakers' player being smooshed against the glass—which rattled, swaying and bending to physics-defying angles when the player, whose name I didn't know, took a bone-jarring hit.

"Ouch," I muttered, but even before I'd finished the word, the player shoved off the boards, sending them rattling again and was...*gone*.

Just *gone*.

Okay, well, he hadn't poofed away in a puff of smoke. He was still on the ice, just somehow suddenly ten feet away and hauling ass toward the other side of the rink.

The guys were *big*.

And fast.

And did I mention *big?*

And *fast?*

Yeah, I knew that Cas and Smitty and the others were tall and in shape, but adding their pads onto those already muscular bodies and the three or four inches from their skates onto their already taller than normal height made them seem like giants—especially when Ethan and I were so close to the ice.

I was used to watching five-year-olds play—er, fly around, fall down, jab each other with their sticks, and generally spend their time on the ice acting like tiny maniacs with blades strapped to their equally tiny feet.

And barring that, growing up I'd watched middle schoolers and high schoolers and a few players destined for the big leagues zip around the rink. But it wasn't like *this*.

Watching professionals skate and shoot and *hit*, now *that* was a revelation.

My breath caught with every collision. I winced when pucks hit the glass and the boards and the goalies and the play-ers. And, yeah, my nails bit into my palms each time another player got close to Cas, every time *he* was hit with a puck or slashed with a stick. And this was professional hockey. Sticks were cracking all over the place and pucks were flying and...

Shit.

He might get *hurt*.

This was a complication I didn't need.

I had a hundred-dollar bill folded neatly in my pocket that I needed to get back to him. I had a lap full of souvenirs and a belly full of treats. My son was jazzed beyond belief and wrig-gling next to me, absolutely captivated by the game (and with absolutely no wincing or worry in sight). He was hooked and happy and...

Cas had done that.

Made my son happy.

Clink.

The chains around my heart hit the concrete floor at my feet, leaving me exposed and vulnerable and—

"*Oh!*" the crowd gasped.

Every muscle in my body tensed as Cas's big body flew through the air, collapsed to the ice, and...

Didn't move.

He didn't move.

For long enough that my lungs began to burn.

"Mom—" Ethan began, his worried gaze turning to mine, but then the crowd seemed to collectively sigh, and my eyes whipped back to the ice.

Cas was up on his skates and the look on his face...

Sent a shiver down my spine.

He was *pissed.*

Maybe it was a cheap shot—I didn't know enough about hockey to say one way or the other. I hadn't bothered to learn the sport that closely as a kid, nor when I watched the games on TV with Ethan. Mostly I took cues from the announcers and the people around me and, this time, the crowd hadn't gone one way or the other. It could be that Cas was just angry he'd been knocked to the ice. Or maybe he was concussed, and the hit had unleashed his inner hockey demon.

Either way, he was on his feet and his skates were flying across the ice and...he crashed into a player from the other team, knocking his opponent down to his knees, scooping up the puck, and *moving.*

Shit, he was fast when he wanted to be.

And this time he didn't pass the puck to his teammate, not like he'd been doing for the first half of the game.

He just started *skating*, hauling butt up the ice, the puck on his stick, and his legs moving so fast I could barely track them. Out of his end of the ice, crossing the big red line that marked the halfway point on the ice, and...

I clenched my teeth together when a player on the other team careened toward him.

Cas just dropped his shoulder, kept skating, and the other player bounced off him.

Literally, bounced off and hit the ice.

Because Cas was a man on a mission. He kept moving, kept skating, crossing over the blue line that led toward the other team's section of the ice.

It was only then that he lost the puck.

Or rather, that he gave the puck up to his teammate, sliding it across a slice of open space to Raph, who corralled it without missing a beat and started sprinting toward the goal. The other team closed in on him in just a few moments, slowing him down, cutting off his rush.

But Cas had kept moving.

And Raph noticed.

The other team didn't, though.

They were focused on Raph and the rest of the forwards closing ranks around him, taking sticks, bodies colliding, open space being closed.

Except around Cas.

Cas slipped down, paused—all alone—next to the net.

Even the goalie wasn't looking at him.

But Raph had.

And he slid the puck back, passing it between skates and sticks and sending it directly to Cas.

Who, as I'd mentioned previously, was *all* alone.

In front of the other team's goal.

I sucked in a breath, nerves seizing, but I didn't even get to exhale before Cas was moving, whacking at the puck, slamming it home.

For one second, the crowd was silent.

But only for a heartbeat.

Then the arena erupted with cheers.

And I was right there with the rest of the Breakers' fans, jumping to my feet, arms in the air, a scream of "*Yes!*" erupting from my mouth as the refs' whistles blew and the red-light shone, the goal song blared through the arena's speakers.

I glanced down at Ethan, saw he was dancing and cheering, his smile huge as he yelled his head off.

Then I looked back at the ice, saw Cas being mauled by his teammates, a cluster of them hugging him and smacking him on the shoulders and back, their group crashing into the boards in a ball of celebrating, hot, hockey players.

But that only lasted for a moment because then the gaggle of yummy hockiness broke up and they began skating to the bench.

All except for Cas.

He pushed off the boards, separated from his teammates, and turned...

And pointed to me.

And I found I was smiling just as wide as Ethan had been.

Shit.

TWENTY-THREE

Cas

MY RIBS ACHED LIKE A MOTHERFUCKER, but I was still standing in the hall, having practically ripped myself, Hulk-style, out of my pads and scalding myself with hot water so that I didn't smell like sweat and ass and disgusting hockey player.

Because I wanted to be there when Jules came down with Ethan.

Wanted to be waiting by the elevators in case she saw the chaos that always filled this level and decided to make a break for it. Currently, back office staff were running around dealing with the usual post-game stuff—media requests, fan interactions, taking pictures for social media, and much more—while the equipment guys were pulling their normal (and heroic) efforts to organize and clean and pack up all our gear, making sure the players had everything we could possibly need for every game. Then there were all the arena workers—cleaners and security, box office and management—as well as many of the front office people for the Breakers.

It was a madhouse.

Organized chaos, but still a madhouse, and Jules was...well, she was important, and I didn't want her to feel overwhelmed and—

I also didn't want her to escape.

And great. Now I sounded like I was trying to be a dumbass evil villain from a crappy Hollywood movie.

I'll never let her escape, muhaha!

Luckily, me being an idiot in my head meant that I didn't have time to worry about whether or not Jules actually *would* come down.

She would, right?

Right. She wouldn't let Ethan miss out on this opportunity. Not everyone got to come down and—yeah, I was an asshole for using Ethan to get close to her. Except, maybe I was only a baby ahole? Because I wasn't just using Ethan. I *wanted* Ethan to have the best night of his life, wanted to make the kid happy. I just...wanted to make Julie happy alongside her son.

Add in all my plans to make that happen, and I *really* didn't have time to worry.

Because then the elevator doors were opening and Ethan and Jules were inside, and fuck if my heart wasn't skipping around like a motherfucker, slamming against my ribcage, stealing my breath and making me feel lightheaded.

"Cas!"

Ethan's face lit up and he sprinted forward off the elevator, launching himself at me and throwing his arms around my middle.

I stifled a grunt. The kid was strong, and my ribs really *were* fucked. "Hey, bud. You have a good time?"

A nod that threatened to turn Ethan into a bobblehead. "You scored a goal!"

A rare feat indeed for me as a defensive defenseman. I wasn't like Smitty. I didn't often jump up in the rush, didn't join the forwards in scoring opportunities.

Oh, I'd take one, for sure, just like I had that night.

But I wasn't the player to seek those out. My strength was cleaning up shit in my own zone, protecting my goalie, blocking shots, and clearing out the front of the net.

Little arms dropped from around my middle, and Ethan stepped back.

"It was so cool!" he exclaimed.

"I'm glad you were here to see it," I said, ruffling Ethan's hair. "I don't do that all too often." I glanced up at Jules, saw that her face was gentle, that there was no anger in her eyes, not any longer anyway.

"Nice game," she said softly.

"Thanks," I murmured, and hell if my voice wasn't gravel. I cleared my throat, focused back on Ethan, focused on my plan to give this kid the best night ever. "You want to go and see some stuff?"

Ethan pumped his fist. "Yes!"

So, I walked him around, showing him the training suite (complete with our intensely focused on her job head trainer, Sam). Then I showed them the family rooms, where kids and spouses could hang out and watch the games on huge flat screens mounted to one wall, play with the provided toys, or use the copious craft supplies. Beyond the training suit was the gym and the hot and cold tubs, including the new machine that players were strapped into while cold air was blown over our bodies (and wasn't *that* a fucking joy?). But it was supposed to help with healing by shocking the body in a way that was similar to the ice baths of old.

There were also massage rooms—though Ethan was definitely more wowed by our Rec Room, which was basically a huge room with a small kitchen, its cabinets jam-packed with food. The rest of the open space was filled with leather recliners and televisions hooked up to different video game consoles, along with several coffee tables where feet could be propped up. Basically, it was a space where the guys could hang out and chill. Though, this was typically before games and in between warm-ups or after the occasional morning skate that Coach had us come to, rather than after games when everyone was tired and wanted to just go home and sleep.

After that, I took him to the locker room. Note: this was last because I didn't need Jules and Ethan scarred by Smitty walking around with his dick out. Even though this was the public-facing room and we weren't really supposed to be walking around with dicks out, Smitty really liked being naked, so one never knew with him. Once I had deemed it was safe, we slipped in through the open door. Also note: this was done after I poked my head in and made sure that everyone was clothed (e.g. that Smitty was decent) and after I'd fixed the remaining members of my team with a death glare to threaten them to behave before I'd actually stepped aside and let Ethan walk inside.

"Whoa!" Ethan said, rushing in and running over to the Breakers logo that was printed on the carpet in the middle of the room. "*Whoa!*" he said again, spinning in a circle, seemingly taking in the stalls where the guys got dressed—many of which were still filled with players who were wearing skates and shin guards and hockey pants, their shoulder pads hanging behind them, their elbow pads on the shelves, plopped next to their helmets.

Jerseys went into the rolling bin in the middle of the room.

Gloves were dropped in the cubbies in the hall to be dried

and cleaned (this was also done in between periods because there was nothing worse than trying to control the puck with wet gloves and slick palms).

"Who's this?" Marcel asked, the quiet captain smiling.

"Ethan!" Ethan filled him in before Jules or I could answer. "And you're Marcel Aubert," he went on, his voice filled with awe—and hell if I wasn't a little jealous. "And you're Connor Smith," Ethan said, turning to Smitty. "And Raph Gomez and—"

That was the point that Ethan short-circuited, going mute, his eyes wide and he seemed to lose his confidence.

I moved toward him, crouching down and wrapping an arm around his shoulders. "Did you know that Smitty once tripped over Raph's stick on the ice and sprained his wrist?"

It was still one of the best days of my life, watching that sequence of events.

The big, bulky defensemen tap dancing on the ice before going down.

Once I knew that Smitty wasn't badly hurt, anyway.

"Really, man?" Smitty boomed. "You're gonna do me like that?"

Hell yeah, I was.

Payback for all the shit I had been on the receiving end of.

"Did it hurt?" Ethan asked, and—damn—my heart squeezed. There was real concern in the kid's voice.

Nice. *Really* nice.

Just like his mama.

"Not too much, buddy," Smitty said, smacking a meaty fist against his chest. "I'm big and tough."

"And klutzy," Raph said, only halfway under his breath.

Smitty glared as the rest of the guys busted up, but then he was coming over to Ethan, taking him on a tour of the rest of the room, showing him sticks and his helmet and generally showing his good (instead of evil) side. This was the side that had endeared him to each and every one of the members of this organization.

Smitty cared, and he did it big.

Even if he was annoying a lot of the time.

"What about you?"

"What's that, gorgeous?" I asked, pushing to my feet with a grunt, biting back a wince when the movement made pain shoot through my ribs.

Yeah, my ribs were definitely not going to be my happy place for the next few days.

"What about you, honey?" she repeated, albeit with the addition of the endearment that sent my pulse skittering through my veins. And I was reeling from the *honey* when she came close, when she gently smoothed her fingertips over my side.

Over my ribs.

"What's that?" I asked again.

"Are *you* big and tough?" Another smooth of her hand. "Big and *tough* enough that you'll ignore and fight through whatever is making you wince?"

"I'm fine, gorgeous." I shrugged, and newsflash, *that* was a mistake. I went on anyway. "Hockey is a contact sport and a lot of time that means it comes with bruises."

A tilt of her head, concern in her deep chocolate eyes. "You're hurting," she said softly, fingers lightly brushing over my aching side again. "You should be resting, not showing us around."

See?

Nice.

Just like her son.

"I'm fine," I said. "Promise. And anyway," I added, feeling oddly shy and nervous. "We should go get Ethan. I'm sure he'll want to see the ice from down here." That was the only stop we hadn't made on the tour yet and Jules's hockey crazed kiddo would love it. "I know it's getting late, and you hardly slept last night and—"

She leaned a little closer, cheeks flushing, eyes warming.

My heart squeezed.

Hard.

Those nerves flared.

"Cas," she whispered. "Honey, you should—"

A child's shriek had us jumping apart.

TWENTY-FOUR

Jules

I DIDN'T MISS the wince cross Cas's face as he jerked away from me, even as Ethan's shriek of joy reminded me we had an audience of very nosy hockey players.

Who would gossip.

And pry.

And would want to know every detail—each of which would be shared with their equally nosy significant others.

I loved the guys—and their significant others—who came into CeCe's.

I really did.

They'd always been fun and kind and had made me feel like I was part of something, even when I was more comfortable (and determined) remaining on the sidelines.

But I didn't want to be in the glare of all that attention.

There was a reason I'd kept a fine line between myself and them.

I couldn't risk letting them in, not deeper than superficially, anyway. I couldn't risk getting hurt.

Couldn't risk *Ethan* getting hurt.

All of which was well and good to say and think and *believe*. Except for the fact that people—*cough* Smitty and Beth and *Cas*—had decided that they were going to walk right over the line in the sand I'd drawn.

That they were going to wriggle in behind my defenses, bury themselves deeply into my heart.

So, despite my best intentions, I wasn't on the sidelines.

And that meant when it all went wrong, it was going to *hurt*.

And Ethan would hurt.

My heart, that bruised, wounded organ, squeezed hard. My baby, my *son*. I should have protected him from this, should have—

Laughter boomed behind me.

Jerking, I took another step back, turned away from the sexy man who was making himself at home in my heart, and saw that my getting close to Cas had definitely *not* been missed (this fact obvious because of the many pairs of interested eyes focused on me and Cas).

Right. Okay, then.

The gossip patrol for the Breakers had been activated. There was nothing to be done about that.

Ethan...he would have a great night, the *best* night. And I would protect him, no matter what. Exactly like I had from the time he'd been growing in my belly.

I would keep him safe.

I'd done a good job so far, and had confidence that I would continue to do so.

I had to believe in that one fact.

Otherwise, I was going to bundle Ethan up in my arms and

run screaming from the room because between my need to protect my baby and the fact that I was very much *not* on the periphery, I was nearing panic.

Fingers on my cheek, a warm chest close to my back, lips I knew could *kiss* and reduce me to a bundle of aching nerves whispering in my ear. "Breathe, gorgeous."

Air hissing out of my mouth.

My body aching to relax, to melt against him.

Not going to happen.

And as for the eyes, they would see soon enough that there wasn't anything between me and Cas—minus a few kisses and some apples and pancakes—and those were nothing (insert my slightly hysterical laughter here). Cas was just doing a nice thing for my son, *all* of them were, so none of this meant *anything* (and yeah, there was more laughter here, this time of the delusional variety).

Speaking of my son, I should probably be paying attention to Ethan.

Yup.

I definitely needed to watch my kid—while at the same time avoiding getting even closer to the sexy hockey player who was standing close, the smell of soap and spice filling my nose. I needed to avoid that sexy hockey player who was pretending not to hurt while he showed my son around and generally made Ethan's night, his year, his *life*.

The thing was...I knew too much about buried pain.

Which meant, as much as I knew I *needed* to retreat to the sidelines, I also knew...I was going to be an idiot.

Because I wasn't going to retreat.

Because I *hated* that Cas was hiding his hurts.

Of course, I could hate it without doing anything about it, without crossing my own line, without being an idiot and risking my and Ethan's hearts.

I could do that.

Sure.

"Whoa! You're so tall, Smitty!" Ethan said, and I shook my head (shaking the tangled thoughts right out of my brain) and focused on the scene that was unfolding in front of me. Just in time to watch my son six-plus feet in the air. Literally. Because he was sitting on Smitty's shoulders, and the tall hockey player was inexplicably jumping straight up and down. Repeatedly.

"Um..." I whispered, thinking that if this was how professional hockey players passed their time on this team, then they were a hell of a lot tamer than I'd previously thought.

Fried cheese. Excited jumping. A maniacal, blue-furred stuffed creature propped in a place of honor on a shelf by the door.

These guys were *weird.*

"He's trying to touch the lucky spot."

I blinked. *Okaaay.* That explanation wasn't any better.

"Um..." I whispered again.

Cas set his hand on the back of my neck, tilted my head slightly up and to the side. "Right there. See?"

I squinted, saw there was a...*oh*, I saw it then. There was a sticker with the Breakers logo stuck to the ceiling, almost hidden between two of the industrial tiles that formed the top of the room.

"I almost..." Ethan grunted and stretched as Smitty jumped again and his fingertips just brushed the sticker. "Got it!"

Smitty whooped.

Some of the guys cheered.

Ethan pumped his arms like he'd just completed a herculean task.

Cas chuckled, called in a voice that sent warmth flowing through every single cell in my body, "Nice job, buddy."

Ethan, still on top of Smitty's shoulders, turned and smiled at Cas, and that smile told a truth that smacked me hard enough to make me see stars. Ethan had that same warmth flowing through him. My kid was in deep too.

Panic, writhing and choking, swept through me.

"Breathe, gorgeous." Another whisper. Another touch of his fingers to my cheek.

How the fuck was I supposed to breathe?

This was all wrong.

And...this was so fucking right, more right than anything I'd ever felt in my life.

This was...almost a fairy tale.

Except, my life didn't bring me happy endings, so I needed to stop that shit right here.

Right here.

I bundled that determination close, glanced up at Cas, lips parting to pass along my decision, but my words promptly stoppered up in the back of my throat. Because the look on *his* face as he watched Ethan hit me. *Hard.* And then he glanced down at me, gave me that same warmth and affection and—

My brain short-circuited.

My big, dumb heart took over.

I found myself reaching up, smoothing my thumb over the prickly hair on his cheeks that was hiding a taut jaw, the lines fanning lightly out from the corners of his eyes. Cas was hurting. He was here giving me and Ethan *warm* while he was hurting. And throughout it all, he wasn't impatient, wasn't annoyed.

He was just...Cas.

Click.

More armor unlocking.

More of my heart exposed.

"We should let you get back to the trainer," I murmured, gently brushing the creases near his eyes again. "You really need to get those ribs looked at."

His big, warm palm was still resting on the side of my neck. My words had his fingers flexing, turning my head toward him now, and—oh look—his face was *right there.* And his lips were *right there.* And the memories were *right there,* flowing through my mind, making me remember exactly how it felt to kiss him, how it felt to touch him, how it felt to see him in my kitchen making pancakes, how it felt to have his warmth shining on me. "I'm fine, gorgeous." Another squeeze before his hand slid down, smoothing between my shoulder blades, settling at my lower back. "Promise."

"But—"

"Smitty!" he called, and I jumped again, my body brushing against all the hardness of his, and hell if I didn't feel that right between my thighs.

Smitty turned, Ethan still on his shoulders. "Yeah?"

"Let my guy down." Cas's hand slipped around to hook on my hip, tugging me close to his side. "I have more to show them."

Yeah.

That was what I was afraid of.

TWENTY-FIVE

Cas

I WAS BREAKING THROUGH.

I could taste it on the back of my tongue, could feel it in the imprint of her fingertips on my skin, could sense it in the way her body had finally relaxed against mine.

The rink itself had been the final thing I'd showed Ethan and Jules, even though I would have continued to find shit to extend the tour if not for the fact that the late night seemed to have finally caught up with Ethan.

When his yawns had punctuated his excitement, I had called it.

Now I'd walked Jules and Ethan back through the arena and out into the cold night air. And when Ethan had stumbled as we made our way up the long flight of stairs leading to Jules's car, I had scooped him up, carried him to give his little legs a breather, and fuck, the little boy had sewn himself even tighter into my heart. Because within a minute Ethan had been *out*, his head dropping to my shoulder, one arm around my neck, the other hanging at my side.

"I can—" Jules began, probably because my arms were also laden with the bags of souvenirs I'd sent them earlier.

"I got him, gorgeous," I said. "You just get your keys out, yeah?"

She bit her lip—which had the side effect of making me want to kiss her—but then she nodded and dug through her purse and pulled out her keys.

"Did you have a nice night?" I asked softly, finding that with Ethan asleep, I needed to fill the silence, needed to hear her voice, needed to know that she was here with me and not thinking about something else.

Footsteps halting, her body spinning toward me so fast I barely processed it. "Are you serious?"

"Yeah." I cleared my throat. Her tone was full-on porcupine, and I decided to proceed with caution. "I mean, I know that it was just a game and looking through a bunch of rooms, but—"

Her fingers touched my jaw. "It was the *best* night of my life," she whispered, and then she smoothed her hand over Ethan's head. "Because I got to see him have the best night of *his* life." She looked up, held my gaze, her voice so soft I could barely hear it. "So, thank you for letting me be part of giving that to him."

Then she was spinning away from me, walking with near furious speed, but not before I'd seen that soft voice of hers on her face...and not before I'd watched all that soft disappear, chased out by panic.

I felt a bit deflated, if I was honest. Losing that soft was like losing a limb.

But then I saw my name on her back.

And instead, I knew I needed to focus on the fact that I was making progress.

She'd shared her past. She was letting me hold her son. She cared about my bruised ribs enough to bring it up several times. And she was wearing my name on her back.

So yeah, progress.

Jules unlocked her car when we got close, tugged open the back door, and through some maneuvering that had my ribs reminding me angrily that they didn't like me bending and twisting, I got Ethan into his booster seat and carefully straightened, stepping back so that Jules could check to make sure his belt was buckled correctly.

Then she was quietly shutting the door and turning to face me.

Yup. All panic. No soft.

Two steps forward. One step back.

"You okay to drive, gorgeous?" I asked, giving in to the urge to touch her and smoothing my fingers over her cheek.

She blinked wide eyes. "What?"

"It's late. We had a rough night last night"—I brushed her forearm, below the spot where my bitch of an ex had hurt her—"and it's late again tonight. So, I'm asking, sweetheart, are you okay to drive?"

A shrug, which had the bonus side effect of rubbing her body against mine. Not as good as holding her, but still, feeling any part of her was fucking incredible. However, then her response permeated my tired, hurting, sleep-lacking brain. "I'm used to it."

Anger prickled at the base of my spine, alertness sliding through me. "What do you mean?"

Anger that apparently permeated my tone and face and body, if her eyes skittering away from mine and her taking a step back were any indication.

Cool it, dumbass.

"I should let you get home," she murmured. "You've had a couple of late nights, too."

I was wiped, yes, but didn't want to say goodbye, didn't want to go home to my empty house, didn't want to sleep in my bed alone again, and I didn't want to leave her, not with that look in her eyes, not with her telling me she was *used to it.*

The fatigue? The staying up late? The rough nights?

All of the above?

"Gorgeous," I said, stepping closer, boxing her in, her scent in my nose, all those soft curves against my body. "What exactly are you used to?"

"I..." She bit her lip, looked away. "It's late. I should get going."

Fingers in her hair, tilting her head back, locking my gaze with hers, needing to know what the fuck was going through her head, what was putting that look on her face. Was it the past? Because then I'd do my fucking best to make it so that those memories didn't intrude on her present. But if it *was* that present, was in her life *now,* then I was going to lose my mind... and then I was going to fix it.

"Spill, Jules," I ordered. "Is someone hurting you?"

Her brows dragged together. "No one is hurting me," she said, that frown still in place. "Well, outside of last night." Her soft addition fucking eviscerated me.

"Fuck," I whispered, dropping my hand, stepping away.

I'd gotten it in my mind that *I* was going to fix her life, going to make things right for her.

But she'd already built out her life into a good one, already had a job and a son and a place that was more like a home than my empty ass house. And what did I bring to her? A psycho ex who'd hurt her, who'd kept her up, who'd—

Her body was suddenly against mine, hand resting on my jaw. "I didn't mean it like that."

She wouldn't.

Jules was nice. She didn't drive the knife home, didn't twist it and try to wound in the biggest, most painful way.

She stroked gentle fingers through my beard, said softly, "I really didn't."

"I know," I said, covering her hand with my own, peeling her fingers back and pressing a kiss to her palm.

"I just meant that I'm a single mom," she explained. "One who works the closing shift at a bar. I'm always tired and I'm equally used to not getting enough sleep."

I hated that for her.

Fucking *hated* it.

"But the hurting stopped when I left California," she whispered. "Matt—you know, the owner of CeCe's—I got lucky when I applied. We clicked, and he watched out for me until I got settled. He and his partner found my apartment, and they were great when Ethan was little." Her tone held love, and fuck, I was jealous of a gay couple again, jealous of the way they'd taken care of *my* woman. "They're still great," she whispered. "But they have their own lives, especially now that they adopted their little girl. We're still close, but I'm not at their place all the time anymore." Her lips turned up. "Something they probably prefer."

They'd be idiots if they preferred that.

Jules was fucking beautiful—and not just on the outside. She had an inner light that shone brightly, that filled the space around her.

I craved that light.

Needed it.

But I needed to know *all* of her. Including the heavy parts she might want to keep buried.

"Was your dad physical with you?"

In other words, who in the fuck did I need to kill?

That froze her, set her light dimming slightly. "No," she whispered. "His expertise was hurting me by not giving a fuck about me, emotionally, bodily, or otherwise. Oh. And eviscerating me with words on the odd times I deigned to notice me."

"And Nate?" I ground out.

A flash of pain in her eyes. "Nate didn't get physical either. He just...manipulated me, made me feel safe, and then the moment I dared to step outside the tiny, lidded box he wanted to keep me inside, he smashed my heart." A breath. "He was really good at eviscerating me with words too." Her throat worked. "And, of course, he hurt me when he decided that he wasn't going to be a father to Ethan. Mostly because I knew that one day it was going to hurt Ethan, hurt the little baby that I already loved even though he hadn't even been born yet." Another breath, a deeper, longer sigh, sad in her eyes. "Which, I think, is his worst crime of all. How"—she gestured to her sleeping son—"how could someone not want *that* in your life?"

"I don't know," I answered honestly. "How he could not understand the gift that Ethan is—the gift that *you* are..." I shook *my* head this time. "Miller is a fucking idiot. And the same goes for your father. You are both fucking *wonderful*."

Her eyes went glassy. "Cas..."

I cupped her cheek. "You are beautiful and bright, a good mom, smart as hell, and *bright*, Jules. I mean it, sweetheart. You fill every room you're in with all that bright inside you."

"Honey, I—" She shook her head again, watery eyes drifting over my shoulder. "I'm just...me."

"And you just being you is fucking *beautiful*."

Her eyes shot back to mine, held for a long moment, emotions swirling in her pretty brown eyes.

And then she lost it.

TWENTY-SIX

Jules

YOU FILL *every room you're in with all that bright inside you.*

How did I respond to that?

Not with tears.

Not like I was doing in that moment, the burning beginning in the backs of my eyes, a prickling moving forward, surrounding them on all sides as moisture pooled, and blurring my vision and...

Letting go.

The dam had broken, and the tears escaped, clinging to my lashes, dripping down my cheeks.

And then there were warm arms around me.

And maybe that was why I found that I could cry.

Because I knew those arms would catch me, would wrap around me, would hold me tight, whisper kind words to me, would wipe my tears.

"It's okay, gorgeous," he murmured, smoothing his palm up and down my back, tugging me against him, holding me so tight that one second, I felt as though I were crumbling to pieces and the next moment, I was put back together, the cracks filled in with superglue. "I'm here. I've got you."

Which was what I was afraid of.

Because he wasn't telling me to not cry, wasn't telling me to stop.

He was letting me lose it while he held down the fort.

While he held *me* together.

That was what finally made my tears dry up, finally had me stepping outside of that beauty he'd just given me, and back into reality.

A breath. Two.

"Sorry," I whispered. And then I was reaching for my cheeks, wanting to wipe the tears away.

But he beat me to it, gently brushing the tears from my face, and then leaning forward, his head dropping, he kissed the skin beneath my eyes, kissed away the remnants of my waterworks.

And just that quickly, I was ready to start sobbing all over again.

Luckily, I wasn't a *total* melting pot and despite his beautiful words and his gentle touch and the fact that right then he cupped my cheek and told me, "Let it out, gorgeous. I've got sisters, and I'm used to tears," I managed to pull it back together.

A nod, remembering what he'd told Ethan in the park. "You have two sisters."

"Yup," he said on a beleaguered sigh. "Both younger." His lips twitched. "Needless to say, I've waded through my fair share of drama and tears."

"I always wanted a big family," I whispered.

"It's great," he said, the truth in the frankness of his tone. "Even with a pesky annoying younger brother and two baby sisters who spent their formative years hogging the bathroom."

I felt my eyes go wide. "You're one of *four?*"

A grin that made me want to taste his smile.

"Trust me when I say it's both fun and torture and"—he wrinkled his nose and that might have been the cutest thing I'd ever seen—"maybe a little more on the torturous side because my parents are in love." Humor twinkling in those green eyes. "And by in love, I mean *in love.* They hold hands and make out and I swear to God, I've seen them sneak off in the middle of a party to go find a closet."

My mouth dropped open.

Cas ran his thumb along my bottom lip. "Yeah. I know."

I giggled. "That's amazing."

"It is," he said softly. "But it's a bit of a curse."

That was...weird. "Um...why?"

"Because they set this standard for me. They showed me what I want to find in a relationship, and it's so fucking great and perfect and"—a sigh—"it's also been *impossible* to find." Another brush of his thumb over my bottom lip. "At least, until I walked into CeCe's and saw you."

I sucked in a breath, decided that I couldn't touch that, not if I didn't want to end up in tears again. "So, you want to settle down?"

Which wasn't much better to ask.

Because—with his fingers on my skin, with his body close— it implied too fucking much.

"Yeah, gorgeous," he said. "I want to settle down."

And the undertones in that...*fuck.* They hit hard and heavy and deep and *fuck,* they made me want *all* the things I shouldn't. Again. Which was why I was standing with my body pressed to his from chest to thighs, Cas's arm around me, his other hand on my face, stroking my skin. All that wanting. All that buried need.

All that stupidity.

Step away. I should step away.

It was late and cold, and I was wrapped in a pair of masculine arms when I should be in my car, driving away from the temptation of Cas.

A brush of his fingers across my cheek, sliding up toward my temple, tucking a loose strand of hair behind my ear.

An ear he bent toward.

An ear he whispered in.

"You, gorgeous. I want to settle down with *you*." His tongue flicked out, grazed my earlobe, making me shiver. "Just in case that wasn't clear before."

My chin dropped to my chest.

"Fuck it," I whispered.

Fingers tracing the shell of my ear. "What's that, sweetheart?"

"Fuck *it*," I whispered again.

"Jules?" he asked, concern entering his tone.

My head shot up. I rose onto tiptoe.

And...I gave in.

Arms around his shoulders, my body pressed tightly against his. So tightly that my nipples were happy being in contact with his chest, that my skin tingled just from feeling the heat of him, the *strength* of him.

"Jules?" he asked again, his hand flexing on my jaw, confusion in those striking green eyes.

And...

I. Gave. In.

Lifting higher, slanting my mouth across his.

Fuck. It.

Because that was good. That was fucking *perfect*.

And just like before, there wasn't the slightest bit of hesitation. Our lips met and our bodies knew exactly what to do. It was almost as though we were made for each other—a thought, when combined with Cas's talk of settling down—that burned through me.

Wanting.

More wanting.

Fear in my belly. Indecision in my mind.

But then Cas's tongue was sliding along the seam of my lips, silently asking me to open, and I *did* open.

My mouth, my mind, my *heart*.

Because the touch was so gentle, because he was holding me close and tight and *carefully*.

Because he made me *feel* and...because he made Ethan smile.

Heaven help me.

But I *opened*.

In the physical world, his groan rumbled through my body, teasing my nipples, sending a gush of moisture between my thighs. One sound, one touch, one kiss, and I was mush, my knees shaking, my legs jelly, my body leaning heavily against him.

Something that wasn't exactly conducive to kissing the man who was so much taller than me.

Something that became a nonissue when he lifted me up and set me on the hood of my car. Suddenly, my back was on the cold metal and my front was pressed to his hot, hard body, and...

He took off the kid gloves and really *kissed* me.

Tongue and teeth and hands stroking all over my body, up along my side, dancing over my ribs, tracing the bottom curve of my breasts, then down again, spreading my thighs, stepping between them, and giving me a whole different kind of hot and *hard*.

Unfortunately, not *all* the hot and hard I wanted because just as my legs wrapped around his hips, just as my hips began rocking, pressing myself against all that hot and hard, Cas reared back, breaking the kiss.

"*Fuck*," he growled, bracing himself on one hand next to my shoulder, head hanging, lips swollen, and hair mussed.

I lifted a trembling hand up to my own lips, still able to feel his mouth on mine, able to feel his hands on my body. "Did I—" I pressed lightly, sucked in, and released a breath. "Did I hurt you?"

His head tilting.

His gaze coming to mine.

Then he gently peeled my hand from my lips and brought it...

Oh.

He brought it to the hot and hard currently straining against the fabric of his pants. "Oh yeah, gorgeous. You hurt me." A nip to my bottom lip. "Because you kissed me like that, and you didn't do it while you were naked."

I sucked in a breath.

But he was already pushing off me, hauling me to my feet, bundling me around the front of my car and to the driver's side door.

A moment later, I was inside on the seat, and he was pulling the belt across my body.

Click.

His hand on my cheek. His lips brushing mine. His eyes locking with mine, molten and swirling and making my mind go hazy with need all over again. "You working tomorrow night?"

I focused on the words, managed to nod.

"I'll come by for dinner."

More focusing. More nodding.

"Ethan with the sitter?"

"No...uh..."

Shit. I'd forgotten that Mary had a date the following night. I was supposed to have called my backup sitter.

Fingers on my cheek. "What's the matter, sweetheart?"

"My normal girl has a date tomorrow," I whispered. "I forgot that I was supposed to call my backup sitter today and—"

"I'll watch him," he said instantly.

I blinked.

"What time are you on at the bar?"

"Um..."

"*Gorgeous.*" A thumb running over one cheek. "What time are you working tomorrow?"

"Six to close," I whispered.

"I have practice tomorrow. Bring Ethan to CeCe's. I'll meet you there. He and I will eat dinner together and hang out with you for a bit and then I'll take him home and hang at your place until you get home."

"Um..."

A tug on a strand of my hair. "I'll be at CeCe's at six tomorrow."

"Um..."

"Goodnight, sweetheart."

He straightened, closed my door.

And then he walked away.

And then...I *drove* away.

Because I couldn't sit in my car, staring at where Cas had disappeared.

Not for more than a few minutes, anyway.

TWENTY-SEVEN

Cas

"AND THEN I'M going to reverse." Ethan slapped a card down on the stack in between us. "And skip and then I'm going to..." The little guy made a flurry of movements and before dropping a final card on the deck. "Uno!"

And yup, that was the moment I realized I'd seriously underestimated the tiny human sitting across from me.

"Your turn, Cas!"

My mind was still spinning from the sudden turn of events, and I randomly set a card from the ones I was holding onto the pile between us.

The *wrong* card, apparently.

Because Ethan slammed down his final card. "I win!"

He *didn't* just win.

He'd absolutely destroyed me.

Holy hell.

Setting my mass of cards down—yes, *mass*—on the table, I

extended my fist across the table for Ethan to bump. "That was well played, bud."

Bubbling hope and joy in Ethan's eyes. "Yeah?"

"Yeah, bud, for sure." I stole a fry from his plate, grinned when Ethan stole a tot from mine. "Next time we do this, we'll have your mom drop you at the rink so we can get a skate in first."

"*Really?*"

I ruffled his hair. "Really. But I think for tonight we're going to have to call it."

Ethan's brows pulled together, and fuck if he didn't look like his mom when he did that. It was cute as hell—almost as much as the question he asked. "What do you mean, *call it?*"

"I mean, it's late, so we've got to get out of here, do your homework, and then head off to bed."

Now nose-wrinkling joined the frown.

Fucking cute.

"I don't like homework," Ethan muttered.

"I didn't like it when I was in school either, buddy, but it's important."

"Why?"

Well, that was a good question. "Because it reinforces what we learn in school," I said, thinking that was a damned good answer. Ethan made a face—whether that was because he didn't know what *reinforce* meant or because he wasn't buying my explanation, I didn't know, but I quickly added, "I have homework too. We can do yours and mine, then go to bed."

Wide eyes. "*You* have homework?"

"Yup." Video to watch, plays to go over. "Think you can help me with it?"

Wider eyes. "You need *me* to help with it?"

"Yeah, bud."

"Okay! Then you can help me with my math and reading."

I was hopeful that I could swing kindergarten math (though I definitely knew that I could crush kindergarten level reading).

I lifted my fist so Ethan could bump it again, left enough money on the table to cover the tab and a tip (though not the hundred-dollar one we'd been passing back and forth because *that* I'd found shoved into my pocket the night before, the sneak). "Let's go say goodbye to your mom, yeah?"

"Okay!" Ethan clambered down from the stool and beelined for Jules, who was filling cups with ice and soda.

I followed with less clambering and speed, but I still made it in time to watch Ethan wrap his arms around her waist and squeeze her tight enough to make her grunt. "We're going home, and I'm gonna to help Cas with his homework," Ethan declared.

Jules' lips turned up as she bent and kissed the top of his head. "You are, honey?"

"Yup." A pop on the p at the end. "Then he's going to help me with mine."

Her eyes lifted to mine, held long enough that the warmth there, the brightness and light inside her was focused solely on me.

My pulse picked up.

"He is?" she asked softly.

"Yup." Another pop at the end.

"Well, that sounds like a plan," she said, pulling her eyes from mine and glancing down. "And then you'll go to bed without giving him any trouble?" Now Mom had entered her tone, and it was a side that I hadn't seen before. A side that had my lips twitching, not only because of Ethan's immediate reaction, but because I was stifling the same response.

That being to straighten and nod in agreement.

Mom Voice meant business.

"We'll be fine, gorgeous," I told her. "Ethan and I are set."

She started to turn for the hall. "I'll get you my keys so you can get his booster seat out."

I cupped her jaw. "I grabbed one from Target today, sweetheart. Ethan's covered."

Her eyes flared. "He's covered?"

I leaned in closer, pressed my lips to the spot on her cheek which was just in front of her ear, into which I whispered, "He's covered, and *you're* covered."

"I'm...covered?" she whispered.

I tugged out the hundred-dollar bill and slid it carefully into her apron, disguising the action with a brush of my lips over hers. "Text me when you're on your way home," I ordered quietly as I straightened. "Or call if you feel tired and need to talk to stay awake."

Teeth pressing into her bottom lip, making me want to kiss her again, and not just a brush this time. Longer, deeper, and without an audience of bar patrons and five-year-olds.

"You with me?"

She nodded. "Thanks again for doing this—I know you're busy and—"

Fuck it.

I kissed her, and it was a little more than a brush that time, though less than I'd wanted. And yeah, maybe I had an ego, but I couldn't help that I liked the slightly dazed way she stared up at me when I pulled back. "No thanks needed," I whispered, brushing my hand over her glistening bottom lip. "Okay?"

She nodded again. "Okay."

"All right, gorgeous," I said with another brush of my thumb over that tempting, *tempting* lip. "I'll see you later." A glance down showed me that Ethan was looking up at us curiously—and with an amount of bright in his deep brown eyes that rivaled his mom's that hit me *hard*. "Ready, bud?" I asked, though my heart was pounding against my ribs.

"Yup! Love you, Mom!" he declared with another squeeze to his mom's middle before he took my hand. "Ready, Cas!"

My heart kept pounding.

This kid.

God, he was *such* a good kid.

Jules glanced at me and then at Ethan, and then her face got soft. "Love you, honey," she whispered, and then her eyes came to mine.

"See you later," she whispered.

"Yeah, you will."

And then Ethan tugged on my hand and we walked out of CeCe's.

And then we went home and crushed that homework.

Both Ethan's *and* mine.

TWENTY-EIGHT

CAS'S CAR was parked at the curb in front of my apartment.

My heart was in my throat.

I was *nervous*.

It was after two and I'd texted Cas thirty minutes before, telling him I was heading home. I'd half expected that he would be asleep, that he wouldn't text back.

But...he was Cas.

So, of course, he'd texted me back.

> See you soon, gorgeous.

Gorgeous.

That still sent a flutter through my belly each and every time I heard it—or saw it in a text, I supposed.

But now I had pulled into my parking spot and was sitting in my car, and I was trying to work up the courage to get my shit together and walk inside.

Except...Cas was in there.

And I'd made some decisions in the last twenty-four hours.

Had decided to take a tentative step—or maybe *ten* tentative steps forward—and now those decisions had led to this.

To Cas in my house and me being awake and no drama surrounding us.

Just me and him and—

My car door opened.

I stifled a shriek. Because it was Cas. *Of course* it was.

"Come inside, sweetheart," he whispered.

"I'm not used to this," I whispered back instead of moving, instead of getting up, instead of launching myself into his arms like I really, *really* wanted to.

"Used to what?" he asked, fingers drifting down my throat. "Someone having your back?" A beat. "Or someone being nice to you?"

Either.

Both.

All of it.

Cas not blinking about playing babysitter. His guilt for being a small part of me getting hurt two nights before. The food. The kisses. The gentle way he touched and talked to me.

"Yeah," he murmured. "I know you aren't, gorgeous, but I'm going to keep on giving it to you. Because you deserve nice. You deserve someone to have your back. You deserve *everything*."

Shit.

Now my eyes were stinging.

"Hey," he whispered, pushing the button to unlock my seat belt, reaching over the console to snag my purse. "Let's go inside and get you warm, yeah?"

Luckily, he didn't wait for me to answer, just tugged me out of the car.

And hell, if him cupping the back of my head, protecting me from hitting it on the frame of the door, didn't send me all that much closer to tears.

I was falling for him.

Deep.

And I knew that I wasn't going to *stop* falling.

That, heaven help me, I was going to ride this out.

A breath.

Several blinks as he closed the driver's side door and locked my car, as he walked me up to the front door and let us inside.

Click.

That lock was engaged too.

"Ethan's out," he murmured, setting my purse on the table in the hall. "So, let's get you to bed, gorgeous." He reached for my jacket, tugging it down my arms, hanging it on the hook by the door.

And that was when I kept on falling.

More care.

More gentle.

More *Cas.*

So, this time...well, *this* time I was going to leap both mentally *and* physically.

I launched myself into his arms, wrapped my arms around his shoulders, my legs around his middle, and then I lowered my head, slanting my lips over his.

"Jules?" he asked against my mouth.

"Bed," I whispered back.

To his credit, he didn't hesitate, just carried me down the hall and to my bedroom.

But he didn't close the door.

Which meant he didn't lock it either.

Instead, he kept carrying me across the room before he bent and laid me on the bed.

When he didn't come over the top of me, didn't pin me to the bed and commence with the kissing and touching—and hopefully, the fucking—I frowned, started to sit up, wanting to kiss him again, wanting to touch him. Only, when I reached for him, he was already moving away, shifting to the foot of the bed, tugging off one of my shoes and then the other.

Okay, *that* was fine.

His fingers trailed down my calf, to my foot, started to rub, and—*oh*—that was better than fine. That was nice. *Really* nice. My feet always hurt like hell after a shift and—

I moaned.

His eyes went hot. "I'm going to make you do that again."

My breath caught. Yes. *Finally*. We'd been dancing around this for so freaking long.

But then he added, "When you're not so tired."

Air rushing out, disappointment coursing through me. "Cas—"

His hands went to my other foot. "Just relax for a few minutes, gorgeous," he murmured. "Then you can get to sleep."

"I don't—"

Oh, holy hell, his *fingers*.

If they were that good on my feet, how good would they be in other places—*in* other places?

Right.

That thought had me freezing, had me focusing. And I knew that he was going to have me reduced to a lump of goo if I let that go on much longer. Which was the only reason that I was able to tug my foot free. Then I moved quickly so he couldn't distract me again, darting to the door, closing it quietly, and engaging the lock.

Yeah, that *click* was satisfying.

Worry in his eyes. "Jules—"

I stopped thinking, concentrated on moving back to him

quickly. A second later, I was in his lap, arms around his neck. "We're alone. Ethan is asleep. And I want *this*." My lips hit his for a kiss that was hard and hot and with copious amounts of tongue. "And"—a breath, pushing through my nerves—"I think that kiss means you want it too."

He groaned, one hand weaving into my hair, the other gripping my hip, dragging me close enough that I felt all that *hard and hot*. "I *do* want it. But it's late, sweetheart. You've worked a full shift and hardly slept the last couple of nights—"

"And Ethan is asleep," I said. "And I'm *used* to being tired. And, I'll repeat, *Ethan is asleep*." My words came quickly, countering the fury that had begun to gather in his eyes as I spoke. "I'm a single mom with a five-year-old who's beyond curious and never stops moving when he's awake. Free time without my kiddo is a premium." My hand on his jaw, feeling the bristles of his beard on my palm. "I..." Here was another leap, another step onto the bridge that suspended me over a gorge when one wrong move would send me careening to the bottom.

But...all the right ones might take me—

Hell, this was the first time I'd even allowed for this possibility.

That being...that the right moves might take me safely to the other side.

"I like you, Cas," I whispered. "And I like the way you make me feel and how you touch me. And I'd like you to touch me more and—*ah!*"

It was a shriek, one that hopefully wouldn't wake my dead to the world son, and one that was accompanied by my body flying backward, my head landing on the pillows...

And Cas's big, hot, *hard* body was on top of mine.

TWENTY-NINE

Cas

SHE WAS BENEATH ME, staring up with swollen lips and hooded eyes.

And we hadn't even gotten started, and I was already walking the razor's edge of retaining control and blowing my load.

"Fuck," I hissed, clenching my jaw, trying to summon my patience.

This was not the time to rip off her clothes and fuck her.

Uncertainty crept into her eyes, and that had me uttering *fuck* again—though this time it was only in my head because I wasn't frustrated with Jules, wasn't angry or pissed off at all. *What* I was...well, I was fighting for control and my woman was sexy as shit and...I repeated, I was *fighting for control.*

Thankfully, I summoned a modicum of it.

"You're so fucking gorgeous," I murmured, bracing myself up on one hand and tracing up her side with my other, loving that she shivered, her body melting with just that touch, her back arching, hips bucking against me.

Strip her naked.

Fuck her fast and furious.

But she deserved more.

More dredges of control being summoned, and I managed to give her more, bending and kissing her until my lungs screamed for air, until her arms and legs had wrapped around me, and she was grinding against my dick. That was dangerous. Especially as her moans kept coming, and she continued to rub against me. I dragged my mouth along her jaw, kissed my way down her throat, traced my tongue along her delicate collarbones.

"Cas," she moaned.

"Yeah, gorgeous?"

Her fingers in my hair, holding her against me.

"*Cas.*" Another moan.

"I like the way you say my name," I muttered, nipping her collarbone, palming her breasts, running my thumbs over her nipples, and then, needing skin, reaching for the hem of her CeCe's-branded shirt and tugging it off over her head.

Pretty.

So *fucking* pretty.

No.

Gorgeous.

"Fuck," I whispered, mouth watering. "You are so *fucking beautiful.*"

She inhaled sharply, breasts jiggling in her plain cotton bra that barely contained her breasts. Not lace and satin, but utilitarian and simple...and still the sexiest piece of clothing I'd ever been lucky enough to lay eyes on. "Cas."

I bent, pressed a kiss to the spot between her breasts,

running my tongue over one plump globe and then the other. When she inhaled again, hips rolling needily against me, I tugged one cup down and—hell—my cock jerked *hard*. A puffy pink nipple, just begging for my mouth. "So *fucking* beautiful," I whispered, flicking out my tongue, dragging it around the sensitive peak, watching it tighten in response. Then I took that hardened bud into my mouth, gently at first, and when her hips jerked and her hands came to my hair, winding firmly through the strands again, holding me tighter against her, I drew harder and deeper.

"*Cas!*" Her fingers tightened almost painfully, but she could rip it the fuck out for all I cared because the feel of her in my mouth, on my tongue, my lips, made that small pain worth it. So much so that I kissed my way to her other breast, yanked that side of her bra down, and gave her other nipple the same treatment.

Her moans were music to my ears.

Her body was the stuff of dreams.

Her there with me right then, allowing me to touch her, to be in this bed—

That was *every-fucking-thing*.

I kissed the underside of her breasts, shifted down further, nipping at her ribs, at her hip bones. My hands curved over her belly, tracing the faint marks there, the ones that proclaimed to the world that she'd helped to create something wonderful, that she'd carried her son, protected him in her body.

And then I was moving lower, circling the faint indent of her belly button, allowing my mouth to drift toward the button of her jeans.

She inhaled sharply when I flicked it open, when I started dragging the tag of her zipper down, so I paused, glanced up at her.

But her eyes told me that had been a good inhalation, a good reaction.

Okay then.

I shifted, tugged her jeans off, tossing them to the side, leaving her in hedgehog-printed panties and a bra that was doing nothing to cover those luscious breasts. The latter probably wasn't comfortable, though, so I slipped a hand beneath her back and undid the hooks, and so sad for me, but then she was topless.

And a moment later, she was fully naked, after I'd whisked her underwear down her legs, threw it to the side so that it joined her jeans on the floor.

"Cas," she whispered, and I realized I'd frozen, that I'd been staring at the gloriousness of all that naked, curvy, *beautiful* woman beneath me for who knew how long.

Though, for long enough that a blip of insecurity had entered the edges of her eyes.

"Don't," I ordered, cupping her cheek. "Don't for one second think that you like this, you in this bed with me, you naked and beneath me, isn't the most beautiful gift you could *ever* give me."

"Cas," she whispered again, but it wasn't insecure, not this time.

It was paired with glassy eyes and a soft expression.

I'd give anything so that I could see that look again and again and *again*.

"You with me?"

Teeth in her bottom lip.

My fingers slid into her hair. "Gorgeous." It was a warning and a statement.

Both of which she seemed to pick up on because amusement slid into her eyes as she nodded. "You're not going to let me believe otherwise, are you?"

"Nope." I kissed that abused bottom lip of hers. "Now, as you're sitting in the truth that you're fucking beautiful, is there anything you don't like? Anything that's off-limits?"

Pink on her cheeks before her brows formed high arches on her forehead, but even though that incredulity (and the giggle that followed) were at my expense, it was better than the insecurity from moments before. "Off-limits? It's our first time together. What kind of crazy sexcapades are you going to bust out?"

I'd do pretty much anything to make her come, so the list was long.

But I didn't tell her that. Instead, I said, "So, no limits then?"

"I—" More pink on her cheeks, her teeth digging into her bottom lip again. And more heat in her eyes.

Hey now.

That was interesting.

It was also hell on my razor-thin control.

"How about we talk about your limits later?" I said, bending to take her nipple in my mouth again—only this time my ribs decided to be assholes, picking that goddamned moment to send a shock of pain through me.

"What?" she asked, unfortunately not missing that fact. "Oh, shit," she whispered. "Your ribs and I made you carry me and—"

A long, wet kiss.

"You didn't *make* me do anything, gorgeous," I told her. "I've been wanting to fuck you from the first moment I saw you."

"I—" She froze. A shake of her head. "We'll talk about that later, too."

Her hand on my chest, coaxing me back, and truthfully, I didn't fight her too much, not when the movement made her breasts jiggle, not when the movement brought her on top of me, her legs straddling my hips, her hands going to the hem of my shirt.

A gentle movement brought the material up and over my head.

Which, admittedly, didn't feel all that great.

But I'd had worse.

"Shit, honey," she whispered.

I blinked, both hated and loved the concern on her face.

"God," she whispered, gently running her fingertips over the large bruise on my side. "This has to hurt."

"I'm fine."

"It's *huge*."

I grinned.

She froze again, only this time amusement warred with annoyance. "Seriously?"

"Is this where I shouldn't say, words a man lives to hear?"

A sigh. A roll of her eyes.

"Gorgeous?" I asked innocently.

"Yeah?" And hell, if I wasn't making progress—if only because she didn't hesitate to respond to the nickname I'd given her.

I crooked a finger. "Come here."

"I'm naked and on top of you," she replied tartly. "How much closer can I get?"

Sass.

She was giving me sass.

And I fucking *loved* it.

More progress.

But I didn't focus on that, just filed it away to celebrate later as I settled my hands on her ass, as I coaxed her up my body.

Higher.

Higher.

Until she was hovering over my ribs, my shoulders, my... face.

"You can get closer," I rasped.

And then I tugged her down.

THIRTY

Jules

I WAS SITTING on his face.

Oh lord, I was *sitting* on his face.

"I—" Um, did people *do* that?

I was going to suffocate him...with my pussy. The thought of which had another hysterical giggle bubbling up inside me—shock and amusement and more *shock,* which was apparently the theme of that evening.

Shock that I'd made the decision to leap.

Shock that he looked at me like I was precious, that he'd told me I was fucking beautiful, even with my baby pouch and the stretch marks on my belly...and my thighs...and my breasts.

Shock that I was there. Now.

Sitting on his face.

"Cas—"

His hands tightened on my ass and his tongue flicked out.

And shock turned to *fire.*

His lips worked my clit, the rhythm of his flicking tongue joining in and—

"Oh God," I whispered, my hands flying forward, gripping the top of the headboard, fingers digging into the dark wood. "Oh *God.*"

He groaned, the sound vibrating through my slick pussy.

"*Cas,*" I moaned, desire pooling, need ratcheting up as he worked me, as his fingers joined his mouth and tongue, as his teeth showed up to the party mid-celebration. Fuck, that was good. Heat was spiraling through me, pleasure filling every cell, firing along every nerve.

And then he found a spot.

Found *the* spot.

And my hips ground down, rubbing against the stubble on his jaw, finding that his beard provided the perfect amount of friction.

Needing the roughness. Desperate for his touch, his teeth, his tongue.

I was close. *So* close. My hips grinding. My hands gripping the headboard—

But I stopped...

Because suffocation.

I was suffocating my man and—

Cas tore his mouth from my pussy, lips shining when he asked, "What the fuck are you doing?"

My lungs were working hard, my breaths in rapid puffs of air. "I'm going to hurt you. Or—" He exhaled and, fuck, *that* felt good, too, the air puffing against my sensitized clit, making it hard for me to think, to form words. "Or you're not going to be able to breathe and I'm going to suffocate you and—"

"Gorgeous." His fingers flexed again, tugged me close once more. "When a man wants you to sit on his face, he wants you to *sit on his face.*"

"I—" A shake of my head. "But—"

"You like what I'm doing?" he asked, flicking out his tongue, a bare inch between my pussy and his damp beard.

Well, that was easy to answer. I liked it. Liked it better than anything any man had ever done to me. *Ever.*

"Yeah," I whispered.

"Then sit on my face, sweetheart."

And then he didn't give me a chance to say anything else because he'd tugged me down again and this time I wasn't just sitting on his face, I was *sitting* on his face. No, I was *riding* his face. And he didn't stop. And he didn't get suffocated. Instead, his mouth worked my pussy, my clit. His fingers slipped back inside, flexing, spreading, sending shivers of pleasure through me.

Pleasure that sparked and grew into a full-blown fire that consumed me.

Then I wasn't thinking about anything except that impending orgasm, the all-encompassing bliss that was barreling down on me.

And if it felt this good with just his mouth, just his fingers, what was it going to feel like with his cock inside me? Which was a thought that had my orgasm coming closer, fluttering at the edges of my consciousness.

Right there. Right *there.*

His fingers flexed again.

My pussy convulsed around them.

And Cas groaned again, clearly having felt that, but thankfully, he didn't stop all that glorious suction and finger action. He kept going, kept taking me closer to that edge.

And then I was there.

Then I was *there.*

Sparks exploding through my mind, my body going taut, *taut*...and then limp, my hands relaxing on the headboard, my body slumping as the world's best orgasm burned through me, pleasure flowing and filling me and making it so I couldn't think or see or...keep myself upright.

Thankfully, Cas had me, wrapping his arms around me, shifting and rolling us so my back was on the mattress and he was on top of me again.

That was nice.

That was *nice* enough that as the pleasure ebbed, I was able to feel him.

All of him.

And he was hot and hard and—

I wanted him inside.

"Honey," I whispered, hand lifting and cupping his jaw. "Now."

A shudder through his body, his eyes blazing hot—a forest fire amongst all those pine trees—but he didn't shove down his sweats and plunge home. Instead, he paused. "You sure, gorgeous? Because I don't need this. I can wait until—"

Now *I* was moving, pushing him to *his* back, crawling over him. A few precise tugs had his sweats and underwear down his thighs and—holy hell, that was a glorious cock. One that I wrapped my fingers around.

"*Fuck,*" he gritted out.

Hearing *that,* in that tone, and yeah, I might finally understand the power of femininity, the power of my body, the power of giving myself to a man who cared for me, who was kind to me, who meant more to me than any man had meant.

Ever.

And I understood how good it felt to give *him* something.

I wanted to watch his muscles tighten as I sucked his cock, to see sweat break out on his skin, for it glisten in the overhead light. Wanted to feel his thighs, the big and strong muscles there, flex against me as I rode him. Wanted to feel his dick, rock-hard and thick, sliding into my mouth, hitting the back of my throat.

I leaned in.

"You don't have—"

His words cut off when I wrapped my lips around the rigid length of his erection.

And then I was giving him something, reveling in the taut muscles, but getting lost in the other things—in his touch and words, his tone and the gentle way he'd weaved his fingers into my hair. Hot and hard was incredible. Hot and hard had my pussy aching and moisture pooling.

But gentle and sweet was better.

Because it was beautiful and told me exactly what I meant to him.

Cas didn't play games—he had made his feelings clear from the beginning, had told me he liked me and then had showed it with every word and action and—

The truth slammed into me.

I'd been the one who'd been playing, who'd been messing around, who'd been wishy-washy.

I needed to do better.

And I would.

Starting with giving the man I liked beyond measure the best blow job of his life—which was something, I had to face it, I didn't exactly have the skills for. I'd only been with a couple of people before Nate and that experience had consisted mostly of fumbling and bumbling and them blowing their loads after a couple of licks. Nate had been more confident, more demanding, but he'd been more of the yank at my hair and fuck my mouth until I gagged variety.

Neither was particularly pleasant.

But, luckily for me—and him, I supposed—I read a lot of romance novels. And repeat, I read a lot of *dirty* romance novels. As thus, I would approach this with enthusiasm and my brainful of fellatio knowledge from my dirty books, and hopefully Cas would like what I did.

Stroking up, I bobbed my head down, flicked out my tongue.

A tight grip.

Plenty of suction.

Taking him as deep as I could.

And Cas liked it, if the curses tumbling out of his mouth, if the sweat sheeting his body, if the way his muscles were flexing and his cock was growing even harder, straining at my lips was any indication.

Because I didn't get a lot of time down there.

Maybe two minutes. Tops.

Then his hands were under my armpits, and I was beneath him again and he froze—

"Fuck," he hissed. "I don't have a condom."

"Top drawer," I whispered, having made a promise to myself after Ethan that I would always have protection on hand.

His hand shook as he jerked open the drawer, pulled out the box I'd never opened.

Then he was tearing the cardboard, ripping one square off from the string of condoms, and using his teeth to open it.

A moment after that, he was rolling it down his cock.

And then he was between my thighs. "Hurry," I whispered, trembling as he spread my legs.

"Are—"

"*Hurry*, Cas."

Then he was pressing home and—oh my, *that* was fucking good. He stretched me wide, hit all the spots deep inside me.

"Tight," he grunted, slowly working himself in, his chest

coming over mine, his forearms braced on either side of my head.

My breath caught as he bottomed out. "It's—*ah*—been a while. Not since Ethan—" My words cut off when he reached beneath me, wrapping my leg around his waist, changing the angle and—*oh* yes, that was somehow even better. *Better* enough that my explanation was forgotten, that I stopped thinking, my brain short-circuiting further when he pulled out and slowly slid back in.

And did it again.

And again.

And—

That was when I started talking.

No. That was when I started giving him orders.

"Harder."

"Faster."

"*Deeper.*"

Thankfully, Cas obliged, and soon, he was pounding into me, stroking deep and hard and fast, and I was flying toward release all over again, flying with a speed that shocked me, with an intensity that was a little scary.

Except, Cas would catch me.

I knew he would.

And...he did.

Just like I caught him when my name rolled off his tongue on a growl and he flew over the edge right behind me.

THIRTY-ONE

Cas

FAINT VOICES PENETRATED my sleep-hazed mind, but it took a minute for me to realize where I was.

In Jules's bed.

Luckily, not naked.

I'd cleaned up the night before, then tugged on my sweats, unlocked the door as Jules pulled on my T-shirt to sleep in. Then I'd crawled back into bed with her, needing to hold her, promising that I'd head home in, "Just a little while."

Well, clearly that hadn't happened.

Probably not the best example to set for Ethan—being in that bed—but, for now, the door was closed, and I'd gotten more sleep than I had in days. And Jules...

Holy fuck, but she'd been hot—shy and sweet and demanding and needy.

The best sex of my life, hands down.

But now, her kid needed to go to school, and I was still half asleep and wasn't helping her, and she'd gotten even less sleep than I had.

Asshole.

Grunting, I tossed the blankets to the side, spent a few moments making the bed, double-checking that the box of condoms—of which we'd used three—was stashed back into the nightstand drawer.

Then I slipped into Jules's bathroom, started to do my business...and froze when I saw the note. It was tucked beneath an unopened toothbrush.

Hope you slept in, honey. Taking Ethan to school.
-J

My heart thudded hard.

And it wasn't hope in my veins. It was happiness.

Finally.

Finally.

Hell, if my eyes didn't sting a little bit, but thankfully, before I could really lose it, I heard Ethan's voice rise in excitement—

An emotion that almost immediately cut off—Jules probably quieting him—but, thankfully, it was enough to snap me out of my moment and send me on to my business of using the toilet, washing my hands and face, and brushing my teeth.

Then I was back in the bedroom, the hall, and heading to the kitchen listening to the sounds of Jules and Ethan talking.

"And then Noel said..." He trailed off as I strode into the room. "Cas!"

Up off his stool, running across the room, throwing his arms around my middle. "Are you going to take me to school?"

Jules winced. "Cas is probably busy, bud—"

"Your mom and I are going to drive you to school," I said.

"Cas!"

"And then I'm taking her for pancakes."

Ethan paused, brows furrowing. "Will you take me for pancakes sometime soon?"

"Ethan!" Jules cried.

"Yup," I said. "Though it'll have to be next week sometime. I have a game tonight and then I'll be out of town for a few days on a road trip." I smoothed my fingers over Julie's nape, loving that she was wearing one of the sweatshirts I'd given her all those weeks before. "We'll go to skate and shoot on one of your free afternoons and get pancakes afterward."

Jules sighed, shook her head, and moved to pull a piece of toast from the toaster.

"What days is Ethan free, gorgeous?"

A scowl in my direction, and she made Ethan his toast and set it on the plate in front of him. "Oh?" she asked archly. "Are you including me in this conversation now?"

"Yup." I took a page out of Ethan's book and popped his p.

Which made Jules smile and soften. "You don't have—"

"I *want*," I said quickly, moving toward her and cupping her jaw. "Now, what days is Ethan free?"

"Tuesdays and Fridays."

"Good," I murmured, brushing her lips with mine. "Friday," I told her and Ethan, turning back toward her kiddo. "I'll pick you up at school, we'll hit the rink, and then load up with pancakes afterward."

"You'll pick me up at school?" Ethan's eyes were wide. "Really?"

"Yeah, bud." I spun back to Jules, slid my palm from her jaw to her throat, held her gaze. "You good with that?"

Her brows lifted, tart in her tone and sass in her eyes. "Nice of you to ask."

I smirked, brushed her lips with mine again. "You're good with that." I straightened. "You work that night?"

As far as I knew, she worked every Friday and Saturday.

A nod that told me I was in the doghouse. Luckily, I had pancakes on the agenda and the deliciousness from Donna's would go a long way to soothing her annoyance.

"Yeah," she muttered.

"Cool. Ethan and I will hang out at my place afterward. You can come over after work and we'll all have a sleepover."

Another flash of irritation in her eyes. "Cas—"

"A sleepover? Really?" The excitement in Ethan's voice couldn't be missed.

Which was probably why she sighed, closed her eyes, and dropped her chin to her chest.

"I've never gotten to do a sleepover before," Ethan said, and I glanced over, unable to bite back my smile. Not in the face of Ethan's happy dance. "Can we watch movies and stay up late?"

"Sure."

Jules groaned softly and I felt that in my dick. "Don't do that, gorgeous," I murmured, stroking her side.

"And popcorn?" Ethan asked.

"Yeah, bud."

Jules's head shot up. "Do what?"

"Moan like that." I bent, nipped her earlobe. "Not unless you want to skip out on pancakes and end up here afterwards."

"And use sleeping bags to camp out on the floor?"

I glanced at Ethan. "We can camp out until your mom gets home, then we'll go to sleep in actual beds." I was way too fucking old to be sleeping on the floor.

Plus, I needed Jules in my bed.

"Maybe I'll bring you back here after we drop Ethan off, tie you up, and torture you for your attempts at manipulation," she grumbled.

"So long as that torture is with your hands and mouth," I said. "I'm down."

Her lips parted, eyes filling with shock—and *fuck me*, with heat. "You're *down?*" she whisper-shouted.

A light kiss to those lips. "Yup."

"And we can have candy?" Ethan asked.

"Yes!" we both called this time.

"You're *down?*" she whispered again, eyes wide.

I kissed her nose. "Anything you want to do to me, anytime you want to do it."

Her mouth dropped open. "I—"

"And will Sparky be there?" Ethan asked.

"Yes, bud," I said again before focusing back on Jules. "This surprises you?" I asked softly, running my thumb over the faint pink that had appeared on her cheek.

"Yes," she whispered.

"Anything for you, gorgeous," I murmured. "*Anything.*"

She was quiet for a long time, then whispered, "You might regret making that statement."

"Why, sweetheart?"

I expected her to say something about her being a single mom with an asshole baby daddy and a job in the bar.

I didn't hear what I expected.

"I read a lot of dirty books."

I blinked.

Once. Twice.

"Um. *What?*"

That pink on her cheeks flared brighter.

"I'm gonna go brush my teeth!" Ethan announced, and then footsteps pounded down the hall.

The kid had impeccable timing.

"Jules."

She bit her lip, released it. Then her chin came up. Her

shoulders straightened. "I'm a single mom. I go to school and work the night shift. I'm not exactly in a dating...*mode* right now."

"Good."

Her head jerked, brows drawing together. "Good?"

"Yup." I smoothed my thumb over her abused bottom lip. "Because that means I get you and your dirty mind all to myself."

"I don't have a dirty mind," she protested.

I lifted my brows.

"I just read dirty books."

I grinned.

Pink, pink cheeks. "It's not—"

Another kiss, this one deeper and wetter, but not longer... because footsteps began pounding on the floor again, only this time they were coming toward us.

"We'll argue about this later," I said, releasing her.

"You—"

"We've got to get Ethan to school, gorgeous." A nudge toward the fridge. "You get his lunch. I'll grab his backpack. Then you can give me a piece of your mind over pancakes at Donna's."

"Donna's?" she whispered, and the awe in her tone mirrored Ethan's when I had mentioned the sleepover.

"You ever been?"

A shake of her head. "No, but I've heard it's good."

"It is, gorgeous." Another nudge. "And you'll find out today."

"I've—" She shook her head again.

"Don't hold back, sweetheart. Not with me."

Her throat worked. "The only one who's ever taken me out to eat is Lake."

I clenched my jaw. Not because Lake Jordan had been the

one to give that to her, but because Nate hadn't, because her father hadn't. And because even though *Lake* was the one to give it to her, he was still a pain in the ass on the ice and I wanted to hate him purely on principle.

Yeah, yeah. None of that was fair.

Which was why I shoved the thoughts down, told her, "I'm glad Lake was good to you, sweetheart. Glad he gave that to you." Then I leaned in pressed a kiss to her forehead. "And I'm glad that *I'm* going to get to give Donna's to you today."

"Cas," she whispered, eyes all soft, mouth so fucking kissable.

Focus.

"Lunchbox, gorgeous. We've got to get Ethan to school."

Her hand lifted and she ran her fingertips through my beard. "Okay, honey."

Fuck, I liked that—the touch, the way she called me *honey*. So, I had to kiss her one more time before I let her get the lunchbox, went to the hall for Ethan's backpack.

We drove him to school, walked him in, and left him at the gate, exchanging hugs, and waving goodbye.

Then I got to take my woman to breakfast.

And I got to give her pancakes that made her moan.

And *then* I got to take her back to her place and make her moan for a whole different reason.

THIRTY-TWO

Jules

I'D BARELY ACCEPTED Cas's place in my life.

And now he was gone.

And now I was *missing* him.

It was freaking awful.

Two days without him—unless I counted catching glimpses of him on the TV screen at CeCe's and random text messages and a few video calls (which, for the record, I *did not*)—and I hated that he wasn't there.

But if I was going to do this with him, then I had to get used to it.

Because his job took him away from Baltimore regularly for half the year.

But I couldn't deny that he was making an effort.

Not just with the calls and texts, but he'd sent me dinner at CeCe's the night before. That morning, as I'd walked Ethan out to the car to take him to school, I'd almost stumbled over a vase of flowers.

Pretty, *gorgeous* flowers.

I'd never gotten flowers before.

And the *clinking* all around my heart as the remnants of my armor dropped away was cacophonous.

I was out there, fully exposed, and...not terrified.

Maybe I'd regret that in the months and years to come, but I *wanted* Cas—in my life, in Ethan's life.

Forever.

Which was a scary fucking thought.

But I'd tabled all the fear to be dealt with later.

Right now, I was enjoying pancake dates and flowers and sweet text messages and video calls that took a sexy turn right at the end.

A scream pierced the air, and I jumped, nearly impaling myself on the stack of freshly sharpened pencils I'd just finished running through the sharpener.

Right.

Right *then* I was volunteering at school and needed to focus on the fact that I was handling sharp objects around small children.

"Julie."

And on avoiding Mr. Philips, who I'd misjudged, considering what he told me weeks ago and the subsequent conversations—yes, conversations—I'd had with Ethan, none of which I was sure that had really taken.

But he was still too familiar—only now I had to wonder if it was because I wasn't used to men being nice to me, especially those in positions of authority.

I didn't trust it.

I trusted Cas.

Though that was probably because he'd worked so hard to earn it.

I forced a smile, glanced up at Ethan's teacher. "Almost done, Mr. Philips."

"Randall, please."

I nodded, not willing to give verbal agreement to his request because it just felt too weird, and then began moving around the space, filling up the organizers in the middle of each container with the sharpened pencils.

"Can I get you a cup of coffee?" he asked.

Too familiar. Too nice.

It made my shoulders hitch up.

And...yeah, it was definitely my past coming into play. Ethan loved him as a teacher and he hadn't come close like he had that day, had seemed to make a conscious effort to keep his distance between us.

Like he knew that I'd been uncomfortable and was trying to ensure I knew I had an exit route.

Yup.

Definitely my past creeping in.

"Julie?"

I blinked, glanced up and safe he was at the Keurig. "Coffee?"

"No, thanks." Normally, I'd never turn down coffee, even if it felt weird drinking it with "someone in charge." But I was in my usual end of volunteer session sweat that had me asking why I did this. Every. Single. Week.

Then I saw Ethan's nametag taped on his spot and knew it was because of the smile it put on his face.

"Sure?"

A nod at the clock. "The kids will be back from recess in a few minutes, and I should finish this before they do."

"Okay." He plunked a pod in, closed the lid, and put his mug under the stream that began coming out. Then he spoke again, and it set my insides going tight. "Ethan hasn't been talking about…" A wave of his hand. "The situation with his dad."

Thank God for *that*.

Hopefully, my gently conversations with him had stuck.

"Glad to hear it," I said, moving to the far side of the room and starting to organize the kids' work into their respective folders. "I talked to him after the last time you mentioned it."

Mentioned the fact that my *baby* had written a letter to himself for a class assignment and that one of the questions he'd asked his future self was if he was bad and *that* was why he didn't have a father.

"I'm glad you straightened a few things out," he said. "And I'll let you know if I see anything else concerning."

Concerning? Yeah, it had been concerning.

But, more, it had been eviscerating.

My *baby* thinking that…

My eyes slid closed.

"It's not your fault." Soft words. Not from too close. And, yeah, I'd misjudged the teacher. "This kind of stuff happens in complicated relationships."

But not with *my* baby.

I opened my eyes, shoved a drawing that looked like a combination of the Grinch and a pile of horseshit crossed with a radiated fish into the proper folder, and flicked my gaze up to Mr. Philips. "I'll keep talking to it."

He held my eyes and I say that, yeah, my past had *definitely* come into play with him. "I know you will."

Then he moved away, sipping his coffee and watching his students play through the open classroom door.

I kept filing. I hadn't mentioned the letter to Ethan as we'd talked, had just tried to gently navigate to the topic of his father.

It might have been easier to address it head-on, and I might have to if it came up again. But he was five years old, and I hadn't wanted to invade his privacy that way.

But I *had* made it clear that it wasn't his fault that his dad wasn't involved.

And seriously, I hated Nate Miller.

It wasn't enough for him to fuck me over, now he had to fuck over my kid?

But if I allowed myself to think that, to be upset about my idiocy, then I'd get bogged down in it. Right now, I needed to focus on giving Ethan the best life he could have.

"He *has* mentioned someone name Cas a few times."

This was a tricky statement, from the teacher whose gaze was still on the playground, and it was tricky mostly because I'd already shared far too much with Mr. Philips. We weren't friends or acquaintances, and I didn't want to discuss my love life with anyone, let alone Ethan's teacher.

And yeah, I was calling it my love life—and not freaking out over the L word.

Miracle of miracles.

And also...maybe it was the miracle of video call sex.

"Ah," I said in response (or maybe, it would be better described as in *non*-response).

"Someone you're dating?"

Now he was going to get more *non*-response.

I'd barely gotten it straight in my own head. I couldn't talk about it out loud. So, I shoved the final paper in my stack into the proper folder and then glanced over at Mr. Philips. "Did you have any other tasks for me today?"

A glimmer of amusement in his eyes. "Message received, loud and clear," he said softly. Then that amusement grew. "Will you organize the leveled reading books?"

Oh man, *that* was mean even as I said, "Sure." Mostly because it was a lesson in futility—the books promptly became *un*organized since the kids never managed to put them back in the "proper" order.

"I'll just say one more thing."

My shoulders inched up.

"I'm glad you're dating. Ethan needs a good man in his life."

My shoulders inched up further. That was *two* things.

"And you do, too."

Three. Shit.

That was *three.*

"And—"

The bell rang.

Saved by the bell. Literally.

Kids began pouring into the classroom, settling at their desks, the noise inside the room increasing exponentially as they got ready for their next subject—art. But I got my reward for the sweat and the uncomfortable conversation with Ethan's teacher—and that was in the form of two little boys who didn't go straight to their desks.

One belonged to me and wrapped his arms around my middle, hugging me tight enough that I struggled to breathe.

The other was Finn—Ethan's teammate that I was just starting to know.

"Hi, Ms. Blackstar," he said, screeching to a halt.

"Hi, Finn."

"Can Ethan come over this weekend after our game?"

Game being Ethan's team's first hockey game. At nine in the morning. On Sunday after I'd schlepped drinks and food until three in the morning.

I couldn't wait to watch him play, especially since he'd been working so hard at practice. However, I wasn't looking forward to getting him up and to the rink and getting him dressed and ready for the ice (since five-year-olds weren't great about getting their own hockey gear on) for a game that began at nine in the morning after my shift the night before.

Alas, such was the life of a single mom.

And I thought that I might be able to rope Cas into the gear wrangling. A professional could do it faster, right?

And God, I missed him.

"Mom?"

Right. Two boys were looking at me, eyes pleading, and it was almost impossible to resist their adorableness.

"I'll talk to your mom at practice tonight," I said and then added because how could I *not* add more to that in the face of so much childlike hope and potential disappointment, "But it's fine with me so long as it's fine with her."

The boys turned toward each other, huge smiles on their faces.

Then Ethan was hugging me again, his smile pointed my way. "A sleepover and hockey *and* friends! This is going to be the best weekend ever."

I squeezed him back before nodding toward the table where both of the boys sat. "You should get ready for art," I said, playing it cool even though I was thinking the same thing, thinking that it absolutely *would* be the best weekend ever.

"'Kay," he said, releasing me and racing over to his table, Finn on his heels.

As I watched them, lips curved up, I saw Mr. Philips had been watching us.

Being *familiar*. Or maybe...it was just that he saw too much.

Damn.

I avoided his eyes.

And then I went back to organizing books.

THIRTY-THREE

Cas

THE KID WAS A MOVIE TALKER.

Normally, I hated that, hated when people talked during a movie, especially when they could just *watch* the actual movie and find out answers to all the questions they had and get more material for the pithy comments they found it necessary to impart on the world—and do it *after* the movie.

But Ethan was cute as fuck.

So, I didn't mind his questions.

And neither did Sparky, who was curled up on the sleeping bag with him, softly snoring.

Plus, I had prepped for the sleepover by buying the kid-sized sleeping bag, a shit-ton of junk food (and some veggies and fruit) and by bingeing a shit ton of *How It's Made* YouTube videos while I'd been on the road trip.

Loaded up with interesting random facts. Ready to answer *all* the questions.

And so far, we'd had a great time. We'd watched *The Lorax*

and then *Up*. Now we were moving onto *Home Alone*. Which was significantly more violent than I had remembered.

Hopefully, Jules wouldn't be pissed at me for corrupting her kid.

My only consolation was the fact that Ethan was looking tired.

It was nearing ten o'clock, and it was well past Ethan's bedtime, so hopefully the kid would pass out before the real violence began and I had to explain to Jules that I'd corrupted her son with hot irons and tarantulas and swinging paint cans.

"Do you think I'm bad?"

I was getting used to questions flying out of left field, but that was next level.

Frowning, I hit pause on the movie and turned to Ethan. "What do you mean, bud?"

His little hands were in fists, his eyes on the screen. On the paused movie that was showing a scene between Kevin and his dad—and one that wasn't going well for either of the characters in the film.

They were fighting and angry and—

Shit.

Then came Ethan's even quieter words.

"If I was good, my dad would want me."

Shit.

I was not equipped to properly handle this conversation. This was something that Jules should be talking to him about, or a discussion that—at the very least—the three of us should be having together.

"If I'm really, *really* extra good," Ethan said so quietly that I had to strain to hear it, "will you be my dad?"

I inhaled sharply.

Seriously, *not* equipped to have this conversation.

But I wasn't going to give some off-the-cuff answer, wasn't

going to bullshit Ethan or put him off. The kid was five years old, but he was smart and funny and kind, and he deserved someone to take care with his emotions.

And that someone had to be me.

Because, right then, I was the only one who was there.

So, girding my proverbial loins, I shifted from my sleeping bag, crawling over to sit with my back against the couch on Ethan's. And watched Ethan's fists get tighter, his knuckles pressing tightly against his skin. "Look at me, Eth." It took a moment, but Ethan did eventually glance up at me. With eyes far too serious for a five-year-old.

Damn.

"It would be an honor to be your dad, bud," I said. "And I hope we'll get to have a relationship like that someday, but your mom and I just started dating, and being a dad is a big responsibility."

A long beat of quiet then, "What does that mean?"

"That means..." A breath, and I gave Ethan the truth. "To me, being a dad is something that is very important. Dads are important in general and yeah, you don't *need* one, but they can make your life good. And sometimes they can make your life tough, too." Ethan's head jerked. "So, it's important that *you* think about what you might want. I hope that one day, it's me in your life like that, but right now, we're friends and I care about you a lot, and I want to keep hanging out and getting to know you." I carefully draped my arm around Ethan's shoulders, used my free hand to smooth out Ethan's fists, hating the tension in his little body. "I want to be here so that if you decide that one day, I'm worthy of that role, I'll be here and ready for it."

Ethan was still. Quiet.

"Would that be okay with you?"

Silence.

Long enough that I found I was holding my breath.

"Yeah," Ethan eventually whispered, finally looking up at me again. "That would be okay with me."

"And I don't know why your father decided that he wasn't able to be a dad to you"—other than the fact that Nate Miller was a *fucking* asshole—"but I *do* know that it has nothing to do with you and everything to do with him. You are an awesome kid. *Awesome*," I repeated when Ethan started to look away. "And your dad is a dumbass to miss out on all your awesomeness."

Ethan's eyes went wide, and I realized that I probably shouldn't be calling Nate Miller a dumbass to his five-year-old son, but that didn't change the truth.

Nate *was* a dumbass, amongst other things.

"*Really* dumb," I said again—sort of, anyway. Minus the *ass* part, in deference to Ethan's five-year-old ears.

More silence, but at least the tension had left Ethan's body at that point.

Then he broke it, and what he said made me fall for the kid even harder.

"He's dumb to miss out on my mom, too," Ethan said, fierce protectiveness in every word. "Because she's really awesome, too."

"She is," I agreed. "And, I agree, he was dumb to miss out on her, too."

"Do you love her?"

Another question from left field, but there was no point in denying it. I'd loved Jules for months.

"Yeah, bud."

Ethan grinned.

But that wasn't what kept my focus.

Nope.

What *stole* my focus from the adorable little boy next to me and yanked it to the hall was the gasp. I looked to the wide opening that led to the space and saw that Jules was standing there, the keys I'd loaned her hanging from her hand.

Her mouth had dropped open. Her eyes were locked on me, and even from the distance I could see the panic on her face.

Fuck.

But then she blinked, and it was gone, and she was moving toward me, toward Ethan.

Her hand landed on my knee, squeezing hard, and then she was taking Ethan in her arms, holding him tight. "I'm so sorry, buddy," she whispered.

"For what?" Ethan asked.

"For making you think that your dad didn't wa—" She broke off, words growing more than a little choked up.

"Cas says my dad is a dumbass for missing out on me," Ethan said, squirming slightly so that Jules would release him. "Because I'm awesome."

Jules froze, dropping her arms when Ethan straightened away from her. "That's true," she said, recovering quickly. "You are *exceptionally* awesome." A breath. "And while I don't think that cursing is the answer"—slightly narrowed eyes in my direction—"he *is* a dumbass. Mostly because how could anyone live with not having you in their life?"

A blip of quiet, and I wondered if Jules was holding her breath as she waited for Ethan to reply.

Because *I* was.

And then Ethan did reply, and it was a fucking knife to the gut. "Because I'm bad."

"Oh, buddy," she said on a rush of air, confirming that she *had* been holding her breath, but her tone was calm and steady and gentle when she said, "We talked about this before. You didn't do anything wrong, remember? Your dad wasn't ready to be a dad. It had nothing to do with you. In fact, he never even met you, so it *really* didn't have anything to do with you."

Tiny hands clenched into tiny fists again. "Why didn't he want to meet me?"

"I don't know," she whispered, and I wanted to pummel Nate *fucking* Miller all over again. "I really wanted him to. Because I knew that he'd love you. But sometimes people can't be what we need them to be, and we have to stop asking them to." A beat. "Otherwise, we're the ones who get hurt."

One of Ethan's hands relaxed. "Like how Finn isn't good at four square?"

Jules's tension flowed out of her, her relief palpable in the air. "Yeah, bud. Exactly like that."

"Okay," Ethan said, curling into her.

"Do you have more questions about your dad?" she asked, hugging him close. "Or other things you need to talk about?"

"Nope." He was back to popping his p's, which meant that I found the tension flowing out of *me,* and it flowed faster when Jules ruffled Ethan's hair, sprawled out onto the sleeping bag and made it clear she didn't care I'd corrupted her son with tarantulas and paint cans.

"Now," she said, "should we watch Kevin get those robbers?"

THIRTY-FOUR

Jules

"HOW ARE YOU HERE SO EARLY?" Cas asked once Ethan had lost his battle with sleep and passed out on the sleeping bag, curled around Sparky, his fingers in the dozing pup's fur.

"Power went out at CeCe's, so Matt sent me home." Good. That sounded casual.

When, truthfully, I was falling apart inside.

Because of the conversation I'd walked into.

Because of what I'd heard Cas say.

Because of my son going to Cas for help and Cas handling him so gently, so carefully—like the care and gentle he'd shown me.

Because of how that had *finished*. Before I'd gotten his shock at seeing me out of the way and joined the conversation, anyway.

"Ah." His fingers smoothed over my cheek, and he got right to the crux of the issue. "How much did you hear?

Right.

Um. I should probably lie, or at the very least, prevaricate.

Instead...I just gave him the truth.

How could I lie? Prevaricate?

When he'd given Ethan—*me*—so fucking much.

Cas might not know it, but listening to him talk to my son, hearing him treat Ethan so sweetly, explaining things in a way I never would have, but also with a gentleness and honesty that I felt in my soul was exactly *right* had reinforced everything.

This was right.

This was special.

This was...something I was never letting go.

A hand on my cheek. Cas's brows lifting in query when I didn't immediately answer.

So, how could I *not* give Cas the same gentle and honest he'd given my son?

"All of it," I whispered.

His fingers flexed. "And are you panicking because I love you or because of what I told Ethan?"

"Neither," I whispered. "I'm not panicking. I'm *falling.*"

His brows drew together.

"No," I corrected. "I've *fallen.*"

That didn't have his brows relaxing. If anything, he went even more still.

"I've fallen for you and the way you look at me. I've fallen for the care you take with Ethan. I've fallen for the man you are and the way you smile and how it feels when you hold me." He inhaled sharply, but I kept going. "I was scared, so scared to let go, to let myself have you—to let *us*—have you. Because I knew —*knew*—you would hurt me—hurt *us*—eventually, and I had to protect him. But you won't, will you?" He took another breath, but I was on a roll and kept going, kept giving. Because it was my turn to give. Because he'd spent the last weeks and months *giving.* "I know you won't hurt us because I know you now." A beat. "And...I love you."

My entire body was trembling.

This was about as far out of my comfort zone as I'd ever stepped.

But it was the truth—one that had been circling around my mind for a while now and I'd been avoiding it, even as Cas kept winding himself tighter and tighter around my heart. Welding himself to it. *Tattooing* himself on it.

It was time to stop denying that.

And it was time to stop playing Chicken Little, bracing for when the bad might come.

Because it *might* come. I couldn't prevent that, and neither could Cas.

But I could trust that he was going to continue to treat me with care, treat Ethan with care, and trust in myself and my spine and the strength I'd gathered over the years to know that I would accept nothing less.

Ethan was blooming.

Part of that was because of Cas.

Part of that was because of how Cas was with *me.*

Because I was more awake, more *alive* now than I'd been in years. Not since I'd first felt Ethan move, not since I'd first held him as a newborn in my arms, covered in blood and goo and screaming his head off—the only people in the hospital room with me the nurses who'd held my hand and my legs and the doctor who'd played catcher—had I felt this much love, this *alive.*

And it was Cas who'd woken my shit up.

Cas who'd showed me what potential looked like.

Not me scrabbling to hold on to the tiniest bit of good, dropping to my knees and scrounging for the crumbs tossed there.

Cas hadn't given me crumbs.

He'd given me everything.

And he wasn't going to stop.

So...I was going to do the same.

"Jules?" he whispered.

"Yeah?" I whispered back.

"Did you just tell me that you love me?"

The surprise in his tone was beyond cute. I'd befuddled my big, sexy, *gorgeous* hockey player. "Yup." And I popped the p.

"I—"

His eyes went damp, and I froze.

Because he was giving me that—letting me know how important those words were to him.

I carefully shifted, moving around Ethan, not wanting to disturb Sparky, and closing the distance between my body and Cas's by crawling into his lap, wrapping my arms around his shoulders. "You're different, honey," I murmured. "And I'm sorry it took me so long to recognize that, to crawl out from beneath my shell to recognize the gift you were giving me." He jerked, but I kept going. "I see it now," I whispered. "I see *you*. And I'm going to protect it and work for it and—"

That was clearly the moment that Cas lost his patience.

Because his lips hit mine, cutting off the rest of my words. Which was fine. I'd gotten to the important parts. I could tell—or rather, take a page out of his book, and *show*—him later.

Now...

His tongue was in my mouth and he was kissing me in a way that set me on fire.

Luckily, he had the presence of mind to hold me close and stand, to carry me out of the room—

Which sparked my conscience, and I tore my mouth from his. "Your ribs, honey."

"Better," he grunted, dropping his head and nipping at my jaw, my earlobe, my bottom lip. "Now kiss me, gorgeous."

I could do that.

I could do *that*.

So, I did.

I kissed him as he walked me down a hall I hadn't had the chance to explore yet, into a room I didn't know because I'd spent all of forty-five minutes in Cas's place and five minutes had been spent standing in the entry, just inside the front door, and the other forty sitting next to my son, watching *Home Alone*.

Now I landed on something hard and cold and I had just a couple of seconds to process it was a dryer as Cas moved away from me and closed the door.

"No lock," he muttered, shoving a large hamper in front of it, eyes blazing as they latched onto mine. "Gotta fuck you now." Rough words that sent a shiver right through me. "So, you need to keep that gorgeous mouth of yours shut and not wake Ethan and Sparky, yeah?"

Oh my.

I shivered again, loving the growly, demanding side of him.

"Jules?" he pressed, prowling toward me, hands reaching for my T-shirt, yanking it up over my head. "Can you do that for me so I can fuck you, sweetheart?"

Truthfully, I probably couldn't.

But I wanted him.

Needed him inside me.

So, I nodded.

A flash of a smile. "Liar." A nip to my earlobe again. Then hot words in my ear, his hand wrapping around my back, flicking open my bra. "Guess I'll have to keep your mouth occupied with other things."

"Yes, please."

It slid out of me before I could think.

Then he was chuckling and lifting me off the dryer, yanking my pants and underwear down my legs, tossing them aside.

"Or maybe," I whispered while he was kneeling before me, "you need to keep *your* mouth occupied with other things."

His eyes hit mine.

Then his lips curved.

And while he occupied *his* mouth, I wasn't very good at keeping quiet.

But neither was he when I occupied mine.

Luckily, Ethan slept like the dead.

THIRTY-FIVE

JULES WAS SLEEPING in my arms.

Ethan was across the hall, tucked into the bed in my guest room.

Both the doors were open, just in case Ethan woke up and got scared, and the nightlights I had bought to make sure Ethan could find the way to my room were switched on. Jules and I had also both gotten dressed.

The life of a parent, I supposed.

I wasn't complaining. The woman I loved and the woman who loved me back was in my arms. The kid I'd fallen for just as deep was sleeping soundly across the hall.

Life was fucking *sweet*.

And I got to enjoy it while I was awake, sunshine glimmering through my bedroom windows, the slow and steady breathing of my woman on my throat, my pup sleeping at my feet (because Sparky might be getting older, but he sure as fuck made sure he made it up the pet stairs that I had bought and kept at the bottom of my bed to sleep at my feet any time I was home).

And I got to enjoy all of that for approximately five minutes.

Because then I heard my front door open.

And my mom's voice echo up the stairs.

"We're here!"

Fuck.

I'd forgotten they'd invited themselves over for brunch.

Because, like an idiot, I'd let it slip that I was dating someone.

Okay, well, it was less idiot and more that I'd forgotten my mom had scheduled a family dinner because Sam and Margot were in town until my mom had called with the details yesterday. At which point, I'd tried to flake since I'd offered to watch Ethan, but my mom could sniff out excuses and deceit like a bloodhound. She hadn't bought the pretext of me bowing out. Not for one second.

With those sniffing skills she'd obviously come to the right conclusion—that I was dating someone and it was serious—and had invited "my woman" to join in on the family dinner.

At which point, I'd had to confess that I really couldn't join in because Jules was working and had a son, and Ethan and I were having a sleepover.

This hadn't garnered any protests.

In fact, my mom had been in rapture.

My mom liked kids (obviously, since she had four of her own), and she couldn't wait to meet Ethan and finally be a grandma. She even had her Grandma Name picked out already.

Because apparently *that* was a thing.

Anyway, my mom had decided to come over and cook us brunch. Well, she'd decided on breakfast first, because she could hardly wait to meet Jules and Ethan, but when I'd mentioned that Jules worked late, breakfast had become brunch.

Which was something I'd been planning on telling Jules last night.

Because I didn't care how ramped up my mom was, if Jules wasn't ready to meet the chaos that was my family, then I'd put my mom off.

Only we hadn't spoken.

Because that conversation with Ethan had happened, and then the *laundry* room had happened, and then we'd tucked Ethan into the guest room, and then we'd gotten naked in *my* room.

And I'd figured we had time to talk about it that morning. After all, my family wasn't coming over until—

I rolled, Jules making an adorable sound of protest as I moved, and saw that—

Fuck.

It was eleven-thirty.

"Oh. Hi, buddy," I heard my mom say. "I'm Luca's mom."

"Who's Luca?" I heard Ethan ask from downstairs. Apparently, the kiddo had gotten up already. Then again, it was eleven-thirty, so that wasn't too surprising. Also, a fact that had me moving, slipping out from beneath the blankets, grabbing my phone from the charger. A glance at the screen showed that my mom had texted and said they were on the way over.

Fuck.

Julie was going to kill me.

"Luca is Cas," my mom said as I was rounding the bed, kneeling next to it, and gently shaking Jules, really wishing my parents didn't have a key to my place to take care of Sparky when I was out of town.

"Do you like Cas?" Margot asked, and heaven help me with annoying sisters.

"Yup! We watch movies and eat popcorn and stay up late." A beat. "Oh, and he takes me skating, and I got to watch him play once!"

"You did?" my mom asked.

"Yup." Complete with that pop at the end. "It was the best day ever."

Fuck. The kid killed me.

"Who are you?" Ethan asked in the semi-polite way of five-year-olds.

"Margot. I'm Cas's sister, and this is Sam and Kathy, his brother and other sister."

Jules. Was. Going. To. Kill. Me.

"Jules, sweetheart," I urged, shaking her shoulder. "Wake up, gorgeous."

She buried her face in the pillow. "Mmm? Just a few more minutes, baby."

God, I'd love to wake her up slowly, to kiss her gently and—

"Is your mom around, honey?" I heard *my* mom ask as I called Jules's name again.

We didn't have time for slow.

"Yup." A beat. "She and Cas are upstairs sleeping."

Shit. Fuck.

"We stayed up late last night watching movies and my mom works late and needs sleep"—something that I had mentioned the day before when we'd planned on letting Jules sleep in while we took Sparky on a walk (this was supposed to have happened *before* my family came over for brunch)—"and Cas works hard too, so I figured he needs sleep too."

"Jules," I said more firmly this time, and finally—thank God, *finally*—her eyes peeled open.

"That's really kind of you, honey," I heard my mom say, her

voice echoing up the stairs, right into the open door and making my woman's eyes go instantly alert. "Do you want to help me make some cinnamon rolls while we let them sleep?"

"Okay!" Ethan said.

Which was the point that Sparky finally seemed to clue in that the house was currently full of people he hadn't gotten the chance to sniff yet—and that some of those people were his *favorite* people (those favorite people being my mom and Margot). As such, Sparky popped up like the puppy he hadn't been in years, bounded down the stairs at the bottom of the bed and took off down the hall.

A soft *woof*.

Skidding feet and claws.

My family and Ethan greeting my pooch.

Then I was turning back to Jules, whose face was pale and eyes were wide. "Who's talking to my son?" she whispered.

I winced. "My family," I whispered. "With everything that happened last night, I kind of forgot to mention they were coming over for brunch."

"Brunch—" She glanced to the side and then her eyes widened further. "It's eleven-thirty."

"I know, gorgeous," I said, smoothing my hands up and down her arms. "And I'm sorry to spring this on you, especially with them already here—"

"It's *eleven-thirty*."

"I know—"

Her hands came to my cheeks as she sat up, the blankets falling to her waist. "No, honey," she said. "It's eleven-thirty and I—" A shake of her head. "I've never slept that late," she whispered. "Not *ever*." She jiggled my head. "Never, honey, and I don't think I've felt this rested in...well, probably since I was old enough to start working."

A bolt of anger through me.

I hated that for her.

But I didn't have time to express that hate.

"You're not freaking out," I pointed out, needing her to focus on the situation at hand.

She still held my cheeks. "You love me. I love you. I think your family will see that." She sent me reeling with *that*, from her calm acceptance of my family's invasion. *Reeling* considering how long it had taken for me to get her here—and how much her calm, *quick* acceptance of my family being there *today* meant for us and our relationship, how much it meant to *me* in that moment. Then she stood up and took my hand.

"Come on, honey," she said softly. "Let's go downstairs."

I found I couldn't move.

Not when my love for her was expanding to epic proportions, not when it was *burning* through me.

She leaned in, touched her lips to mine. "Ethan is down there."

"Yeah," I whispered.

"And he's making cinnamon rolls with your mom."

"Yeah," I whispered again.

"And..." Her eyes went hopeful even as her expression became unfathomable. "And I've never made cinnamon rolls with a mom, honey."

I inhaled.

Then I whispered "Yeah" for a third time before releasing her and going to my closet, pulling down a sweatshirt for her (another she would probably steal). It was cold in my house in the mornings.

Since she'd followed me in, I tugged it over her head, then took her hand, led her downstairs.

"Let's go make cinnamon rolls."

Because Jules deserved to do *everything*.

But she especially deserved to make cinnamon rolls.

THIRTY-SIX

"NO, MOM," Ethan said, his butter-covered hands coming over mine and grabbing out a huge handful of sugar and cinnamon mixture from the bowl I'd been put in charge of. "Nonna JoJo says you can't have too much cinnamon and sugar."

"Except Nonna JoJo doesn't have to deal with a sugared-up five-year-old," Cas whispered, making me giggle, even as he scooped *his* hand into the bowl, and since it was significantly larger than Ethan's, it provided significantly more sugar to spread onto the dough that had been buttered by Ethan.

With Ethan's bare hands.

Because, apparently, cinnamon rolls tasted better when made with bare hands.

This was a statement Ethan could get behind.

My kid loved getting messy.

And since Nonna JoJo—aka Joanne—was clearly the

cinnamon roll expert, and thus, all things cinnamon, sugar, butter, yeast, or dough-related deferred to her.

But it was something that I had embraced as well, and although I was covered in flour and sugar and butter and cinnamon, I was having the *best* time.

Partly because I was hanging with Ethan and Cas and making something together, but also because Cas's family was like him. Nice and kind and thoughtful and Joanne hadn't even blinked when Ethan had given her a hug and had gotten butter on her jeans. For that matter, neither had Cas's dad—also Luca, though he actually went by Luca (or as he'd advised Ethan to call him, Ace)—when Ethan had high-fived him and he'd ended up with a glob of butter on his pale green polo.

Margot and Sam and Kathy had joined in on the mess just as eagerly, each assigned a job they'd clearly done for years and each gentle and sweet and patient as they'd showed Ethan how to do their tasks, not seeming to mind that a five-year-old was making a mess of it.

They were laid back expert cinnamon roll makers who didn't care that the butter was going to leave grease stains on their clothes or that the rolls were uneven and maybe a bit lumpy or that—

Cas kissed the hinge of my jaw, murmured, "Spread the sugar, gorgeous."

It was hard to concentrate with his big, warm body pressed to mine, even harder to concentrate with Ethan making a mess. But, frankly, all of that was not even *remotely* as challenging as trying to concentrate when his siblings were watching me and Cas like we were scientific experiments, while also being extremely funny and cool and welcoming to Ethan.

And to me.

Asking me about school—and commiserating how hard it was to work and study at the same time. Talking to Ethan about his interests—which, unfortunately for me, now included breaking down every single trap that Kevin from *Home Alone* had laid out for the robbers. The movie had given him *ideas*—and sweet baby Jesus, that was terrifying.

Ideas that were only slightly less terrifying than the curious looks that had greeted me when Cas and I had strode through the doorway that led into the kitchen, holding hands.

I'd apologized and fussed over Ethan—tried to make it clear that he didn't spend time awake without me and I didn't want Cas's parents to think I neglected my kid.

A worry that had lasted approximately ten seconds.

Because then Joanne was wrapping me in a tight hug—a *Mom* hug—and then she'd pulled back, studied me closely. "Look at those dark circles you both have." A shake of her head. "You should have had us come earlier. We could have watched Ethan while you both got more rest." Another squeeze. "Feel free to pop up for a nap later. I know how hard it is trying to do everything."

I figured, with four kids and a job, that Joanne probably *did* know.

"Now," she'd said, drawing me further into the kitchen. "Cas has told us next to nothing about you and Ethan"—a glare at her son—"which means that I need to know *everything*."

Said not in a scary, demanding way.

But rather, in a kind, friendly, *maternal* way.

And the front I'd pulled up in Cas's bedroom—about there being nothing to worry about because we loved each other—had clicked into place. Only it wasn't a front, hadn't been me holding it together because he was clearly worried.

Not any longer.

Because one hug and a short conversation, and I'd known it would be the truth.

This was going to be okay.

We were going to be okay.

And bonus, it came with butter and sugar and cinnamon.

"So, what are you studying, darlin'?" Luca asked, sitting next to me.

I'd plunked down onto the couch, was watching the action in the kitchen while eating my third cinnamon roll.

They were delicious.

Nonna JoJo was right. There was no such thing as too much sugar.

Especially when I'd eaten bacon and eggs alongside the baked goods.

Definitely not a healthy meal. Nor one eaten remotely near brunch time. They'd become early afternoon cinnamon rolls (because it took a long time to make cinnamon rolls with a five-year-old who had a ton of questions—not to mention a grown woman who had an equal amount of very similar questions).

But no one seemed to mind—the timing or the questions.

So, we'd all eaten and then did dishes and then I'd gone back for seconds—or thirds, I supposed.

But it was cold and overcast outside and the meal was warm and spicy...and felt like home.

I felt home here in Cas's place, surrounded by his family, by the laughter and easy acceptance.

But...I couldn't lie and say I didn't feel a *bit* intimidated being near Luca, and so I hadn't really put myself out there with him. He hadn't given me any indication he wouldn't be open to conversation. It was just that I was more comfortable with Margot and Sam and Kathy and Kathy's husband, Tim, who teased each other and bantered just like the Breakers' players and their significant others did when they came into

CeCe's. And obviously, Joanne was amazing—sweet and bubbly and giving me major Beth vibes, so I was feeling right at home with her too.

Interacting with Luca, though?

Well, that had been...hesitant.

Mostly because—in *my* experience—dads were scary and not nice and—

Right. *Crap.*

He was waiting for me to answer a question. And dads got impatient, and he might think I was dumb and—

His hand came over mine, squeezed lightly before letting go. "It's not a trick question, darlin'," he said gently. "I promise."

"I know," I whispered after a moment, holding very still. "I just—"

I bit my lip, knowing I had a choice here—one I knew that Cas would make for me if I let him. He would step in, make the call to protect me from this conversation because he knew it wasn't the most comfortable place for me. He'd done the same thing throughout the entire visit. Like when I'd been vague about some of the details of my childhood, and he'd given his family pointed looks so they'd accepted that vague without further explanation.

Because of Cas, they'd taken my benign explanation about my mom dying and my father not being currently in my or Ethan's lives at...well, maybe not at face value. But they hadn't pressed for anything further...and then they'd gone back to baking.

Similar to how they'd accepted my short explanation about Ethan's dad—though that had, luckily, required *fewer* vague comments and euphemisms and pointed looks from Cas.

Because Ethan was nearby, and they were careful with him.

I knew that part of Cas stepping in was that he was

protecting me and Ethan, saving me from dredging up painful shit, but I also recognized that his family had left it alone because they were nice people, and they'd picked up on the fact that it wasn't a comfortable conversation for me.

So yeah, as the afternoon had rolled on, it was clear where Cas had gotten the Nice Trait.

From a good family.

Good siblings.

A good mother.

A good *father*.

The last of which was why I released a breath, shoved down the prickling instincts that told me nothing good could come of this conversation, met Luca's eyes, and said, "I'm not used to this."

It was a soft admission.

"Not used to what, honey?" he asked kindly.

Another breath and then I gave him more honesty. "I'm not used to a father who's interested in my life." I cleared my throat, tone a little quieter. "I'm not used to a father who *likes* his kids, let alone one who looks at his kids like you do."

Silence.

Long. Not particularly comfortable.

Then, "How do I look at them?"

My throat was tight, but I pushed the words through. "Like you love them."

He inhaled sharply enough that Cas called out, "Gorgeous?"

Seeing me. Watching out for me. *Protecting* me.

I turned, forced a smile, and directed it at him. "I'm good, honey. Promise," I added when he didn't look convinced.

"I hate that for you."

I blinked, glanced back at Luca, met eyes that were *Cas's*

eyes. And just like Cas's, they were warm and gentle and kind. "Sorry?"

His hand came back, only this time it wasn't just for a light squeeze. He covered my hand with his and left it there. His skin was a little rough, but the hold was all gentle. "I hate that someone as deserving as you didn't have something good at home."

His tone was gentle, too.

And comforting.

And I didn't know what to do with *that*.

So...I just breathed and held very still and deep down I hoped that one day it wouldn't be so hard to accept that fathers could be kind. That one day I could accept it without a second thought. Then I slipped my hand free, having reached my limit of Dad-ness, and managed to pull myself back to today, to focus on happier topics.

"School," I said, and he nodded approvingly as I got our conversation back on track. "The hope is that one day I'll go to nursing school," I told him. "But right now, I'm just slowly plugging away at all of my general ed requirements."

He didn't reach for me again, and he didn't seem upset that I'd pulled back.

Patient.

Like Cas.

And maybe he liked me.

Like Cas.

"That's good, darlin'," he said. "Gotta take it one step at a time, especially with a little one at home and a full-time job."

"Yeah," I whispered. Then paused, stymied, not knowing what to say next.

Though I didn't have to fumble for long. Luca filled the silence by asking, "Nursing, huh?"

Instinctively, I braced. Cas's dad had been nice so far, but, in my experience, father figures tended to strike out at the time I was the most unprepared. For all I knew, there was a snarky comment about me not being smart enough to go into a field like nursing coming my way.

But when Luca just nodded, and I saw that same kindness Cas had demonstrated over and over again, I knew that bracing and preparing wasn't something that I'd have to keep on doing.

Because Cas had to have gotten his kind and soft from somewhere—and it was clear the man sitting next to me had played a huge role in it.

Especially when he smiled and said, "I can see you as a nurse."

My brows lifted.

"You've got a good heart." A wink. "Plus, you'll look good in scrubs."

My lips curved, the past fading and amusement crowding in. "That factors?"

"Gotta look good to play good—" He shrugged. "Or *medicine* good, as it is."

I giggled.

Giggled.

And then, oddly, my eyes stung. Because I'd never had anything close to this with my own dad.

And that *hurt.*

But I kept it together...at least until there was a cheer and I turned and saw Ethan, Cas, his mom, and all his siblings sitting at the kitchen table playing UNO.

My son...he was *shining.*

Part of this was normal for him—we played UNO a lot.

But part of it was completely out there.

Because he'd never had *this.* He'd never had the chance to bask in the positive attention of a family. But Cas—and Cas's family—had given him that.

And *that* was when I lost it.

"Excuse me," I whispered, jumping to my feet.

"You okay, darlin'?" Luca asked, following me up.

"Great." *Shit*. My voice had cracked on that lie. "I just need some air," I managed to croak out. Then I hurried to the door, avoiding Cas's eyes.

His *concerned* eyes.

And the concerned gazes of his family.

"Jules?" he asked, and I heard his chair slide back.

"I'm good," I called, still beelining for the front door. "I just need some air." There. That sounded a little more normal.

I turned the handle, yanked open the door, and froze.

Cas's voice was close to my ear, having already come to me. Because...he was Cas.

But he didn't sound like my Cas when he growled,

"You *have got* to be shitting me."

THIRTY-SEVEN

Cas

CHELSEA WAS STANDING on my porch, her fist raised, poised to knock.

Chelsea.

Jesus fucking *Christ.*

And when she saw Jules, her face hardened.

"You are *not* here," I said, pulling my cell out of my pocket. "Please tell me that you're not dumb enough to actually be *here.*"

More anger transforming her once-pretty face.

Her lips parted. "You—"

"Mom?"

Fuck.

But before I could ask someone to occupy Ethan and to get him away from the psycho that was Chelsea showing up unwelcome on my porch—after having shown up unwelcome and getting rebuffed on various occasions since I'd unleashed the power of my attorney and the Breakers' security team on her, and *still* not getting one fucking clue—Jules's son was there, trying to squeeze past me and get to his mom.

"Hey, buddy," I said, holding Ethan back and carefully tucking Jules behind me. "This is an adult conversation. Can you go with Nonna JoJo and pick out the movie we're going to watch tonight?"

A long look, holding my eyes.

Then that stare shifting to Chelsea's, and I bit back a curse when Ethan seemed to pick up on too much. His body went stiff, and he grabbed his mom's hand, holding it tightly, silently telling me he wasn't going anywhere.

Okay, normally, that would be extremely touching, Ethan standing by his mom, protecting her. But it couldn't happen in this situation. I needed to make sure that Ethan could be a five-year-old, instead of the kid standing in front of me with old eyes and a tight expression.

"Eth?" I said as my dad stepped up next to me, correctly assessing the situation in a few seconds and blocking Chelsea's view of Jules as I crouched in front of Ethan. "I've got this," I said softly, resting me hands on Ethan's shoulders and holding the boy's gaze. "I love your mom, and I love you, and I won't let anything happen to *either* of you. I promise."

Ethan's eyes went wide, his mouth falling open.

"And promises are meant for keeping, right?"

Ethan looked down, mouth closing, free hand tightening into a fist, and it took everything in me to wait it out, to shut up and wait, to not blabber the fuck on and beg this kid to trust me.

Then he was releasing his mom's hand and wrapping both arms around my neck. "Yes," he whispered. "Promises are meant for keeping."

"Exactly, bud. Now," I said, nudging Ethan toward my mom, "can you go with Nonna JoJo and trust me to have this?"

A nod. Ethan turning away.

Pausing. "Cas?"

"Yeah, bud?"

"I love you, too."

Fuck.

That hit hard.

But what hit harder was that the first time Ethan and I shared that was on the front porch of my house while my dad was playing interference with fucking *Chelsea.*

"Movie, yeah?" I said quietly.

A nod and then Ethan was gone, my mom corralling him into the family room.

My siblings, though, they were gathered around the front door and spilling out onto the porch. A wall of Castillos.

"You have a son?" Chelsea snapped.

"Yeah," I said, straightening and curling an arm around Julie's shoulders, tucking her close. It was decided. Ethan was mine, same as Jules was. Biology didn't matter in this, and frankly, Chelsea wasn't owed any further explanation.

Chelsea froze. Then, "You have a son with *her?*"

Which was the point that my dad lost patience.

"Woman," he snapped. "*Look* at them, at us, at him."

Chelsea's eyes flashed, and she opened her mouth, no doubt to spit some vitriol.

"*Look,*" my dad said again. "And get a fucking clue. You never had this and you never will."

Her body rocked back as though those words were a physical blow.

"Luca?" she whispered.

"Cas," I corrected, sending a prayer up to the hockey gods that she would get it this time. "And my dad is right. You know that. I've made that clear. *Repeatedly.* And I'll continue making it clear. Because you'll never be my family, Chelsea,"

I said, and my tone wasn't gentle, not in the least. "*Never.*" I held up my cell. "Now, I can call the cops and have you arrested for trespassing and violating the restraining order and you'll be dealing with more charges"—besides the assault ones from the incident at CeCe's—"or you can stop fucking around, leave, and live your life, getting a clue and understanding that what I have with Jules is far more than I ever had with you."

"Cas," Chelsea whispered, and I almost snapped at her, ordered her to leave again. But my name was paired with a trembling hand dragged over her face, her feet moving, taking her back down the steps and onto the walkway.

"Now I see that you're finally *looking* at them," my father said.

Another rock back onto her heels, more words that were a physical blow.

A jerky nod.

"I—" she whispered. Then she glanced at me, at Jules. "I'm sorry."

Chelsea didn't get to see my reaction to that statement—and it was definitely shock, albeit with a dash of pity thrown in, because she *did* seem to be looking, did seem to be *finally* seeing.

She didn't get any of that.

Because she'd spun on her heel and run.

"THEN SHE DISAPPEARED, MAN," I told Smitty. "I reported her to the detective in charge of the restraining order, but she'd already reported herself, said she wouldn't do it again."

The ref blew the whistle, and both teams began getting ready for the pregame festivities.

"And you think she'll get a clue and finally leave you the fuck alone?" Smitty asked.

I wasn't sure of anything when it came to my psycho ex.

Which was why I just shrugged. "Fuck if I know." I chugged some water. "All I *do* know is that it's been two weeks and I haven't heard a peep from her. She hasn't come to my place or CeCe's or the arena or the practice rink or anywhere that she used to show up before." I chucked the bottle back into the holder. "And all I can do is hope that she's finally gotten that clue."

"Damn," Smitty muttered. "And I thought *my* girl had it bad." He tossed his own bottle back into the rack. "At least she never had to deal with any psycho exes."

Unfortunately, my teammate had a point.

Unfortunately, that point did little to distract me from the fact that we were playing the Sierra.

Lake Jordan was the captain and apparently also the only person who'd been nice to Jules growing up. He was also a pain in the ass on the ice and had left Jules to work her ass off in Baltimore, her rebuffing his help or not, so he had a hit—or a plethora of them—coming.

But it was Nate Miller who was going to get his ass handed to him.

H.A.N.D.E.D.

"Asshole," I muttered.

"You love me," Smitty said with a smirk, wrongly assuming I was talking about him.

Not that I hadn't uttered the moniker at him enough times before for Smitty to make that assumption. Clearly. So I didn't bother to correct him.

"You sure about that love?" I asked dryly, watching as the guy who'd sung the national anthem left the ice and they rolled out the red carpet for a ceremonial puck drop.

"Pretty sure you're going to *love*"—Smitty waggled his brows—"that I gave your woman and her kid tickets to the game so they could watch you—"

Ice through my veins. *"What?"*

Smitty ignored the interruption and continued, "Watch your cute little butt skate around the rink."

I grabbed the water bottle again, clenching it so that I didn't wrap my hands around Smitty's neck and squeeze.

And *squeeze.*

"What?" I repeated icily.

"Are you asking about your cute butt or—"

"You gave *my* woman tickets without talking to me first?" A quiet question, but even I could hear the edge of danger in it.

"Hell, man, it's not like that," Smitty said. "It was all on the up and up. She asked and wanted to surprise you, and I know you liked the last time she came to watch you and—"

I lost it, shoving the bottle at Smitty's chest, hard enough that water squirted everywhere. Then I did my best to corral my temper and to not do it by punching the fuck out of my teammate and have *that* particular action be caught by fans' cellphones and broadcast on social media—or on *traditional* media.

Ethan might see it.

And then what would my kid think of me?

"What the fuck, man?" Smitty growled, chucking the bottle into the holder, and wiping a hand over his dripping face.

I inhaled. Exhaled.

Struggled to not throttle my teammate.

"The fuck, *Smitty*," I gritted out, "is that I didn't ask Jules to come to this game"—one of only a handful of matchups we had against the Sierra this year—"because Nate Miller is Ethan's dad."

And for once—and for all the wrong *fucking* reasons—Smitty didn't have a response to *that*.

A fucking miracle.

A fucking *disaster*.

THIRTY-EIGHT

Jules

IT WASN'T until we'd walked down the concrete stairs and taken our seats that I realized I'd made a big, big mistake.

And that happened when I'd looked up at the scoreboard.

Breakers on the left side with their cute little wave-shaped logo.

On the other...

A logo of mountains.

My stomach clenched as I read the team name—The Sierra.

No.

I couldn't be this stupid, couldn't be this unlucky. This just...this couldn't be *right*. It had to be a mistake, *had* to be. So, as calmly as I could—since Ethan was next to me—I reached into my pocket to extract my cell with shaking hands.

Called up the tickets Smitty had sent me...still with shaking hands.

And actually *reading* them this time, not just skimming over the details and looking for row and seat numbers, but reading the game time and the team names.

Breakers versus Sierra.

Christ almighty.

I *could* possibly be this stupid. And unlucky.

If I'd been by myself, I would have hopped right out of this seat, walked my butt up the concrete stairs, fled to my car, and surprised my hot hockey player in his bed later that night.

But I wasn't alone.

I was with my son, who was firmly entrenched in the hockey bug and loving every part of playing, practicing, and watching the sport.

No surprise since he'd been adopted into the hockey fold—hell, he'd even gotten to hang with Cas and the rest of the Breakers crew last night at CeCe's for a little while before Cas had taken him back to my place.

Mary was still babysitting semi-regularly, and I had been worried about the *semi* part of that fact, since Ethan had also spent time with Nonna JoJo and Ace—aka Luca—and one night with Kathy and Tim (Sam and Margot were back at school) but then Mary had told me that her coursework had gotten really intense and she was overwhelmed and that while she loved Ethan, she was glad to have some extra kiddo free time to study.

My guilt was assuaged—somewhat, because Mary had also confessed that she'd felt overwhelmed for a while but hadn't wanted to leave me in a pickle. So, since I was saving a lot of money on babysitting fees (though I had offered to pay both Cas and his parents and they'd both declined), I vowed to do something nice for Mary as soon as the semester ended. A spa day, or a gift card toward books in the campus bookstore.

God knew I *felt* down to my bones how expensive text-books were.

But...maybe a spa day.

Because Mary was like me.

She didn't have a lot of family, didn't have a lot of friends.

And since I was no longer on the outside, no longer relegated to the sidelines (and it felt fucking great), I was going to bring Mary along with me.

I'd totally bet that Beth, Kailey, and Hazel would be down for a spa day. Pru was a bit more of a tomboy, but I thought that even with that being the truth, she would still be down, too.

All of which was a good thing, something I was looking forward to.

But it wasn't something that was going to help me take care of *this* situation.

We'd arrived later than the last time we'd come to a game—having zipped over straight from Ethan's practice and making a pit stop for some grub on the way. Yeah, I was saving on babysitting, but wasn't going to go crazy with spending, especially with arena prices (though I *had* promised that Ethan could pick something here for dessert and, for the record, he'd gone with cotton candy, which was currently smeared like bright blue lipstick around his mouth).

The game was starting in just a few minutes, the national anthem had just finished and a player from either team had gathered around a few people standing on a red carpet that had been rolled out on the ice.

The Breakers player was Marcel.

The Sierra player...was Lake Jordan.

God, I hadn't actually *seen* him in years, and...he looked good. Bigger and stronger and happy, standing there smiling next to the group of people, pausing to ruffle the boy's hair.

I could almost hear his voice, since it hadn't been all that long since we'd talked (though in my darker moments, I had preferred texting, because it had been less personal and more comfortable and...easier for me to remain on the sidelines).

I needed to reach out to him.

Connect.

Tell him how much his help had meant to me. Tell him how much it had meant that he'd...well, that he'd been good to me when no one else had been.

So, now that I wasn't on the sidelines any longer, I needed to own that, to let him know how much it meant then *and* now, and...it was just that I'd prefer to not do it anywhere in the vicinity of Nate.

For one, my lawyer had advised me long ago to not communicate directly with my ex.

For another, I hadn't seen Nate since he'd turned me away and broke my heart and...I wasn't sure how it would feel to see him now, after all this time.

Last, and more importantly, I didn't want to expose Ethan to his vitriol.

Didn't want my son *anywhere* near him.

But how could I pull Ethan away from something he loved?

I tried to breathe, to think. We weren't going to go anywhere near the Sierra's locker room or players—yes, I'd planned on heading down and surprising Cas after the game, but I could tell Ethan that something had come up and that we couldn't go down and visit today. I'd soften the blow by telling him that we'd meet Cas at his place. That way, it would still be a surprise for Cas, and it would definitely still be fun for Ethan. That had pretty much been the original plan Ethan and I had before I'd gotten the bright—dumbass— idea to ask Smitty if he happened to have any spare tickets for the game. Until then, we would watch the game and enjoy ourselves.

Until then, I would avoid looking at Nate, at Lake, and instead focus on my man, my friends.

It would be easy to stay under the radar.

Ethan and I were just two faces in a crowd of twenty-thousand people.

It would all be okay.

"That's Lake Jordan, Mom," Ethan breathed with almost as much awe as he'd had when first meeting Cas and Smitty and Marcel and the others.

"Yeah, bud," I said, forcing my tone to stay neutral. "I grew up with him, remember?"

They'd had conversations about Lake when Ethan had first gotten into hockey.

A nod, his eyes glued to the ice. "But you haven't seen him in a long time."

"Right." I smiled down at him.

"He's *big*," Ethan said.

Lake was. He'd always been tall and solid, but now he was muscled, and in his gear, on his skates—even across the ice he was approaching giant status. Not to mention that *face*.

It was...pretty.

Too pretty to risk being sliced open with skate blades and whacked with sticks.

"Yeah, he is," I said. "Almost as big as Smitty."

Another nod, still watching intently. "Do you think he'll recognize *you*?"

"Well," I teased. "I didn't get *big*. But I doubt it," I told him. "It's been years, bud, and we've only texted and talked on the phone—"

Tap. Tap. Tap.

My head jerked up at the sharp sound.

Jerked up...and saw Lake standing there.

Waving at me. *Grinning* at me.

"Whoa," Ethan murmured. "I think he recognizes you, Mom."

Shit.

Shit.

I couldn't form a response, not to save my life.

Because who was standing behind him?

Nate Miller.

THIRTY-NINE

Cas

THE GAME WAS fast and furious and *bruising*.

But I never got close enough to Lake Jordan to warn him to lock down his teammate and make sure the fucker kept his distance from Jules during and after the game.

Every shift was moving too fast, too filled with contact and rushes and skating my ass off for me to get that chance.

When the buzzer went off after the third, the teams returned to our respective locker rooms, exited out separate corridors (because things often got intense during professional games and that separation was good...even *if* I had friends on other teams, a cooling down period was often required to leave hockey on the ice and return to friendship off it).

But all of that meant it still wasn't easy to get Lake alone, to warn him that Jules was here, and he needed to help me run interference between Jules and Ethan and Nate.

So now I needed to run interference between Jules and Ethan and Nate by myself.

Except, she wasn't picking up her phone.

Christ.

"You good, bud?" Smitty said, and for once, his voice wasn't a boom, wasn't blaring across the room.

It was quiet and concerned.

"What do you think?" I muttered, jabbing at my phone to call Jules again as I tore at my laces.

Thank fuck, I didn't need to do press today—or rather, thank fuck that my teammates had stepped in to take over the interview requests so that I didn't have to.

"Hand it over," Theo said, putting his hand out. "I'll keep calling. You get changed."

I didn't bother arguing, just slapped the phone into my friend's hand, who immediately tapped at the screen and lifted it to his ear.

"I'll call security," Smitty said, still quiet and not like Smitty. "She was going to meet me by the training suite. I'll get them to meet her and bring her and Ethan to a room well away from—" A shake of his head and he didn't finish that statement, just stood up from the bench and walked from the room, still fully dressed.

I got my skates off, tore off the rest of my gear, yanked on a sweatshirt, and shoved my feet into my shoes.

Ridiculous to wear dress shoes with my tight under layers and sweatshirt, but I wasn't bothering with anything else, especially as the press were starting to come into the room. Marcel stood up, meandered over to one man, intercepting him when he seemed intent on coming for me.

Thank fuck for my captain.

Shoes on, I glanced at Theo, brows lifting in silent question, asking for an update.

Theo pulled the cell from his ear and shook his head.

"Nothing," he muttered, ending the most recent call, and handing the phone over.

"Fuck." I shoved it in my pocket, then thrust a hand through my hair.

"Go, man. Start at the training suite," Theo said. "Smitty and security and the rest of us will help."

Right.

I began to leave, but Eva Moreno—sports blogger, smart and talented journalist, and a woman who was able to sniff out a story (and especially a scandal, no matter how small)—stepped into the room right as I hit the door.

Fuck.

But then Theo was there.

Theo was there. Theo, who *hated* Eva, not only because she wrote no shortage of snarky stories about him and his exploits. Theo, who couldn't stand Eva because she was immune to his playboy charm and never failed to ask him questions that left Theo—and, frankly, *all* of us—scrambling for good answers. Theo, who despised giving interviews in the first place—and who especially despised giving them to Eva. It was *Theo* who voluntarily intercepted Eva, engaging her quickly despite *all* of that.

Despite the fact that they were oil and water and constantly tried to one-up each other's snark.

That probably wasn't going to go well.

But I had bigger issues.

I exited the locker room, taking the quickest path to the training suite, which happened to take me by the elevators...

And by Lake Jordan.

"What the fuck are you doing here?" I snapped.

Irritation in the big fucker's eyes. "Don't come at me, Castillo. I've got a friend coming down and then I'll be out of your hair."

Okay, yeah, our battles on the ice tended to be contentious.

But *this* was more important—Jules and Ethan were more important than any interaction on the ice, even *if* Lake was one of those guys everyone hated playing against (though they didn't mind if he was on their team).

"Who's your friend?" I demanded.

A laugh that was less amused and more pissed off. "None of your fucking business, that's who."

And that was when I lost the thin tendril of control that was keeping my temper in check. I flew forward, gripping Lake around the throat, shoving the other man into the wall. "Who. The fuck. Is. Your. *Friend?*" I growled.

"What the fuck, man?" Lake snapped, grabbing at my wrist, trying to yank my hand off.

Wasn't going to happen.

Wasn't going to happen.

"*Who* is your friend?" I gritted. "Is it a woman?"

Lake froze, hand tightening enough around my wrist that swear to fuck, I felt my bones practically grinding together. "What the fuck, man?" he said again.

"Is it *Jules?*" I growled.

Lake's fingers spasmed, sending a bolt of pain up my arm, but I didn't release him, especially when Lake asked, "How do you know Jules?"

My response was visceral. "She's *mine.*"

Another spasm. Another jolt of pain. "What?"

"*She's mine.*"

Lake moved then, breaking my hold like it was nothing, and I was reminded all over again that he was a big fucker. A *strong* fucker. "How is she yours?" he asked, frost in his tone and his face in mine.

"I love her," I snapped, shoving him back. "And Ethan, too."

"So why the fuck is she *here?*" Lake swept a hand out.

I clenched my jaw and did some sweeping of my own. "The bigger question is why the fuck are you bringing her down *here?*" I snapped. "Closer to that *asshole?*"

Lake went still again. "Nate is so far up his own ass that he couldn't be bothered to pay attention to anyone but himself." His big chest rose and fell on a breath. "And I asked her down here because I needed to make sure she and Ethan are okay, and"—he stopped, his tone less granite and more controlled—"I need to give her something."

Yeah, I bet he did.

"She doesn't need your money," I snapped.

She didn't need any other connections to Lake, to Nate, to that whole fucking team.

I had her now, had them both now.

"She's on her own—"

"I know you helped her five years ago," I said, taking a breath and trying to find my control again. Lake—asshole or not—had helped Jules. That was fact. Jules cared about Lake. Also, fact. But neither of those mattered in this moment because I needed to end this conversation, stop fucking around, and *find Jules.* "But I have them both now, so you need to back the fuck off."

"Look"—Lake took his own breath—"I can appreciate that you care about her, but she's important to me, Cas. I need to talk to her."

"She needs to leave that shit in the past." A beat. "Including you."

"If she wanted to leave it behind—leave *me* behind," Lake said, "she wouldn't return my texts and calls, wouldn't have come to the game tonight."

There was a point to that.

One I didn't want to hear.

Not right then.

Not without knowing where Jules was. Not without knowing where *Nate* was.

Jules would come down. I knew it. Not just because she'd made arrangements with Smitty, but because she wouldn't take this away from Ethan—a chance to meet a player he liked, a chance to be in the mix of all this hockey atmosphere.

The kid was hooked.

And Jules wouldn't hesitate to give that to her kid, no matter what it might put her through.

"This isn't a safe space for Jules," I said, "and you know it."

For the first time, a glimmer of uncertainty hit Lake's expression.

But we didn't have time to explore that, to continue the conversation.

Because a voice came from behind us.

"I had that pussy." A laugh that was cold and cruel. "And let me tell you, it was nothing to fight over."

"Nate," Lake began.

But he didn't get to finish.

Because that was when the elevator doors dinged, opened...

And Jules and Ethan stepped off.

FORTY

Jules

ETHAN WAS CHATTERING, excited about descending into the depths of the arena, barely able to contain himself because a woman in a Sierra shirt had come during the third period and said Lake Jordan wanted to meet us and had given us passes to the Sierra side of the arena (taking away my ability to avoid that part of our evening).

He'd been beside himself.

Seeing the Sierra *and* the Breakers?

Nirvana for a hockey-crazed five-year-old.

So Ethan was about to meet Lake Jordan *and* see the people he liked most in the world (and no, I didn't include myself on that list, not when it came to a comparison between me and *his* hockey players).

And yes, he thought of them and called them *his* hockey players.

But I'd barely been able to smile at his description, had barely been able to file it away to tell Cas later because one second, he was chattering, and the next, the elevator doors were opening and I was stepping off onto the floor and...

Into a fucking nightmare.

Lake was standing outside the door. But he wasn't the nightmare.

Cas was standing next to him, looking pissed. But he wasn't the nightmare either.

Nope.

That bad dream of all bad dreams was...Nate standing behind them both.

I knew I shouldn't have come down here.

I *knew* it.

But Smitty had made plans and then Lake had sent the passes and Ethan had been excited and they'd come with a note promising to be discreet (something that I was realizing now was too little too late, considering the fact that he'd singled me out with that tap on the glass before the game and had smiled at me several times throughout—despite the fact that his team was losing).

Ethan had wanted to go.

And I'd done my best over the years.

But for so long, it had been difficult to give my son what he wanted.

I knew that he wouldn't have thrown a fit if I'd told him that we couldn't go down, that we needed to go home.

But the light in his eyes would dim...and my heart didn't have that in me.

Not right then.

Not when things had been so fucking great over the last couple of weeks.

So...we'd gone down.

And now I'd stepped off the elevator and walked straight into my worst nightmare.

"Hey, Cas, I haven't—" Smitty's voice preceded him as he came around the corner and cut off when he finished walking into the lobby area. Or maybe when he processed the shit show that was taking place in front of him.

"Smitty!" Ethan cried out, running toward him.

The big man recovered impressively quickly, moving forward and scooping up my son and then putting plenty of distance between them and Nate. Thank God he wasn't frozen like I was. That he seemed to know what to do, *unlike* me. "Hey, bud!" he said, settling Ethan on his shoulders. "I have something cool to show you." Smitty's remorseful eyes hit mine and he mouthed, "I'm sorry."

"It's okay," I mouthed back.

But we both knew it wasn't okay. Not in the fucking *least.*

But Smitty was getting my son away, making it so that he wasn't going to be exposed to this scene, and however shitty it turned out.

Because every part of me knew that it wasn't going to go *well.*

The sneer on Nate's face and the glimmer of *mean* in his eyes told me that much.

He'd had that *mean* the last time I'd seen him. I'd felt that *mean* in every interaction we'd had since—and those interactions had been limited to some texts, a handful of phone calls (and nasty voicemails left on my phone, for his part), and later, through our own attorneys (on the advice of *my* attorney) with terse emails and letters and faxes.

"Wait," Nate said, grabbing for Ethan's arm. "What's *your* name, kiddo?"

"Don't—" I began, but then Cas was there, his body between Smitty and Ethan and Nate. Who didn't like Cas's interference, not in the freaking least.

Which he showed by shoving Cas hard enough to send him back a pace.

"That's my—" Nate hissed.

"Shut it," Cas said, the tone fierce enough to cut Nate off, though my ex took a step closer, got even more in Cas's face.

Then Cas had the assistance of Lake, who stood shoulder to shoulder with him, arms crossed, face thunderous.

Lake.

God. My *Lake*.

I'd pushed him away for more than five years and he still had my back.

And *that*—as I stood smack dab in the middle of my worst nightmare—was when I understood why I'd been able to trust Cas, how I'd been able to do it so quickly after everything had happened.

Because despite everything, I'd had one good man in my life growing up.

And he was standing next to the man I loved now.

Nate's voice rose. "Get the fuck out of my way and—"

"Don't do *that* in front of Ethan," Cas snapped, fiercely enough that miracle of miracles, Nate shut up again.

"Mom?" An uncertain question from my son.

I turned, plastered a smile on my face. "It's okay, honey. But we do need to have an adult conversation"—a snort from Nate—"so why don't you and Smitty go have fun and I'll catch up with you in a little bit?"

He bit his lip, clearly not buying my explanation *or* my fake smile. "I'll be right there." I called on all of my limited acting skills and added, "Promise."

"And promises are made for keeping," he said, his expression relaxing.

I saw Nate jerk out of the corner of my eye, but didn't turn to look at him. Instead, I just focused on what was important.

Ethan.

"Exactly, bud," I said.

"Smitty?" Cas asked once Ethan had nodded, had smiled back at me. It was less question and was more like an order, and a sharp one at that.

But Smitty didn't rebuke it.

He just said, "On it," and took off back around the corner with Ethan on his big, broad shoulders. Maybe that should have scared me, a big man just taking off with my kid. But I knew Smitty, and I knew Cas, and I knew that they both would do anything to protect my son.

So, I didn't comment on Cas's order or on Smitty's actions.

In fact, I didn't comment on *anything* else.

Not until I was certain that Smitty and Ethan were out of earshot, that my son was safe. Not even when Theo appeared as Smitty disappeared, his expression darkening as he moved toward our trio, making it clear he was throwing down with Lake and Cas.

Only then did I turn to Nate, prepared to confront all that mean.

Cas stepped toward me, taking my hand, tucking me behind him. Protecting. Again. Only this time, it was me and not Ethan.

I clenched at his fingers.

He was calm and steady and *Cas*.

"That's my son," Nate said.

And it wasn't mean.

That alone had me looking through a gap in the broad wall Cas and Lake and Theo were forming, had me studying Nate's face.

"That's my son," he said again.

"No." I pushed between Cas and Lake, fought against the hold Cas had on me. I didn't succeed in breaking it, didn't succeed in getting in front of the only two men in my life who'd loved me.

Lake's love was that of a big brother, a friend.

Cas's was...well, Cas's was everything else.

So, I wasn't surprised that they kept me hemmed in with their bodies, kept me safe. I wasn't surprised when Cas exchanged the grip he had on my hand and slid his arm around my waist, pulled me against him.

What I *was* surprised about?

The expression on Nate's face.

"Promises are made for keeping," he whispered.

And lightning shot through my veins. After all this time... I'd forgotten.

Forgotten who'd told me that the first time, who'd made promises of his own but then *hadn't* kept them.

Nate.

He'd said that. He'd made the promises.

And he'd broken them.

"That's my son," he whispered now.

"No," I repeated. "He's *my* son. *Mine*. You haven't spent a minute with him, haven't tried to know him, haven't provided for him." Nate rocked back on his heels like I'd punched him, but I didn't stop. Not when his expression went stark. Not when his throat worked, and he looked away. "He will *never* be your son. You don't love him. You've never loved *anyone*."

His head jerked up, eyes filled with shadows.

And that had me amending my statement. Slightly. "You've never loved anyone who couldn't give you something," I said, jabbing a finger at him. "You're selfish and an asshole and if you think I haven't seen the way you are in the many dozens of news stories about you, then you're wrong. I've seen them. I've seen *you*. And I know you haven't changed."

This time he took a physical step back.

"So, no," I growled. "You're not going to bring your bullshit into *my* son's life. You're not going to poison the light he has inside him. You're not going to hurt him. Not today. Not in the future." Nate stumbled back another step. "Not *ever.*"

Nate swallowed.

Cas's arm tightened.

And since I was on a roll, I kept going. "What *you* are going to do is sign the papers your lawyer has had for *years* and get the fuck out of Ethan's life. *Forever.*"

"Promises," Nate said again, and—fuck me—but his gaze dropped to his feet, and it made me feel the slightest bit guilty.

When, dammit, I had nothing to feel guilty about.

"*Promises.*" His head shot up, and I couldn't read his eyes, couldn't read his expression.

Because then he'd turned away.

Then he'd *walked* away.

I looked at Cas, at Lake, searched for an explanation, but their faces told me they were just as clueless.

"You have *got* to be shitting me."

I jumped, spinning toward the voice and saw that a petite blonde with deep brown eyes was behind us, teeth biting into a lush bottom lip, her curvy body pressed so tightly against the expanse of wall, it was as though she were trying to disappear.

"I'm sorry," she said, meeting my gaze. "I-I didn't mean to overhear."

Theo glared. "Bullshit, Eva."

I glanced away from the stricken woman, eyes widening at the fury on Theo's face. "Don't tell me you weren't trying for a big story."

That was when I saw the cell phone with the recording app open in Eva's hand.

Fuck.

I really didn't want my story, my face, my *son* plastered on social media.

"I'm not going for a story. I swear," Eva added quickly. "I was just going to head home, and I turned the corner and you guys were—" She bit her lip again, pressed back against the wall even harder. "I promise. I-I—" Her gaze went to mine again. "I'm *really* sorry. I wasn't trying to overhear."

Theo snorted.

And Eva narrowed her eyes.

But then she all but threw her phone at Theo. "There, okay?" she snapped. "You'll see that I didn't record anything." A glance back at me. "I *didn't* record anything."

Theo snorted again. "Right. We all know that you'd do anything for a story."

The emphasis on *anything* made Eva pale.

Another glance at me, her throat working before she said softly, "I know you won't believe me. But I promise I won't report on this."

Then Eva turned on her heel and hurried away.

FORTY-ONE

Cas

"WHAT THE FUCK is up between you and Eva?" I muttered to Theo.

Silence.

Tense enough that I looked away from where my woman was talking to fucking Lake Jordan, gabbing like they were old friends—because they *were* fucking old friends. Ugh. Ethan was glued to her side, hero worship on his face.

Tiny little traitor.

But seriously, trust that *my* woman would be friends with a pain in the ass like Lake Jordan.

Even if the man *had* stood by my side during the shit that had gone down with Nate fucking Miller.

Nate Miller, who'd disappeared, looking wrecked by the things Jules had—*rightfully*—laid on him. I was so fucking proud of her, had agreed with everything that she'd said. My woman standing up for herself, being so strong after what that fucker had done to her.

"Nothing's up between me and Eva," Theo said.

Which was a bullshit answer, and my mind was so twisted up by everything that had happened that night, I almost let it slide.

I didn't trust Nate's disappearing act.

Professional hockey was a small circle, so it was a well-known fact that the man was a motherfucking snake, that Miller had made it his mission to be an asshole.

All of which meant that I didn't trust *anything* the man did.

So yeah, I wasn't buying the wrecked expression on Miller's face and I was also thinking that the asshole just being on the same planet as Jules and Ethan was too fucking close, let alone the fact that Miller was still in the same building as my family.

That ate at me.

But I couldn't do anything about it at the moment, other than watch out for them and stay close.

And Ethan and Jules didn't need me to take out that frustration on Lake. I had already done that enough that evening—enough to feel a little bit guilty about it for sure—so I was making amends by giving them space. Because Jules deserved to connect with her old friend, and because I wouldn't burst Ethan's excitement.

But seriously, Lake played with Miller.

I didn't know how the man could stand it. I understood that Lake had no control over the Sierra's roster (and knew that management sometimes kept assholes on that roster because they produced by scoring goals and helping to win games, just like I knew that Miller was good at both).

But I also understood that Lake had made his dislike of Nate clear.

A point in the man's pro column.

Though, the fucker was still a pain in the ass on the ice.

Two more—as much as I hated them—were that Lake was good with Ethan *and* he was clearly keeping his gaze on his surroundings, ready for Miller to make a reappearance.

I wouldn't breathe easy until Miller was back in California.

Which was why I'd only left Jules alone for a minute with Lake while I'd retrieved Ethan from the locker room.

I wanted to sweep them out of here, to take them back to my place where it was safe.

But...old friends and hero worship.

So, I was propping up the hallway's wall—the same wall that one Eva Moreno had tried to disappear into during the confrontation with Theo.

"You were pretty harsh with Eva for there being nothing between you two," I said lightly.

Theo's jaw clenched, a muscle ticking in his cheek, and I wasn't so focused on Jules and Lake and Ethan—and that fucking hero worship—to miss the flicker of guilt cross my friend's face.

Theo wasn't normally an asshole.

Though, no one could argue that I'd been one tonight.

"She's a fucking reporter," Theo muttered. "She spreads bullshit for a living."

"I wouldn't consider the stories that Eva writes bullshit."

Theo grunted but didn't argue.

Mostly because he couldn't—or couldn't without looking like even more of an asshole. Eva was smart and talented, and her blog had become popular—even among the trolly asshole male fans, who liked to discount a female fan just because she was female. But no one could discount Eva. She was a fan, *and* she knew her stuff.

Which was why she'd gotten a media pass.

Which was why she'd been picked to color commentate on the pregame show more than a few times in recent months.

It was also why her social media had exploded.

And it was why I knew that she was under Theo's skin.

Deep.

I didn't know how or why, just knew that I was right. Eva Moreno was smart, took absolutely *no* shit, and was gorgeous.

Which was why I also knew that Theo was fucked.

My friend had hurt a good woman's feelings, and he wasn't normally an asshole so the fact that he'd acted like one was going to eat at him.

So, yup, Theo was fucked...in the best possible way, and I, for one, couldn't wait to watch the show.

The team's most eligible bachelor matched against the league's up-and-coming broadcaster, successful blogger, social media expert, and general Jill of all trades.

Yeah, watching that show from the sidelines was going to be awesome.

I just wanted to watch from the comfort of my own home.

With my woman in my arms and Ethan tuckered out from watching movies and—

"I'm going to shower and get the fuck out of here," Theo muttered.

"And go find Eva?" Smitty asked, proving the big man had ninja skills and could sneak around when he wanted to. Of course, his booming voice made the both of us jump as well as drew the attention of Lake, Ethan, and Jules. "Word on the street is you have some groveling to do."

Theo had started to turn away but froze at the booming voice. Now he swung back, irritation in every line of his face. "You all are fucking annoying."

"But you *luuuv* us," Raph said, joining the party and slinging an arm around Theo's shoulders.

"Fuck you," Theo muttered, shrugging him off.

"You'd be better off asking Eva to fuck *you*," I couldn't resist adding, waggling my brows.

Theo dropped his chin to his chest, sighed. "I hate you all."

"Hate is a bad word."

Theo's head popped up and, for the first time since Eva had walked away, hurt written into every inch of her body, he smiled. "Trust fate to bring him by after all the other bad words," he muttered before crouching down in front of Ethan and lifting his fist. "You're right, buddy. I'm sorry."

"You don't need to apologize to me." A pointed rebuke, brows lifting.

Rebuked...by a five-year-old who had us all wrapped around his pinky finger.

I smothered a bark of laughter—or attempted to, anyway.

Though, I didn't think I did a good job because Theo glared up at me.

Worth it.

Especially when that glare was accompanied by a grumbled apology to all of us.

"Cas?" Ethan asked after Theo had gotten his fist bump from Ethan, made it back to his feet, and then left—though not until after he'd glared at us all (minus Ethan) again, just for good measure.

"Yeah, bud?"

I braced for questions about what had happened earlier, about who the man was, and what the tension was for.

But instead, Ethan just asked, "Can we go home?"

And God, I loved this kid (and especially the fact that going home meant getting Ethan and Jules out of this building).

"Yeah, bud," I said. "We can go home."

I knew that the questions would most certainly come later.

Just like I knew that this night wouldn't leave Jules unscathed.

But, for now, going home seemed like the best fucking idea anyone had had all night.

FORTY-TWO

Jules

"CAN you put those books in the box, bud?" I asked over my shoulder, wanting to finish up the packing before Lake came over, sneaking up from D.C. before the Sierra played the home team there the next night.

It had been two months since that night in the rink with Nate and Lake and my surprise gone very, very wrong.

And, though it had kept me up at night—seeing Nate, seeing his *mean*, watching him walk away and worrying that he was going to muster up that *mean* again and turn it on me and Ethan—I hadn't heard from Nate.

Nothing.

Not for seven full days.

Then, finally, exhaustion had overtaken me, and I'd gotten my first full night of sleep in a week...and I'd woken up the next morning to an email from my attorney asking if I would be home the next day because she needed to overnight me some papers.

Papers that had been drawn up by Nate's attorney.

Papers relinquishing custody and parental rights...and included in the paperwork, hidden at the back of a stack was a check for all the back child support he hadn't wanted to pay.

But what had made my heart squeeze hard was the trust.

He'd set up a trust for Ethan.

For school. For a future. For whatever he might need.

I would be the custodian until he was twenty-five. And then it was Ethan's.

I'd cried and Cas had held me, and though the cruelty and the struggle of the last years hadn't been erased, I had begun to remember some of the good parts.

Like sitting at the rink, watching a game, Nate at my side and talking about dreams.

Like Nate telling me about promises and how they were meant to be kept and how I'd told Ethan that same thing so many times over the years that I'd forgotten where I'd gotten it from.

Like the care he'd taken with my body when I'd first given myself to him.

Like the way he'd buy me a pretzel or a drink or a meal when I had no money and was hungry and had lied about wanting something.

All of that had been lost in the hurt and heartbreak and the bad times, and maybe I wouldn't ever be able to forgive him, wouldn't be able to see the boy I'd fallen in love with, but I *had* remembered some of the good. And remembering that good had soothed something in me.

I'd finally slept.

Because I hadn't picked quite so badly.

I could trust myself.

I—

"Okay, Mom!" Ethan called back.

I blinked, tucked the past away, but when Cas ran his knuckles over my cheek, I knew that later that night, he would coax my thoughts out of me, would get me to talk it out.

Because he'd done it more than once over the last weeks.

Because he cared about every part of me.

Even if he would never find any good about Nate *fucking* Miller.

"Gorgeous," he murmured, pressing a kiss to my forehead. "My gorgeous, *gorgeous* woman."

He wasn't talking about the outside—though, thankfully, he liked the package I came in (because I really liked *his* package). But I understood now that he was talking about what he saw inside me—a light that continued growing brighter every day because I was loved and secure and happy.

It was the same light I was watching grow in Ethan.

My boy, who was so freaking excited we were moving in with Cas.

"I'll help him," Mary said softly, and hell if my eyes didn't tear up. Again. Even though Mary and I had cried plenty over the last few days.

I was going to miss my friend.

Mary had become family and—

I sniffed.

"Oh no," Mary said, her eyes going glassy and shaking her head at me. "I can't function if you do that."

"I'm okay," I croaked, waving a hand in front of my face.

"I'll only be fifteen minutes away," Mary said. "And I'll still be babysitting. And we'll have time to hang out now that you're not working full time at CeCe's."

I was still working, and probably always would. I needed to feel secure in my ability to provide for myself, for Ethan. But when the new semester had approached and Cas had suggested that Ethan and I move in with him so I could pick up a few extra classes, he'd done it telling me that he loved me and that he was sick of the two houses bullshit. *Then* he'd done it, reminding me that I had him and Nonna JoJo and Ace, Kathy, Sam, and Margot, *and* Mary (not to mention Beth, Hazel, Pru, and Kailey and Smitty and Raph and Oliver and even Theo).

He'd gently reminded me that I wasn't alone any longer.

That I had a family and a support system, and I could lean on them so as "not to be in school for the next decade."

It made sense.

I wanted that future.

I wanted that family.

I'd still talked to Ethan first. But considering that Cas had done up a guest room for him weeks before, taking Ethan to Target and letting him pick the sheets and bedspread and lamp and beanbag and bookshelf—basically kitting out Ethan's room into an epic Minecraft slash hockey slash Squishmallow-filled spaced, Ethan hadn't been a hard sell.

Then I'd looked at the class schedule, had gotten excited, and had signed up for *all* the classes.

I'd thought Matt would be angry when I asked to reduce my hours.

But my boss—who'd struggled and struggled and eventually found his own happiness—had just cupped my jaw, looked deeply into my eyes, and wished me all the best.

"It's only fifteen minutes," I agreed with Mary now, mostly because if I didn't, Mary and I would turn into sobbing messes. Again.

Partly because I was so freaking happy.

Partly because this was a big change.

Partly because we'd been reduced to sobbing messes several times already that morning.

"Yup." Mary sniffed, her eyes still glassy.

My vision blurred and the sobbing messes probably would

have made a reappearance if not for the knock on my apartment door.

"I've got it!" Pounding feet echoing down the hall.

"Look out the window first," I called.

A hitch in those footsteps. Then, "It's Lake!"

More light. More bright.

"Go," Mary ordered softly. "I'll finish this box up and then I need to go study."

So bright that I needed sunglasses.

I hugged my friend, whispered, "Fifteen minutes," and then ignored both of our sniffles as I snagged the hand Cas extended, let him pull me to my feet.

He trailed me to the door, murmuring that he'd go back to packing the kitchen and let me hang with my old friend.

Giving me space to rebuild our relationship.

Shit.

I sniffed again.

I just loved him so much.

"Lake," Cas said by way of greeting since Ethan had opened the front door and was showing Lake inside. He kissed the top of my head, started to turn away.

Then he froze. "What?"

The barked-out question had my gaze focusing on Lake instead of my son, who had stolen my attention because he was being fucking cute, standing there in the hallway, hopping from foot to foot in his excitement.

I concentrated on Lake's face, took in his expression, his eyes...and the light inside me dimmed.

"What is it?" I whispered.

Lake came to me, wrapped me in big, strong arms, and whispered softly in my ear. "I'm sorry, babe, but it's your dad."

FORTY-THREE

Cas

SHE WAS ASLEEP. Finally.

I couldn't take the anguish in her eyes, hated that Lake had been the one to cause it and hated even more that I couldn't blame the annoying fucker for having brought it—literally—to Jules's doorstep.

But I would have hated even more if she'd heard it from someone else.

Her father was dying.

Had apparently been doing it for a while—and was doing it painfully.

Good.

What he'd done to Jules—the asshole deserved it.

But my woman, my love, my *heart* didn't deserve another hurt, and despite all her father had done—and, more importantly, all the fucker *hadn't* done—there was a part of Jules who still loved her father, who wished that someday things might turn out differently.

I hoped to fuck that her father would get that.

Because I didn't want to kick a dying man's ass.

Christ.

I bit back a sigh, but Ethan, the smart, kind, sensitive boy who was the son of my heart, sensed it anyway.

"Cas?" he whispered. "You okay?"

And that small act of care had my heart squeezing tightly. Even now, Ethan was kind. Even after the flurry of actions that had been packing for an unexpected trip and buying plane tickets and me getting the okay from Coach to miss a couple of games (and with the back office—not that I thought they'd have a problem with it because family came first with the Breakers, even when the need to see to mine came up at a busy point in the season).

"Yeah, bud."

Ethan was quiet for a moment. Then he asked, "Is my other grandpa nice?"

Well, *that* was a question and a half. As thus, I focused on the easier part of the question to address. "Your other grandpa?"

"Yup," Ethan said, hugging the stuffed avocado he'd become attached to for some reason. "Because I have Grandpa Ace and then I have my *other* grandpa."

"Joe," I said, knowing at least that much.

"Yup." Ethan nodded. "I have Grandpa Ace and Grandpa Joe." A beat. "So is Grandpa Joe nice?"

The first part of that settled deep and warm in my heart.

The second wasn't so easy.

"I'm not sure," I said honestly. "I haven't met him before."

"Oh." Silence for a few beats before Ethan whispered, "I hope he is."

I sure as shit hoped so, too.

"Cas?"

"Yeah, bud?" I replied again.

"Are you going to be my dad forever?"

I froze, every muscle in my body going taut. Now *talk* about a question and a half. Silently, carefully, I inhaled, then just as silently, just as carefully, I released it. "Am I your dad now?" I asked softly.

"Yup."

No hesitation.

No delay.

Just a pop on his p, accompanied by a vigorous nod.

Then Ethan went on. "You help me with my homework and tuck me into bed and watch movies with me and you showed me how to use the toaster. And we play hockey together and you drive me to school and pick me up sometimes and you watch me while Mom works." His shoulders lifted and fell on a shrug. "That's what dads do. So, yup"—another pop—"you're my dad right now."

I had spent the last couple of days fending off female sniffles and tears as Jules prepped to move, but fuck if I wasn't one second away from losing it right there on the plane.

But I didn't want what Ethan had just given me to get lost in that emotion.

"I love you, bud," I said, slipping my arm around Ethan's shoulders. "I'm glad I can do that stuff with you, and I will always do them with you, will always love you. Whether you call me Dad or not."

A frown between Ethan's brows. "But I can still call you Dad, right?"

"Absolutely."

We could talk more about names and biology later.

But right then, Ethan needed a dad.

And right then, I needed to *be* a dad.

A dad fighting back sniffles again when Ethan looked up at

me, smiled his mom's smile, bright shining out of eyes that were just like his mom's. "I love you, too."

I cleared my throat, held Ethan closer. "And you know that Nonna JoJo and Grandpa Ace and Aunties Margot and Kathy and Uncles Tim and Sam do, too?"

"Yup." A pop. "And I love them and Smitty and Raph and Theo and Mary and Hazel and Beth and Pru and—" He broke off, wrinkling his nose. "And Pru and Marcel's babies are kind of scrunchy and cry a lot, but Mom says they'll be fun when they get a little older, so I love them, too."

Then, while I was reeling from all that bright, all that love a little boy felt, was cocooned in, and was thanking whoever was in the sky above that I'd had a small part in bringing that to Ethan and Jules, Ethan smiled, hugged his avocado, curled in, and fell asleep on my other shoulder.

And I knew.

Knew it would all be okay.

No matter what happened when the plane landed.

Because *I* would make it okay.

FORTY-FOUR

Jules

TALL PINES COVERED IN SNOW.

A winter wonderland that had once brought me peace, but as Cas drove us through the roads, the snow piled up high on the sides of the road from the plows, the mountains that were home and life and *pain* grew closer.

And closer.

My dad was dying.

But he still hadn't reached out to me, not even after all this time, not even when he was dying, and I didn't know what in the fuck I should be doing, should be *feeling*.

He'd hated me.

He'd treated me like shit.

And I was dropping everything to run to the airport, jump on a plane, and see a man who hadn't loved me enough...if at all. Uprooting my life, bringing my *son*.

Putting him at risk.

"This is a mistake," I whispered.

Cas glanced in the mirror, probably checking on Ethan. But my boy had fallen asleep almost the moment he'd been buckled into the booster seat at the airport. A moment later, he glanced forward, back at the road again, and reached across the console, lacing his fingers with mine. "I think you need to do this," he said, keeping his voice soft, making certain not to wake my boy. "Not because it'll all work out and you'll necessarily get the father you deserved. There's nothing he can do or say to make up for the childhood he gave you." A squeeze of his fingers. "But I think you need to get closure, need to see him and make peace with it all."

My lungs inflated on an inhale, released on an exhale. "Make peace with what?"

He paused at a stop sign, glanced at me. "That none of what went down in your childhood was your fault."

I froze as the words washed over me, his fingers slipping free to complete the turn onto the even narrower road. The road that was painfully close to my childhood home. The road that I'd walked on and driven on enough times growing up that my body automatically braced for the turns.

But even as I distantly recognized that, the words were...

Something I'd thought before. Something Lake had told me more than once. Hell, even Nate had told me the same during the good times we'd had together.

But there was something about Cas telling me right *then* that struck hard.

Maybe because I was in a different place in my life. Maybe it was because Cas had come into my life and Beth and Smitty and Theo and Ace and Joanne and the others, and I finally *felt* what it was like to be in a family that wasn't dysfunctional.

Maybe it was because I had Ethan and I knew, *knew* I would never treat him the way I'd been treated.

"I don't know what it will be like now," I whispered.

His hand coming back to mine. "What do you mean, gorgeous?"

"I mean," I said, still soft, "I just..." A breath. "What if I walk into that house and I become *her* again?"

That little girl who was broken and vulnerable and took her father's vitriol at face value.

Who thought *I* was to blame for my mother's death, for everything that had gone wrong in our lives.

Cas knew exactly what he meant.

Of course he did.

He'd always seen too much when I hadn't wanted him to, but now that he was in my heart, that thoughtfulness, that insightfulness, the fact that he knew each and every part of me was a gift.

"You won't, sweetheart." A squeeze of my fingers. "Because you're not her. I don't think you ever were—otherwise, you wouldn't be the woman I know and love." I inhaled sharply, and his fingers tightened again. "But I also know that you won't be that girl because Ethan and I are here with you and we have your back, gorgeous."

I shook my head. "He's a baby and I'm potentially exposing him to—" Another sharp shake of my head, trying to clear away the past. "I should have left him at home."

"He needs to be here. Yeah, he's young," Cas said when I started to protest. "But he saw how upset you were. He knew that you were rattled. If you'd come without him, if you'd left him at home, then he would have worried all weekend, sweetheart, worried about you because he's old enough to see that you're upset. Bringing him, giving him that comfort, at least, was the right call." He released my hand again to make a turn, and I saw that we were there, that we were pulling into the long, dark driveway that led up to my childhood home. "And I promise you," he said, slowing in front of the house, "I *promise* that at the *first* sign of this going bad, we're out of there." A beat, his eyes hitting mine. "*All* of us."

"Okay," I whispered.

"And *if* it goes bad, gorgeous," he said, pulling to a stop in front of the garage, "you'll have your answer."

He saw too much.

Knew too much.

Knew even more than I'd known herself.

Because I had held on to a question, buried deep beneath everything else, for a long, long time.

What if my father had changed?

THE *HOUSE* HADN'T CHANGED.

Old leather furniture, the smell of smoke and whiskey. Dark wood and dust in the corners and worn paint covering ancient walls.

Only it was worse than when I'd left.

Because back then I'd been trying to keep the polish on, to make it so that...

My father would love me.

But no one had cared for this place for a long time.

Not the soft-spoken nurse who'd answered the door and then disappeared down the hall to give us privacy, and not my father.

Who was on a big, hospital-grade bed in the middle of the living room.

Looking at me.

I sucked in a breath. He looked *old*. Six years had passed from when he'd kicked me out of this house, left me with a bag of clothes and toiletries on the snow-covered porch.

That night, I'd walked to Nate's place.

Who'd delivered another blow.

Then I'd gone to Lake and—my eyes stung—*he'd* been the one to help me.

But the eyes staring at me weren't the frozen, angry eyes that had glared at me that night, venom having soaked through the blue irises, turning them ice-cold.

They were...well, I didn't get a chance to see *what* they were because then they turned to Cas.

No. To Ethan.

My heart squeezed hard, and I took a protective step toward my still-sleeping son, shifting, putting my body between my father's gaze and my baby.

And that was when I knew that Cas was right.

I wasn't going to turn into a weak, simpering woman. Not now. Not ever.

Cas's fingers brushed my lower back, a slight movement barely discernible because he was holding Ethan and wouldn't risk waking him. I turned, let my gaze show him what I'd realized, felt the warmth *he* had inside wash over me.

It would be okay.

No matter how it turned out.

"You came."

Two words that had my focus swiveling back to my father. I nodded.

"Lake tell you I'm dying?"

I nodded even though I was rooted in place by the dry words tinged with a shadow of cruelty. *God.* His voice hadn't changed, even though his body had. He was thin—so fucking thin—and he looked so frail it was almost shocking that he managed to lift a hand and point it at the couch. "You can put the kid there if you think he'll be more comfortable."

Cas brushed my back again, then moved by me, laying Ethan out and spreading the blanket my son had brought from home over him. A moment later, he was back at my side and I'd managed to shore myself up, to get myself to move closer to the bed.

Another point to the couch. "He looks like you."

Ethan was on his side, eyes closed, body curled up, and my dad was right. Ethan *did* look like me—his face, anyway. His body was all Nate. Which meant that Ethan also looked like Cas. Something that was obviously coincidence and not genetics, but not something that my father knew because he hadn't heard—or rather, listened to—anything more about my pregnancy aside from the fact that I *was* pregnant.

Then everything had exploded.

And I hadn't seen him until now.

"And you," my father said to Cas, clearly noticing the random quirk of genetics. "He yours?"

"Yes," Cas said firmly, and I felt his warmth settle over me. Ethan *was* Cas's. So was I. The man lying in the bed in front of me had no bearing on that.

He'd given up all rights to that long ago.

"I thought you'd die."

That had me rocking back on my heels, my breath seizing in my lungs, making it impossible for me to speak.

My father didn't have that problem.

"Like her."

My throat went even tighter.

"You've always looked like her."

"And I took her away from you," I said. "I know." I pressed my lips together, released them. "There's nothing I can change about that. And I know you were stuck with taking care of the kid who was the cause of your pain, and I looked like her and that must have been hard. But I was a child, and I didn't deserve that."

Silence—long enough that the words formed in my mind

and I was able to unload the rest of the old hurts, the rest of the old pain.

"I was *innocent*," I said, slamming a fist to my chest. "I did *nothing,* and you were a shit father." I swung a hand toward Ethan. "I'd never do that to him, never treat him like you treated me."

More silence.

Cas took my hand, held it tight.

"And he's amazing and kind and bright and full of life and I was those things too—*am* those things—and you missed out on them, on knowing *me* and all the good I am because you were too caught up in the past."

Still more quiet, for long enough I almost told Cas to grab Ethan, almost declared we were going to go.

"I thought I could do it."

That had me blinking, looking away from my son and back to my father.

"She loved you so much," my dad said. "I tried to do the same for you." His eyes held mine. "I couldn't." A beat. "And I still can't."

I inhaled, Cas's hand spasmed, his body going taut, and I hated that my father's words still had the power to hurt.

"Right," Cas growled, drawing me to the couch, scooping Ethan up. "We're done."

My father just said, "I can't love you."

"You're not nice."

Blinking, I realized that Ethan wasn't asleep, that he was sitting up, staring at my father.

"Grandpa Ace is nice," Ethan said, grabbing his blanket and moving to my side. "And he only says nice things about my mom. He says I'm lucky to have her and to be nice to her"—my eyes stung—"and you're *not* nice. You're not like Grandpa Ace."

Something sharp across my father's face, and I opened my mouth, ready to order Cas to take Ethan outside.

"You're right," my father said. "I'm not nice." A beat. "And I'm not like your grandpa."

"Let's go," I whispered to Cas, who nodded, took Ethan's hand, and turned to the door.

"But you're a good boy, Ethan." There was something broken in his voice that drew my gaze. Despite the pain, the old hurts, the shittiness of this situation, the ravaging need to *go*. "I wish I could be that man." His eyes held mine, and for the first time ever, I saw regret instead of anger and grief. "And your Grandpa Ace is right. You're lucky to have your mom." He looked away, gaze going to the wall. "Remember that."

My lungs were tight, heart pounding.

Then Cas's arm was around my waist, drawing me away.

"Dad," I whispered.

He met my gaze. "Don't waste time looking back, Julie. Just live your life." A rasping cough that was a powerful reminder of the cancer riddling his insides. "And let an old man wallow in his regrets."

Said in a cold, harsh tone.

But the words...they didn't undo everything.

Hell, they didn't really undo *anything*.

But they did allow me to nod.

And to walk out the door.

EPILOGUE

Cas, Six weeks later

I WAS glad that the news of her father's death came when I was home.

Jules leaned on me.

Not by curling into my chest and crying, by growing depressed, or losing herself for long periods of time. She went on with her days, with her busy life. But she *was* vulnerable and retrospective and quiet. So, I'd been there to feed her, to watch after Ethan, to make sure she had time to process her feelings rather than burying them and having to deal with life's heavy like she'd had to do way too many times over the last years.

I wanted to make sure she had space for her emotions, that she could cry if she needed.

But all she wanted was time with me and Ethan, time with her family.

Much like she'd wanted in the hours and days after the visit home.

Worried that she'd returned to life—to work and school and our various groupings of hockey and biological families—I'd talked to Hazel. The team's sports psychologist was solid, and while grief wasn't her specialty, she'd advised me to just be there, to lend an ear, and to watch out for Ethan.

So, I had been there.

I'd waited, prepared, but once she'd shed the quiet, retrospective mood, it had stayed gone—even though I'd been prepared for it to come back by reading books, watching a shit-ton of YouTube videos, and keeping the names of several therapists that Hazel had provided close at hand.

All of which was too much worry, apparently, because Jules had pulled me aside, ordered me to relax, and had thoroughly reassured me that she was okay.

"I spent too much time living on the sidelines, honey," she'd said, cupping my face and staring into my eyes. "Now is my chance to *live*."

And she had.

We had.

We'd had Valentine's Day together (where she'd given me the hundred-dollar bill back once and for all, centered in a black frame that I kept on my desk), and we'd celebrated Ethan's sixth birthday twice—once with his school and hockey friends and once with our family of Breakers players, their significant others, their kiddos (including Pru and Marcel's scrunchy-faced twins) along with Grandpa Ace and Nonna JoJo and Kathy and Tim and even Sam and Margot had made it.

Now, it had been several hours since Lake had called, and Jules had retreated into that quiet, and I was prepared again.

Turned out, I didn't need to be. Again.

She came out of the bedroom, her cell to her ear. "Yeah, six is good. We're home, but Cas needs to take off for the rink soon."

I frowned.

I wasn't going to my game that evening. I'd cleared it with Coach already.

"Yup," Jules said with a pop. "I'll meet you at your place when I take off." She laughed. "Yeah, Ethan too. Be prepared because I already packed the UNO cards."

My frown deepened, but Jules had already wandered off, her voice echoing through the kitchen.

I slipped away from Sparky, my pooch having fallen asleep during his daily brushing, followed her, and made it into the kitchen right as she was hanging up the phone. Her gaze hit mine after she'd set her cell on the counter, and I inhaled sharply.

The light was back.

"I'm not going to the game," I blurted.

The light in her grew so bright it was almost blinding. Then she was in my arms. "Honey," she murmured, fingers in my beard, body flush against mine. "I'm okay—"

"Your dad—"

"Not my dad," she told me. "My father. My sperm donor. The person who kept me alive." A shake of her head. "But he's not my dad."

"Gorgeous—"

"So," she whispered, "I'm not taking any more time for him. I got the closure I needed. I got the explanation—or lack of one, anyway. I heard that he had regrets, but that was pretty much it, and even if he groveled or begged my forgiveness—which he didn't—I decided after that trip to not waste my life by looking back on what he did." She leaned more heavily against me, wove her arms around my shoulders. "Because I know now that I'm never going to understand how he could do that to me. It's never going to make sense, but I'm done trying. I'm done taking that on *me*. I have Ethan and you and my family, and that's more than enough."

"Sweetheart," I began.

"And I have a family that is awesome enough to come out and watch the man who loves me play his five hundredth NHL game." She rose on tiptoe, brushed her mouth over mine. "A game that there is *no* way in hell you're going to miss, honey. Not for him. Not for the bad memories. We're going to jump into the light and *live*."

I'd forgotten.

Forgotten that the ceremony was tonight.

Forgotten about the hoopla the team had planned and had run by me earlier in the week. Because nothing was more important than the family Jules and I had built together.

"The game—"

"Before you tell me it doesn't matter"—another brush of her lips over mine—"you've taken care of me so often, honey. Now it's my turn."

"Your father—"

Her eyes holding mine. "Ace will be there if I need him."

Fuck.

That sat heavy on my chest, squeezed my heart, stung my eyes. I knew she and my dad had gotten close, but the fact they had *that*, the fact that Jules saw it that way...

I loved her and was so thankful she had it.

That I'd helped her get it.

"My picker isn't broken."

Her lips curved. "No, honey." One more brush of her lips. Except this time it turned into something more, something hotter and longer and wetter—and for my part *harder*.

But then footsteps echoed our way, and we pulled apart, turning to the hall just in time to see Ethan appear, fully kitted out in Breakers gear. "It's Game Day!" he shouted and turned for the family room, giving me a glimpse of the back of his jersey, showing me my name there.

And that hit heavy too.

And that was...*perfect.*

"Get ready for the game, baby," Jules murmured, nudging me toward the stairs.

I didn't argue further, just got ready, and later that night, when I looked up into the stands and saw my family—*all* of them—cheering like lunatics, I knew my earlier statement was right.

My picker wasn't broken.

It had been a little dinged from misuse, dusty because I'd thrust it up on a high shelf, but mostly it had been on standby.

Waiting.

For Jules.

Eva

I slipped out from the arena, leaned back against the wall.

The playoffs were closing in, and I should be down in the locker room, asking all the questions I'd spent hours preparing.

But Theo was down there.

I'd heard his voice echoing out into the hall.

That I could identify him talking through the din of other noises was concerning, but there had been a lot of concerning things about Theo from the very beginning.

Like the fact that we'd fucked.

And it had been life changing.

The man was built, his cock was magnificent, and he knew

how to use it—and his lips and teeth and tongue and fingers and—

He'd blown my mind.

Then had moved right on.

Ouch, yeah?

But he was a professional athlete. I was familiar with their antics and how many of them had an allergy to committing to one woman.

And I was just one woman.

An average one at that.

And one who was now ruined for all other men. Maybe I'd switch to women. I liked a good set of boobs, could get behind curves—

Ha.

Who was I kidding?

I liked hard and built and *thick.*

And Theo.

I'd really liked him.

But he hadn't called. In fact, he hadn't even let me stay the night. He'd fucked me senseless, sent me on my way and yeah, being blown off hurt, but it wasn't exactly a surprise. I was me. He was him.

And so...I'd gotten over it.

Then I'd gotten on with work—which, uncomfortably, was in the Breakers' locker room.

He'd made his disapproval of that clear, and at first, I'd been determined to prove he didn't affect me, to ignore what happened, to demonstrate that he meant nothing to me, so I'd forced myself to interview him like normal, to report on him like normal.

Were all the stories nice and kind?

No.

I'd sucked the guy off, and he'd still been ready to fuck me senseless. Hell, my pussy had throbbed for two straight days after we'd fucked, and I'd left his bed feeling like I'd run a marathon—something I didn't bother with because *exercise*, blegh.

But that was it.

Nothing else.

No catching feelings. No repeat performance. Just... moving on.

So, no, not all the stories about Theo were nice, but that wasn't because we'd fucked. I just...didn't always shy away from tough questions, and he'd made it clear that my tough questions, that my reporting in general made him unhappy.

But, I repeated, *moving on.*

Making the best of it. Doing my job.

Getting opportunities I'd dreamed of and staying busy enough that dealing with Theo Young had gotten easier.

Until he'd eviscerated me in front of Smitty and Cas and Raph and Julie and Lake Jordan.

That, surprisingly, was harder to get over than never having his dick inside me again, never tasting his skin, or feeling his big body come over mine.

He didn't like me.

He didn't respect me.

And I'd still gotten wet in the face of all that derision.

I *was* despicable. And pathetic. And desperate. And—

The heavy metal door swung open so fast that I didn't have the chance to stop it, to dodge it. The panel of steel slammed into me, nose to toes, and then the pain was flooding my senses, sending me to my knees on the concrete.

More pain.

But then there was warmth—liquid warmth. Blood gushing out of my nose, dripping down...onto my blouse.

Shit.

Not the expensive silk blouse I'd borrowed from my sister.

It cost who knew how much—and I was terrified it would be a *lot*, considering that Dommie had expensive taste.

That wasn't the worst of it.

Nope.

There was something even more terrible than the thought of having to replace an overpriced shirt, than the pain in my kneecaps and my face and my hands and my chest and my toes.

It was the voice.

"Shit, I'm sorry," he said, frantic hands on my arms, my shoulders, my waist. "Are you okay?"

The *voice*.

I heard it in my fantasies, my dreams.

Rough and soft, like velvet sandpaper, if that was even a thing.

And I supposed it was.

At least in Theo Young's world.

Thank you for reading! I hope you loved meeting Cat and Julie as much as I did! The next book in the Breakers Hockey series is BREATHE. **He'd never been interested in settling down...until he met her.**

CLICK HERE TO READ BREATHE NOW>

And if you enjoyed BLOWOUT, pick up book one in my brand new Grizzlies Hockey series, MARRIED TO NUMBER TWENTY-TWO. **I signed the contract. I just didn't expect her to show up ten years later, ready to cash it in.**

CLICK HERE TO READ MARRIED TO NUMBER TWENTY-TWO NOW>

READ on for a sneak peek below!

Aiden

I wake up to a heavy knock on my condo's front door and glare blearily at my phone in the charger.

"Two in the fucking morning," I mutter, grabbing a pillow and clamping it over my ears. "It's two o'clock in the morning on my fucking birthday, and I have to deal with this shit."

This shit being my neighbors.

It's not the first time they've pounded drunk on my door, desperate for their roommate to let them in to what they think is their apartment.

This was sort of funny the first time.

I remember those days, drinking too much, being dumb.

But after the second and the third—where I gained status into the inner circle and a code to the keypad to their apartment door—it was no longer cute.

Now, six months later and countless times of bailing them out, I'm *so* not in the mood.

Especially when it's my fucking birthday.

The knocking cuts off and I think—*pray*—that they've gotten the hint.

But it's approximately two seconds later when it starts up again.

I glance at my phone again, see that really five minutes have passed, making it two-seventeen and officially my birthday.

Some present.

I could try to ignore it—but that just means extending the torture. Sighing, I toss back the blankets and stomp to my apartment door, whipping it open to reveal a slender brunette on my doorstep.

"Ho, mama," she says, gaze taking a slow perusal down my body.

"Who the fuck are you?"

"It's me. Luna."

I stare at her, uncomprehendingly.

"From Rockfield?" she adds.

Recognition begins to dawn. "Luna Maybelle?"

"Yup! That's me." She nods, grinning, and I see it then, the glimpse of my best friend from the childhood rink I grew up playing at come out in her smile. Mischief and life. Joy and hard work.

Summers spent spending every spare moment together— her figure skating, me playing hockey.

But she's not little Luna anymore.

Christ, she's anything but—tall, beautiful, curves for days— and she's staring at me.

Because I'm staring at her.

Fucking hell.

I spur myself into motion.

"Luna! Oh my God!" I pull her into a hug. "What the hell are you doing here?"

"It's your birthday!" She holds up a piece of paper that looks faintly familiar. "And, well, it's mine too, remember?"

That's right.

We have the same birthday.

"We're both twenty-five, single, and—"

My eyes narrow in on the paper. It's crumpled and stained, as though it's years old.

A purple and pink swirl decorates the edges and suddenly I

remember her painstakingly drawing it as we sat side-by-side at one of the high top tables of the ice rink, waiting for the Zamboni to finish cutting the ice.

Her brow had been furrowed. Her movements carefully controlled.

And I had been obsessing over how pink her lips were and what her butt looked like in her skating dress, so much so that I barely remember what we'd been drawing.

No, I think hard, grabbing on to those memories, not what we'd been *drawing*.

The contract we'd put together.

The contract my hormonal twelve-year-old self had signed.

With a sparkly pink colored pencil.

A giant boulder settles in my stomach, but before I can snap myself out of the horror of those memories, she shoves the paper in my hands then throws her arms around my neck.

"We're getting married!"

CLICK HERE TO READ MARRIED TO NUMBER TWENTY-TWO NOW>

BREAKERS HOCKEY SERIES

<u>Broken</u>
<u>Boldly</u>
<u>Breathless</u>
<u>Ballsy</u>
<u>Bewitched</u>
Blowout
Breathe
A Breakers Christmas
Blazed
Bound

Hate missing Elise's new releases? Love contests, exclusive excerpts and giveaways?
Then signup for Elise's newsletter here!

www.elisefaber.com/newsletter

And join Elise's fan group, the Fabinators (https://www.facebook.com/groups/fabinators) for insider information, sneak peaks at new releases, and fun freebies! Hope to see you there!

If you enjoy my series, considering supporting me on PATREON! Get access to early releases, bonus content, character art, audiobooks, special edition covers, swag, and much more!

CLICK HERE TO SUPPORT ME>

I so appreciate your help in spreading the word about my books, including sharing with friends! Please leave a review on your favorite book site!

Gold Hockey (all stand alone)

Blocked

Backhand

Boarding

Benched

Breakaway

Breakout

Checked

Coasting

Centered

Charging

Caged

Crashed

A Gold Christmas

Cycled

Caught

Cap

Covered

Crushed

Changed

Scored

Breakers Hockey (all stand alone)

Broken

Boldly

<u>Breathless</u>

<u>Ballsy</u>

<u>Bewitched</u>

Blowout

Breathe

A Breakers Christmas

Blazed

Bound

Sierra Hockey Series

Over the Line

Caught from Behind

The Big Skate

On the Fly

Rush Hockey Trilogy #1

Big Puck Energy

Filthy Puckboy

So Pucking Over It

Rush Hockey Trilogy #2

Love, Pucks, and Other Stories

All's Fair in Pucks and War

No Pucks Lost Between Us

Rush Hockey Novellas

Puck and Make Up

Eagles Hockey Series (all stand alone)

Broken Laces

Lace 'em Up

Knotted Laces

Loaded Laces

Lucky Laces

***Billionaire's Club* (all stand alone)**

Bad Night Stand

Bad Breakup

Bad Husband

Bad Hookup

Bad Divorce

Bad Fiancé

Bad Boyfriend

Bad Blind Date

Bad Wedding

Bad Engagement

Bad Bridesmaid

Bad Swipe

Bad Girlfriend

Bad Best Friend

Bad Rebound

Bad Romance

Bad Business

Bad Billionaire's Quickies

Love, Action, Camera (all stand alone)

Dotted Line

Action Shot

Close-Up

End Scene

Meet Cute

Love After Midnight (all stand alone)

Rum And Notes

Virgin Daiquiri

On The Rocks

Sex On The Seats

Life Sucks Series

Train Wreck

Hot Mess

Dumpster Fire

Clusterf*@k

FUBAR

Perfect Storm

Free Fall

Lost Cause

Roosevelt Ranch Series (all stand alone, series complete)

Disaster at Roosevelt Ranch

Heartbreak at Roosevelt Ranch

Collision at Roosevelt Ranch

Regret at Roosevelt Ranch

Desire at Roosevelt Ranch

***Phoenix Series* (read in order)**

Phoenix Rising

Dark Phoenix

Phoenix Freed

***Phoenix: LexTal Chronicles* (rereleasing soon, stand alone, Phoenix world)**

From Ashes

In Flames

To Smoke

KTS Series (all stand alone, series complete)

Riding The Edge

Crossing The Line

Leveling The Field

Scorching The Earth

Cocky Heroes World

Tattooed Troublemaker

ABOUT THE AUTHOR

USA Today bestselling author, Elise Faber, loves chocolate, Star Wars, Harry Potter, and hockey (the order depending on the day and how well her team -- the Sharks! -- are playing). She and her husband also play as much hockey as they can squeeze into their schedules, so much so that their typical date night is spent on the ice. Elise is the mom to two exuberant boys and lives in Northern California. Connect with her in her Facebook group, the Fabinators or find more information about her books at www.elisefaber.com.

facebook.com/elisefaberauthor

amazon.com/author/elisefaber

bookbub.com/profile/elise-faber

instagram.com/elisefaber

tiktok.com/@elisefaberauthor

goodreads.com/elisefaber